LOW WATER

JENNIFER LANE

PSYCHED
PUBLISHING

Psyched Publishing

Published by Psyched Publishing, October 2025

The characters and events in this book are fictitious.
Any similarity to real persons, living or dead,
is coincidental and not intended by the author.

ISBN: 978-0-9979970-6-4

10 9 8 7 6 5 4 3 2 1

Cover & Interior Book Design by Coreen Montagna

*Dedicated to my parents, Jan and Roger,
who died at age 87 and 88
during the year that I wrote this story.
Mom and Dad, thank you for instilling in me
a strength of perseverance
as well as passion for sports and psychology.*

*"You are not your trauma;
you are the strength that rises from it."*

Marcus Kane

*"To heal is to touch with love
that which we previously touched with fear."*

Stephen Levine

1. JORDAN

"**A** dolphin!" Kim shrieks.

I stop swimming and pop my head up to scan the turquoise water around my sister. She jabs her finger straight ahead. "He just swam past me, that way!"

Treading water, I frown. "Bummer, I missed him." My disappointment vanishes, though, when a gray triangle rises over the calm sea about thirty feet in front of Kim. Reverently, I watch the dolphin's graceful arc as it slips back into the ocean. I wish I were that smooth and powerful in the water.

Kim's broad grin borders on idiotic. "This is *so* cool."

"Yeah," I agree. The shards of sunlight stabbing into the cool Sea of Cortez almost blind me.

"Thank you, Jordan." Her mirrored goggles block my view of her eyes, but I imagine them crinkling with happiness. "This is such a thoughtful birthday present."

Since she and I both swam at Kenyon College, a small school in Ohio, I knew she would seize the chance to take a swimming vacation with our former teammates for her fortieth birthday. For the past few days, we've camped on a remote island off Baja, Mexico. Twice a day, guides have driven us in small boats called pangas to various locations for a mile or two of open-water swimming. The hidden world of wildlife weaving in and out of the coral below me has stolen my breath more than once.

I shrug. "We had to take this trip before you're too old to keep up."

There's a good chance her eyes now narrow at me, given the tight press of her lips. "Ever the irritating little brother," she says.

"That's my job, to annoy you. Even when you're an old woman." I use eggbeater kicks to keep my head above water as I stretch my triceps. "You're so old, your soccer ball was a dinosaur egg." The peeved pucker of her mouth keeps me going, though I'm only two years younger. "You're so old, you babysat for Yoda."

"I get it," she grumbles. "I'm old."

I shouldn't get this much satisfaction from teasing her now that we're adults. I give her a break with my next joke. "Hey, Kim. What'd the shark say after he ate a clownfish?"

Her mouth is a slash of anticipation, maybe dread.

"This tastes a little funny."

Not even a crack of a smile from her. She shakes her head. "I feel sorry for your wife and kids, having to deal with you. Your team, too."

"Aw, they love me." I coach a club swim team in South Carolina. Though the youth swimmers usually consume me, they're a distant memory right now in this idyllic, fantastical water world. Kim wasn't the only one coveting this swim vacation—I needed a break, too, especially after the awful high school state meet. My burgeoning star, Mason McCall, had subpar swims, and I've been mired in guilt ever since. "Just like you love me," I add.

Kim points behind me. "Watch out for that coral."

The current has pushed me backwards during our conversation, and I spin around to see a slab of reddish-brown rock near my knee. Just before I knock into it, I take a quick pull to move my body away. The voice of Peter, our guide, echoes in my mind. *"Sharks, stingrays, jellyfish—they're unlikely to be a problem on this trip. But please avoid the coral. It's sharp, and it can cut you."*

"Thanks," I say. More evidence that my big sister loves me. I look ahead and notice our teammates are some distance away now. To my right, Peter is on the panga, gripping a pole that supports the boat's canopy. He wants us to swim as a group for safety, and he's already admonished Kim and me for drifting apart while admiring an eel or parrotfish. "C'mon, we need to catch up."

Kim nods and glides into her smooth, strong stroke. I'm relieved that she feels better today. She missed yesterday's morning swim because of seasickness. I'm also grateful that the ibuprofen I took after lunch has lowered my nagging shoulder pain to a twinge.

My sister was a national champion in the freestyle events, and she still has a long extension and powerful catch with each pull of her bronzed arms. Her kick isn't as steady or potent as it used to be, but the ocean helps her out. The high salt concentration elevates her body position. Her success at a small liberal arts college in Ohio led me to join her there two years later, despite my partial swim scholarship offers at larger universities. It was one of the best decisions I've made. Not only was our coach the most effective innovator and stroke technician in the country, but his compassion for Kim and me cemented his role as a father to us. Every day, I try to emulate his brilliance as a coach. I know I fall way short.

By the time our afternoon swim has finished, there's a burn in my arms and a heavy euphoria coursing through my bloodstream, reminding me of the mind-body bliss I used to feel at the end of a tough college practice. I doubt my thirty-eight-year-old body could make it through eight-thousand yards of fast intervals and race-pace repeats. Swimming just shy of four miles in the ocean is the closest I can get.

After Kim is safely on board, I haul myself up the panga's ladder and accept Peter's hand during the disorienting last step onto the deck.

"How was it?" he asks as I shake water out of my ear, mimicking a wet dog.

"Eh." I shrug. "Nothing special."

Wyatt, my best friend, pauses toweling off his hair to look at Peter. "Too bad Jordan's one of your swimmers on this trip."

"Unlucky for us all," Kim adds.

Peter's face reveals nothing, and I hope he knows my comment was a joke.

"Makes sense," he tells me. "Your swimming was nothing special, either."

It's good he can dish it back—makes me like our guide even more.

Wyatt laughs. "Yeah, where *were* you, Jordo? Riding the struggle bus after too many cervezas last night?"

"We saw the coolest dolphins!" Kim says as her head pokes through the black swim cover-up she pulls over her shoulders.

"Oh, me too!" another of our teammates hollers over the din as the motor roars to life at the hands of the Mexican boat captain.

On the ride back, Peter explains that dolphins sometimes only use half of their brains, like when sleeping.

I grin at Wyatt. "Dude, no wonder the dolphin's your spirit animal."

We launch into a shouted analysis of the afternoon's wildlife sightings as the panga cuts through the water back to base camp, the setting sun casting a glimmer of orange and red hues around us.

"Happy birthday to you," we croon to Kim two hours later. I'm grateful the remote island's unseen snakes and scorpions are the only inhabitants to hear our song. Had my sister joined the singing, she would've harmonized the last line and salvaged our off-key rendition. I don't know how she found time in college to sing in an a cappella group in addition to two swim practices a day and volunteering at a local preschool. She's one of those people who's just good at everything.

Her tanned face glows in the candlelight, and I'm not sure which impresses me more—the sheer number of candles our local chef has stuck into the frosting or the fact that he's managed to bake a cake at all, given that we don't have electricity out here. Kim pauses a moment before blowing out the candles. After her robust swimmer's lungs decimate the flames, we all clap, with a few whoops thrown in like we're cheering on a teammate at a meet.

The boat captain turns the battery-powered lights back on, and my eyes adjust to the brightness of the dining-tent canopy. I slap at my neck and wonder why I keep applying bug spray since I'm already covered in bites. Wyatt nudges in between Kim and another teammate to snatch a plate with the first piece of cake she's cut.

"Oh," he moans after taking a bite. "Cinnamon." He licks a creamy blob from the corner of his mouth. "Where've you been all my life?"

Kim recoils. "Gross. Get a room."

"Good idea." Wyatt scratches a mosquito bite on his arm as he extends his plate in front of her face. "Cut me another piece, birthday wench. I'm taking these babies back to my tent to have my way with them."

Another teammate makes a sound of disgust. "Leave some for us, Wyatt!"

She's right—the whole cake will be devoured soon. After burning so many calories, we've all stuffed our faces with tacos, ceviche, and cookies on this trip.

Kim shakes her head, but she serves him another piece. Wyatt graduated the year between my sister and me, and he's become a good friend to us both. But with Kim living in Ohio, Wyatt in Washington, and me in South Carolina, we don't get to spend much time together.

I notice a smear of frosting on the sleeve of Kim's shirt—likely from Wyatt the slob. I'm pleased that she's wearing my daughter's birthday gift tonight, a violet long-sleeve that reads, *My Niece Has the Coolest Aunt.* Hailey pleaded with me to buy it for her after Kim gave her a *My Aunt Has the Coolest Niece* T-shirt for her eighth birthday.

Kim and I finish off the cake while crushing our opponents as euchre partners in our favorite card game, and eventually we're the last ones remaining in the dining area. Though it's only nine pm, most of our tired, sore teammates have already collapsed onto air mattresses in their zippered tents. I hope Wyatt hasn't begun snoring off his sugar coma by the time I return to ours.

Kim and I listen to the constant crash of waves onto the shore mere feet from where we sit.

"What'd you wish for, birthday girl?"

She starts, as if broken out of a reverie. "Isn't it bad luck to say your wish out loud?"

"Is it possible to have back luck in this paradise?" I gesture to the slice of moon illuminating whitecaps on the inky black water. The shine of stars over the dark waterscape adds to the celestial lightshow.

"He's here with us." Kim points at the sky. "He's happy we're swimming together again."

I roll my head back to gaze at the tiny points of light. *Is she right? Are you up there, Dad?* The stars seem to bob and undulate as I stare, but maybe it's the gushing sound of ocean waves playing tricks on my mind.

"Family is everything, Jords."

I study her face, still turned up to the sky. Her serene smile seems incongruous with the glisten of tears in her eyes. She's getting maudlin, and we haven't even consumed any alcohol. "Are you going to tell me your wish, or what?"

After a beat, she sniffs and looks at me. "I wished I could have more time with my niece and nephew." She unzips her jacket and fondly pats her shirt. "This one's almost as good as the *I'm the Favorite Aunt* shirt Hailey gave me."

My wife's sister was offended when she saw a photo of Kim side-hugging Hailey while wearing that shirt. To keep the peace, my wife, Elena, bought the same shirt for my sister-in-law and told her it was from our daughter. Everything turns into a competition in my family.

"And the enhanced-vision goggles Hudson gave me are perfect for this trip," Kim adds. "Too bad I can't call to thank them for their gifts."

We don't have cellular service on the island, which was an appealing aspect of this particular trip. The company hosts swim vacations all over the world, and my teammates and I have already considered future tempting sites like Belize, Croatia, or Mallorca.

She sighs. "I wish I lived closer to watch them grow up."

We've talked about her moving south, but it's tough to find a job as an elementary teacher in my town. And she just met a guy in Columbus she sounds excited about—finally. She has dated so many losers that I can't keep track. Though she adores my son and daughter, I bet her true birthday wish is to have children of her own. She loves kids. She just hasn't found a man who seems worthy as a good husband and father. Her brief inquiry into foster parenting revealed that it's tough to qualify as a single parent. And now that she's forty, having kids probably won't happen.

The next morning, this trip doesn't feel so sublime. Gusts from a westerly wind chop the water, and I fight the waves with almost every stroke. At least the saltwater shooting up my nose clears my sinuses. Kim seemed rather green on the boat ride to the leeward side of the island, where we are today. I'd hate to see the waves on the windward side. She avoided tossing her cookies overboard, but the rollicking swells probably aren't helping settle her stomach during our swim.

My most difficult challenge is the piercing pain in my right shoulder, which makes it even harder to keep up with my speedy teammates. I wish I had trained more before the trip, but the last place I wanted to be was slogging laps in a pool. Between coaching my team and watching my kids' swim meets, I spend far too much time around chlorine.

I see Kim's bright purple swim cap a second before I swim into her, and I flinch back. It's not raining, but the overcast skies limit visibility.

"You okay, bro?" She lifts her goggles to her forehead.

She must have circled back from the lead group to check on me, and she's not even breathing hard. My best sprint times were faster than hers in college, but she's in better shape now because she's on a master's team in Ohio. She hopes this trip will prepare her for a competition in December.

"Just my damn shoulder." I wince as I pull my right elbow across my chest to stretch it. A wave smacks my ear, adding to my irritation.

She shakes her head. "Your right hand's still—"

"I know!" I bark. She's told me probably ten times now that I'm rolling my thumb down as my right hand enters the water, causing unnatural torque on my shoulder, but I fall back into old patterns when I'm tired. As a coach, I should do better. "I'm working on it!"

"Jeez." Her chin retracts. "Just trying to help. You need to pay better attention to your technique."

"Who's the coach here?" I bellow. Her eyes turn down, and I regret my crabby tone.

The approaching hum of a motor interrupts us as the boat captain maneuvers the panga alongside. Peter's forehead creases. "Perrys, do you need help?"

We both shake our heads as we tread water.

"You sure?" Peter gives Kim a pointed look.

I squint at her, and she lets out a breath. "I threw up earlier." Her nose wrinkles. "In the water."

I cringe. Then my chest tightens as I realize she's swimming faster than I am even while battling nausea.

"But I'm better now." She looks at Peter as she thumbs in my direction. "Jordan should get in the boat, though. His shoulder hurts."

"I'm fine," I insist.

Peter glances behind him at the boat deck, then back at me. "Did you bring your fins?"

I blow out a gust of frustration. "Forgot 'em." The truth is I didn't want to take my wussy fins on the boat. I shouldn't need them to keep up with my teammates, especially the women. "Look, just keep going. I'll catch up."

Peter points ahead. "This is our longest swim of the trip — about three miles — and we're almost done. You're doing great."

"So great," I growl.

Kim says, "I'll stay back with you on this last part."

"No!" That came out louder than I intended. I'm the one who should take care of her, not the other way around. "You had to sit out yesterday, and my stupid shoulder shouldn't ruin *this* swim, too. Go on ahead."

She nibbles her lower lip, which looks swollen from the salty sea. I can't wait to slurp electrolyte drinks when we're back on the boat, along with about five ibuprofens.

"Go, Kim." I see her starting to waver. "You'll stress me out if I hold you back."

Peter listens to his walkie-talkie, likely chatter from the other panga that's following a slower group of swimmers who started before us. He leans over the boat. "The purple caps and the yellow caps are done with their swim, waiting for us. Let's go — I'll track you both. Lots of coral in the area, so stay vigilant."

With a sigh, Kim circles her thumbs on the inside of her goggles to clear them.

Before she resumes freestyle, I add, "Just don't gloat to Hudson and Hailey about how slow I swam when we get home."

"Don't worry, I'll preserve your massive ego." She smirks, then takes off.

I groan underwater as I glide into my stroke. My one distraction from shoulder pain is having to weave around coral constellations — the water seems lower in this part of the sea. After a long stretch, I switch to pulling only with my left arm to relieve my screaming right shoulder.

One-arm swimming has slowed my progress, and the panga matches my pathetic pace. I can't see the group ahead, only rolling waves, but I bet Kim has already made it there to join them. Wyatt will give me hell for my grandma speed.

When a big wave lifts me up and crashes me down, I look up to find the panga zooming ahead. No wonder it's extra turbulent, given I'm in the direct path of the boat's wake. I sputter from a spray of water into my nose and mouth. As I bob in the undulating sea, a chill prickles up my spine. I've never seen the panga hightail it like that.

Panicked shouts in the distance direct my vision to the spot where the panga has whooshed to a stop. It takes a second to realize the shouts come from Peter, who stands on the gunwale of the boat with a red lifeguard rescue tube slung across his torso. After he jumps into the water, I grasp the name he's yelled: *"Kim!"*

Kim. Her name propels me into a full-out sprint. What happened? How far away is she? Two hundred meters? Three hundred? Was she bitten by a shark? My heart thunders, and my legs explode with lactic acid, but adrenaline blocks awareness of my throbbing shoulder. Nor do I feel anything when my left hand brushes against an upcropping of dark, greenish-blue coral. Quick head lifts to help my sighting confirm I'm drawing closer, but the blurred chaos near the panga doesn't answer the terrified questions battering my mind.

Panting, I arrive near the panga, rip off my goggles, and whip my head left to right in a frantic search. The water is empty. Above me, Peter shouts something in Spanish, followed by the boat captain's terse reply. When I hear a moan from Kim, I lunge toward the rear of the boat. A slash of blood on the white surface near the ladder shoots my heart into my throat. Shark? Is there a shark behind me? I spin around, but all I see is the other panga speeding toward us. I turn back to the boat and rush up the ladder.

Pink liquid sloshes my bare feet, the color deepening to dark red as my eyes trail along the deck up to Kim, lying prone on her back. Peter rustles around some sort of first-aid kit as he hovers at the right side of her body, while the boat captain speaks rapid-fire Spanish into his walkie-talkie. I peel off my cap and step closer, dreading the aftermath of a shark attack. Thank God Kim still has all four limbs, but one of them—her right leg—sports a long, jagged gash down the thigh. My stomach turns as blood spurts from the wound. A buzz fills my ears, pulsing to the staccato beat of my heart.

Peter pushes a pad of gauze against the top of her thigh, right below her bikini line.

I clutch the gunwale with a desperate search of the rollicking sea. "What kind of shark was it?"

Peter whips his head back to glare at me, and I realize I was the one who just spoke. "Jordan! Get over here."

I stare at him.

"*Now.*"

His order unfreezes me, and I hurry to my sister. The gauze beneath Peter's gloved hand has already turned candy-apple red, in contrast to the paleness of Kim's face. Her eyes are closed, but she grunts in pain when Peter presses another layer of gauze onto her thigh. Too soon, I see red seeping into the new layer.

"So much blood," Peter murmurs.

I buckle to my knees on the other side of Kim and slide a hand under her head to cradle it.

"Kim!" Peter snaps. "Are you on a blood thinner?" When she doesn't respond, he looks at me. "Is she?"

I shake my head. "No?"

The boat captain tears open another sterile gauze package and hands it to Peter. Then he exchanges words with the other captain who has pulled his empty panga alongside ours.

"My teammates!" I look at Peter as I break out of my fog. "We have to get them out of the water! The shark—"

"No shark." Peter tilts his head toward my sister's thigh. "She ran into coral."

My mouth drops open. *Coral* did this?

"She kept apologizing for being careless." Peter grimaces as he opens another gauze pouch with his teeth. "Looks like an arterial bleed—femoral artery. If the bleeding doesn't stop soon, we'll need a tourniquet."

A *tourniquet?* I know nothing about emergency medicine, but that sounds bad. The boat captain's question in Spanish interrupts my freak-out.

Peter shifts his body, still holding pressure on the wound. "Listos—ready." He looks at me as he nods at the deck. "Sit. It's gonna be a bumpy ride."

I can't keep cradling Kim's head if I need to sit, so I grab a folded towel from the bench and tuck it beneath her swim cap. My butt barely has time to find the deck before the motor roars. I grasp Kim's cool hand and silently plead with her to be okay. *I should've let you stay with me. Open your eyes, open your eyes. I shouldn't have abandoned you.* Her hand trembles in mine as blood rolls down the deck toward the engine. I am in another universe—this can't be real. Over the reverberation, I shout, "To where?"

Peter's blue eyes bore into me, and his jaw ticks. "The hospital in La Paz."

It's the closest town to our remote island. But it was a ninety-minute boat ride from La Paz to get out here—does Kim have that long? *Please be okay, Kimmie. I should've kept up with you. Please be okay.* The wind whips around us, and I shiver. Kim's body vibrates as the tremor in her hand quickens.

Peter hands me a larger package, and I unwrap the space blanket. I cover Kim with the silvery material, leaving the red stacks of gauze exposed on her thigh. Blood squeezes out from beneath Peter's hands. "Put on some gloves," he tells me. "I'll need you to apply pressure while I prepare a tourniquet."

It takes longer than it should for me to glove up my shaking hands. I'm a mess, whereas Peter is all cool efficiency. "She'll be okay, right?"

He meets my eyes, and his pause stops my heart.

2. AVERY

"I see we're out of time."

My client jumps as I interrupt her. She glances at the large, round seascape clock on the office wall. "But it's only one fifty-two," she says.

"Yes. Our sessions are forty-five minutes. We started about one-oh-five." I stand.

Janet came to therapy six months ago to cope with conflict in her second marriage. But after a few sessions of getting nowhere, I discovered the true reason she was here: trauma. Her first husband had physically abused and terrorized her. We've completed twelve weekly sessions of a post-traumatic stress disorder treatment that has improved her life in many ways, especially her satisfaction in her marriage. But then her cranky father-in-law moved in, challenging the recent peace at home.

Still seated, Janet frowns. "What should I do about Bob?"

"What about Bob?" I muse, recalling the movie in which a persistent client annoyed the living hell out of a therapist. A woman of fifty-five would likely know a 1990s movie better than I would, but Janet doesn't return my smile at the reference. "I want you to do a

CBT worksheet about your father-in-law for us to review next time," I say as I move toward the door. "You scheduled a follow-up online?"

After a moment, she takes the hint and caps her pen, then gathers her book bag, journal, water bottle, and jacket. I suppress a sigh at her plodding pace. I heard my cellphone vibrate twice during our session, and I'll probably need time to return calls or texts. Also, the blinking blue light on my desk indicates that my next client is in the waiting room, and I don't want to be late. I'm never late.

Janet pauses in the open doorway. "Are you mad at me?"

Now I'm the one who flinches. Confirming that the short hallway outside of my office is empty, I take a moment to search my feelings—much tougher than helping clients sort through theirs. *Am I mad at her?* "Not at all." I shrug. "Maybe my neurotic need to be on time unintentionally showed up as impatience."

"Oh." She smiles. "One of your stuck points?"

I grin back, gratified by her reference to the trauma therapy protocol she's completed. "Yep, I get stuck on the belief that being late leads to tragedy. No evidence for that one!" I tilt my head. "I wonder, what led you to think I was angry at you?"

Her smile drops. "Well, you sounded just like my boss when he cut off our meeting yesterday. I felt...dismissed."

I nod, relieved that her insecurity is more about transference—transferring her feelings about another person to me—than my behavior. She works as an administrative assistant at Parris Island, a nearby Marine Corps base, and she's mentioned her domineering boss before. "You interpreted my abrupt ending to the session as dismissing you like an errant employee."

"Exactly." She pauses. "Come to think of it, Bob did the same thing last week, shooing me out of his room when I was only trying to collect his dirty dishes."

I nod. No wonder she needs to talk about her boss and father-in-law. Both are older men who have berated her. They're similar to her cruel first husband. I try to recall her beliefs about male authority figures, as we may need to revisit them. Her inaccurate reading of my feelings indicates that we have more cognitive behavioral therapy ahead of us. And I definitely want to discuss her relationship with her father in more depth.

She inhales, seeming to arrive at a realization. "But I'm making you late!" As she scurries away, she calls over her shoulder, "Don't

want to activate your stuck points. I have enough for the both of us."
She exits through the door to the waiting room.

I shake my head. Actually, Janet is quite a competent, put-together woman who has healed from trauma and cares for her husband, two children, and now father-in-law, all while working full-time. But I'll have to save my questions about her self-worth for next time. We've already dealt with one doorknob disclosure at the end of the session.

Sometimes I learn more about my clients in the last few seconds of our time together than in the prior hour of therapy. As I scoop my cellphone from my desk, the blinking blue light catches my eye. I can also learn a lot about clients during the first few seconds of an intake.

The missed text is from my best friend and partner in this practice, Nadia:

Ready to get your freak on at speed dating?

I cringe. *Negative.* How she talked me into tonight's nightmare is beyond understanding. She keeps haranguing me about my avoidant attachment style and how I'll never find a man if I don't face my fear of intimacy. Sometimes it sucks to have a friend who is also a psychologist. Since Nadia is home with her sick daughter today, instead of in the office next to mine, I decide I'll answer her later.

The missed voicemail is from an unfamiliar number. "Mrs. Clarkson," a male voice begins, and I scowl. *I'm either Avery or Dr. Clarkson, thank you very much.* "This is Gabe Diaz, uh, I'm a coach, er, assistant coach for the Lowcountry Lionfish? I was supposed to call you a few days ago—my head coach wanted me to reach out to you while he's out of town—but like an idiot, I forgot. I hope to catch you before you meet with Mason McCall."

That's the name of my new client in the waiting room, so this guy has good timing. But he better speed up his message, because it's 1:57.

"Mason is an awesome swimmer. Like, really good. Like, Michael Phelps good—well, he's only fifteen, but there's so much potential there. Mason's a total head case, though. You really helped Olivia Zollinger…"

Ah, Olivia. She's a young swimmer I met with last year. She must be on the team Gabe coaches.

"…and I want Mason to meet with you to get his head on straight. I coach the younger kids, not Mason's group, so I talked to Mason's coach. Coach Perry's a little sus about Mason meeting with you, honestly."

I roll my eyes. The more coaches I encounter, the more they seem like control freaks who don't want psychologists messing with their star athletes. I am familiar with the paranoia, however, after dealing with military commanders who are reluctant to refer their subordinates.

"But Coach agreed to let him see you if I called you first. And I promised you could help Mason."

Holy tacos, no pressure. Gabe ends his call by leaving his cellphone number. I add it to my iPad under my notes for Mason, though I won't be able to return Gabe's call without the permission of Mason's parents.

I walk out to the small waiting room at 1:59 to find a lanky blond boy seated next to a petite brunette. As they stand, the woman appears close to my age of forty-one. She must be Mason's mother, despite their different heights and complexions.

I smile at them. "Welcome, I'm Dr. Avery Clarkson."

"Molly McCall," she tells me as she shakes my offered hand. A few freckles dot the bridge of her nose.

Mason pauses and reddens. When at last his palm meets mine in an awkward handshake, I gawk at the size of it. I look down at his beige deck shoes, which resemble foot-long subway sandwiches. His appendages remind me of Nadia's golden retriever's massive puppy paws. Even the veterinarian underestimated her eventual adult weight of ninety pounds. Mason appears to be only a few inches taller than my 5'9", but I understand Gabe's prediction of stardom. The boy is going to be huge.

"Introduce yourself, honey," his mother instructs.

He mumbles his name as he stuffs his oversized hands into the pockets of his khaki shorts. The fried ends of his disheveled, whitish hair jut out in all directions.

Following ten minutes of clarifying confidentiality limitations and listening to the mother's side of the story (she reported no family history of mental illness, and she didn't know the complete paternal health information since Mason's father was a sperm donor), it's just me and the young swimmer in my office. When I look up from writing on my iPad, his hazel eyes seem to plead with me to say something.

"Your mom said you want to manage pressure better in swimming. Is that right, Mason?"

He nods.

"Coach Gabe left a message for me and said you've had incredible success in the pool." I leave out the bit about being a *total head case.* "What makes you think you don't manage pressure well?"

With a grimace, he looks down. "The state meet."

"The high school state meet?" I ask. After he nods, I add, "When was that?"

"October fifteenth, uh, about a week ago." With a suffering sigh, he rolls his head back, resting his neck on the sofa. "I totally let Coach Perry down."

"Your coach *said* that?" I lean forward. "That you let him down?"

"No…not exactly." Another sigh, and he sits up. "He said my two-hundred free was a painful death, like watching a slow-mo of Bruce the shark eating Nemo, starting with his tail, then fins, then chomping off his head."

My slight amusement shifts to confusion. "I thought Bruce became Nemo's friend in *Finding Nemo?*"

He huffs. "Not in this scenario. In this case Bruce is a boujee, cocky senior named Sean who mowed me down in the last fifty. I should've never lost to that guy."

"You're a freshman, right?"

"Yeah."

"A twelfth grader beat you, meaning you finished second in the state?"

He shrugs like it's no big deal.

"You finished second in the entire state of South Carolina, as a *ninth grader?* And you think that disappointed your coach?"

"I should be crushing these guys!" he roars. "How will I compete on a national level when I'm not even CEO in my own stupid state?"

I feel old trying to decipher this kid's slang, but I know empathy works for all age groups. "You feel so disappointed, and you're worried for the future."

He sags against the sofa.

"Swimming seems quite important to you."

His gaze wanders around my office, pauses on the window overlooking a lagoon, and lands on my bookshelf, where neat stacks of psychology workbooks and framed documents sit. His leg jiggles, then he rises to lift a framed photo off the shelf—my graduating class from Officer Candidate School. "Mom said you were in the Navy?"

"Yes, sir."

"You know anything about sports?" He replaces the photo. "About swimming?" He flops back down on the sofa.

I stretch my neck from side to side, weighing his question. "I specialize in recovery from trauma, especially for first responders. There's *some* overlap between the military and sports. I've met with a swimmer or two from your team, but I'm more of a runner, so there's a lot I don't know about swimming. I hope I can learn more from you."

My answer seems to satisfy him.

"How do you feel about swimming?" I ask.

His squint, followed by a long pause, makes it seem like he's never thought about that before. "You know that book, *A Tale of Two Cities?*"

I nod. "They made us read that in high school a hundred years ago."

"Yeah, us too, last month. I low-key hated the whole thing, except for the first line… That stuck with me."

"'It was the best of times; it was the worst of times,'" I recite.

"That." Mason points at me. "*That's* swimming for me." When I don't reply, he continues. "When the water's cold and fast, and I'm gliding, flowing on top, like there's a surge of energy thrusting me forward, my lats engaged, my elbows high, the only sound is my breath, and nobody can catch me, I'm flying so fast…" His eyes shine in the afternoon sunlight filtering through the blinds. "It hits different."

His voice conveys tenderness and awe, like he's describing a great love affair. His mouth curls up. "And when I drop tons of time in a race, like that time my relay split made Coach's eyes bulge out of his head and he smothered me in a hug—I seriously couldn't breathe, no cap." He shakes his head. "I told him he *had* to stop his cringey dad jokes after I swam that fast, but he still keeps them up, day after day."

"Dad jokes, huh?" I smile at his scoff. "Lay one on me."

"What does a buffalo tell his kid every morning?"

I scratch my chin.

"Bye, son."

I wince. "That's bad."

"Not as weak as, My daughter asked me to stop singing 'Wonderwall.' I said maybe."

I laugh at that one.

"Don't want to drag him, but a new joke every *day?*" He gives me a look. "At least Coach is out of town this week, in Mexico. So I'm getting a break."

Despite his disdain, I read a real fondness for his coach. After a beat, I ask, "So when is swimming 'the worst of times'?"

His dramatic sigh returns a heavy feeling to the room. "When I lose it behind the blocks. I get so nervous that I'm, like, *shaking*—it's high-key stupid. I have to stop this stressy. I need to get it under control."

Ah, anxiety. The more we try to control it, the worse it gets. "You think nervousness interferes with your performance in swimming?"

"Obvs."

I add that to my typed note. "What about school?"

He shrugs. "Nah. School's easy."

"Yeah? What's your GPA?"

Another shrug. "All As. But I haven't taken the hard classes yet."

"Is it difficult to fall or stay asleep because you're worrying about stuff?"

His eyes widen. "All the time. So extra."

"And what do you worry about?"

"Mostly swimming—it's impossible to sleep before a big meet. But sometimes I worry about school or my mom."

I continue with my questions, discovering that Mason has a good group of friends on his team and at school, and he doesn't report symptoms of panic attacks, OCD, depression, ADHD, or trauma.

"I wonder," I say, shifting from assessment to intervention. "What if you *had* held off this Sean dude and won the two-hundred freestyle at State?"

He stares at me.

"Would anything be different now?" When he doesn't answer, I add, "Would your coach still be disappointed?"

He nods. "Probs. We both know I can swim faster."

"Would you stop feeling nervous for your next race?"

A little tension seems to drain away as he exhales. "Nope." His smile cracks through. "If I won, I'd probably be even *more* mental, 'cause then I'd have to defend my state title."

I match his smile. "That would suck. But I hope you *do* feel nervous next time, because some anxiety helps your performance."

A line forms between his eyebrows as he cocks his head.

"Tell me, Mason, have you ever felt freaked out from anxiety and then swam a great race?"

He looks away as he considers my question. "Yeah, at summer sectionals."

"So, you don't need to *stop* your anxiety, just manage it a little better." As I let that sink in, I decide not to share my suspicion that he has an anxiety disorder, likely social anxiety disorder. Or maybe it's an adjustment disorder as he deals with the pressure of his increasing success. I hesitate to arrive at a diagnosis before I gather more data, especially for a client as young as Mason. "Would you like to develop skills for managing anxiety?"

One subway-sandwich shoe taps on the floor. "What kind of skills?"

"Cognitive behavioral therapy. It's a skill to help you talk to yourself in a more balanced way so you feel better. Maybe mindfulness too, as well as some communication skills to help you in your relationship with your coach."

"He's the one who really needs the help." Mason grunts.

I pause. "Are you being sarcastic, or do you mean that? If your coach is putting too much pressure on you, I might need to have a word with him."

His eyes grow big, and he stammers, "Oh, no, uh, Mrs., Dr...., uh —"

"You can call me Avery or Dr. Avery if you like."

"That was dumb, what I said." He chews on his lip. "Coach Perry's the best coach I ever had. He's the reason I've broken so many records. He'd do anything for me. I just, I just don't want to let him down, you know?"

I'm touched by his earnestness. "Clearly, swimming's important to you, and so is your coach. I think training your mind as well as your body could help take your swimming to the next level, and help you sleep better, too. Would you like to meet again?"

He nods, and after we schedule our next visit, Mason points to my seascape wall clock. "Hey, Dr. Avery, what'd the ocean say to the beach?"

I can't come up with an answer. "What?"

"Nothing. It just waved."

I groan. "You're right. Your coach *does* need help."

A few hours later, the speed dating organizer's perky voice grates on my nerves. "Ladies, you'll stay put while the men rotate from one table to the next. You'll have six minutes with each love match before the bell rings, signaling the men to move on to the next lucky lady."

I aim a longing look at the exit, and then my gaze moves to Nadia, seated at a table just outside the ring of high-tops reserved for tonight's event. My friend's strategic placement between me and the exit *has* to be intentional. I tilt down the corners of my eyes and lips in a pleading puppy-dog look, hoping she'll let me leave.

But she lifts one groomed eyebrow and shakes her head. She mouths, "Open mind," as she taps her temples with her index fingers and fans her hands outward in an arc.

Easy for her to say. Nadia's feminine charm scored her a husband years ago. Her long blond hair curls over the collar of a delicate navy blouse adorned with a stylish gold necklace, and her knee-length cream-colored skirt shows off her slender legs. Also, her beige pumps (who the hell wears heels on Hilton Head Island?) put my boyish sandals to shame. I smooth my striped sundress over my thighs and tug at the elastic waist. Is the A/C working? *Please, please don't sweat.* Though it's late October, it reached eighty-five today. This must be how Mason feels behind the blocks before a big swimming race. *Speed daters can smell fear.*

In addition to forbidding me to leave early, Nadia was full of advice at the dinner we just finished. *"You* will *feel uncomfortable,"* she said. *"That's your fear of intimacy—the activation of your avoidant attachment style. But show that anxiety who's boss. Give guys a chance instead of finding their flaws. You told me you're tired of third-wheeling it with Martin and me, right?"* Ugh, throwing my words back at me.

She also told me I have to agree to further communication with at least two men after the speed-dating event.

Bachelor number one slides onto the chair across from me after Perky rings a bell to start the torture. We stare at each other for a moment, and then he looks away as he rubs a hand over his bald head. Seconds tick by, one by one, and after an agonizing pause, he slides his palms up and down the sides of his jeans while licking his lips. Other couples chat easily around us, but he doesn't say a word. When I can't take the nervous silence any longer, I ask, "Do you live on the island?"

"Nah," he booms, and I jump a little at his volume. "Ridgeland."

Ah, a rural area that's more inland. Closer to the coast, where I live, I don't often hear a Southern twang like his. He had to drive over an hour to get to Hilton Head, compared to my thirty-minute trip. When he doesn't elaborate, I squirm.

"Don't interrogate them like they're therapy clients. Give them a chance to ask you *questions,"* Nadia said.

But I search for something else to say to quell the awkwardness. "How do you like Hilton Head?"

He scratches the collar of his plaid shirt as he glances at the modern décor of cherry wood and emerald-green leather seats. The owners converted an old bank into a bar-restaurant, with beer taps shaped like the spokes of antique safe dials and drinks titled Fat Cat and Strategic Risk. "Kinda fancy for me. I'm just a country boy."

Sir, you don't have to shout. "You live in the country? What do you do there?"

"Pig farming."

My eyes widen, and I try to rearrange my face in a neutral expression.

He must take my response as an urge to continue because he gobbles up the rest of our six minutes with a detailed description of his clean, clever, profitable pigs who sometimes escape from their pens.

Recalling Nadia's advice to let the men lead the conversation, I need to ask her: *What if they're so self-absorbed they don't know how to talk about anyone but themselves?*

My relief at the departure of Swine Farmer snaps when bachelor number two swoops in. It seems he has stolen all the hair from the last guy—I can barely see his face beneath his shaggy beard, droopy mustache, and messy long hair, all in shades of reddish-brown. ZZ Top comes to mind. I jolt as he captures my hands between his.

"If I'd known there'd be such pretty women here, I'd have tried this speed-dating thing years ago."

My lips press into a tight smile as I steal my hands back and slide them under my thighs. Again, the man dominates the conversation, but this time he presses me with questions.

Him: "Have you ever been married before?"

Me: "No."

Him: "Why?"

Me: "I guess I've focused more on my work."

Him: "What do you do?"

Me: (bracing myself) "I'm a psychologist."

Him: "Are you analyzing me now?"

Me: (Yep, he went there. How cliché.) "Are you paying me now?"

That response shuts him up for a second, but soon he resumes firing questions. I'm not accustomed to talking about myself, and my frequent sips of gin and tonic during the grilling drain my beverage too soon.

After the blessed bell rings, I see Nadia typing on her phone—the perfect time to make a run for it. But the gorgeous creature who now towers over my table freezes me to my chair.

His black hair is cut short on the sides with volume on top that accentuates his height and the sharp cut of his jaw. Smoldering blue eyes—did I just use the word *smoldering?*—land on my empty glass. He angles his head toward the bar. "Let's get you a refill."

I hesitate. "Isn't that against the rules?"

He tips his head down closer to mine, his deep voice lowering as he takes hold of my glass. "I'm not much for rules."

His aftershave's whiff of musk and bergamot zips up my spine. I find myself following him before I have time to think. The cut of his navy sport coat emphasizes broad shoulders that taper to a lean waist, and I wonder why such a hot man is fraternizing with us speed-dating losers.

When I sidle up next to him at the bar, he doesn't look at me, like he's unsurprised I followed him. *I bet every woman does your bidding.*

Ice tinkles in my glass as he draws it to his face and takes a sniff. His nose is long and straight, about the right size for his build, and there's a scar near his temple. I find his five-o'clock shadow sexy as hell.

"Gin and tonic?" He looks at me from the corner of his eye.

I nod.

"Two G and Ts," he tells the bartender. "Plymouth, if you have it."

As we wait for our drinks, he turns to me. His eyes travel up my body and linger on my unsubstantial chest, leading me to tug up one of the thin straps of my sundress, before his gaze lands on mine. "So, Avery…" he begins.

How did he?—I glance down and remember the nametag stuck to the top edge of my dress. But I feel even more at a disadvantage because there's no rectangular white sticker on his jacket.

He smirks. "Will you give that pig farmer another chance?"

I step back, and his smile broadens. "It's rude to eavesdrop," I tell him.

"Not if the farmer's so loud that you can hear him from two tables away, where my love match regaled me with photos of her *four* children. Ah." He accepts the drinks and slides a fifty-dollar bill toward the bartender. "We're good." He taps the bill.

"Thanks, man," says the bartender.

Was that sizable tip supposed to impress me? Because it does. I've worked hard to pay my student debt, and I don't want a man to mooch off me. His Adam apple bobs as he takes a sip. "Still waiting on your answer." He dips his chin as he looks at me over his glass. "Will Pig Farmer get your email address at the end of the evening?"

"Um…" I scrunch up my nose and try to forget the promise I made to Nadia. "Probably not."

"That's too bad." He shakes his head. "Missing out on free bacon for a lifetime."

My laugh escapes, sounding too loud and high-pitched. I knock back a quick drink to try to appear more mature.

He grins as I place the glass on the bar. "You have the cutest dimples."

I squint up at him. A few of the men I've dated have told me that my height, muscles, military service, and career as a psychologist intimidated them. But *I'm* the one feeling daunted by this guy. "What's your name?"

He twitches and looks down his nose at his lapel. "Where'd my nametag go?"

The organizer taps my shoulder, and I spin around.

"Didn't y'all hear the bell? Time to switch tables," Perky says.

"Oh!" I blink. No way that was six minutes—I need more time with this mystery man. But he probably won't want to share his contact information. He's way too attractive to want anything to do with me. Feeling deflated, I reach for my drink.

But he clasps my arm. "Don't go?" His big hand wrapped around my bare forearm feels warm and comforting.

Perky purses her lips as she looks at her watch. "The others are waiting. Let's go."

"I'm not interested in anyone else," he tells her. "I only want to talk to Avery."

A fountain of delight springs up within me. He's interested in *me?*

"But you *have* to finish out the night," Perky says. "That's what you signed up for. The chance to find true love."

He bristles and seems to grow even taller. "No."

A knot forms in my gut, and I realize I'm holding my breath at the standoff.

She puts a hand on her hip. "You two, let's go."

I step toward the tables, but I turn back when he thumps his glass on the bar.

"No," he repeats, louder this time. "You know what? I'm out of here."

His long strides take him out the door in a flash.

As I allow Perky to lead me back to my table, I look over at Nadia, whose open mouth slowly closes. The tight pull of her eyebrows echoes my own confusion. *What the hell just happened?*

3. JORDAN

Four Months Later

"*Pathetic!*"

My shout reverberates across eight lanes of the indoor pool. The gold-group swimmers freeze—some in the water, clutching the gutter and panting after their timed sprint, and the rest behind the blocks, stretching or talking. All chatter stops as fearful looks turn my way. *Good.* I have their attention.

"Your effort's *pathetic*," I repeat as heat flushes my face. The headache that started an hour ago has taken up full residence in my skull. "Only six weeks till our taper meet, and this is the best you got? Five one-hundreds all out from a dive, and these are your times?" I hold my stopwatch aloft. "Fifty-three in the fly, Mason?"

Still in the water, my star swimmer hangs his head.

"That's right—you should be embarrassed." Furious heartbeats vibrate my chest. Mason is throwing away his future right in front of my eyes. "You won't stand a *chance* at trials with that kind of swim!"

Mason keeps his head down. He has already qualified for six events at US Nationals in June, quite a feat for a swimmer his age. But I'll have to hide from my coaching peers if he's a disaster at that meet.

"You're done, McCall." His head whips up to look at me, his eyes big. "Get ready for dryland," I add. "You're doing extra tonight." I turn to point at the bleachers behind me, only to jump when I find them full of parents and kids from the younger groups that are swimming next. I suck in a breath. *What time is it?* My smartwatch tells me we've run ten minutes past our practice time, and I didn't even realize it.

I take a closer look at the group on the bleachers. A few of the ten-year-old boys laugh as they snap each other with their goggle straps, oblivious to the tension on the pool deck, but more than one parent drapes an arm around their young swimmer, pegging me with hostile stares, as if they're protecting their babies from me. From *me*. The man who started this club. The man who will turn their swimmers into superstars, if they work hard enough.

My gaze then lands on my wife, who stands next to the bleachers with our son and daughter on either side of her. My kids are looking down at the pool deck, but Elena meets my eyes. *Her* stare isn't hostile. Instead, her angled head and hand placed over her heart seem full of concern. A lump lodges in my throat as I remember Kim giving me that same look after our father died when we were kids. Then I realize that Elena's expression isn't one of worry. It's *pity*. Pity for the pathetic man who can't get over his sister's death.

"Coach?"

I spin back around to see a slight sixteen-year-old swimmer raise her hand from the starting block.

"Should we start the next hundred?" Lexi asks.

I blink. This should be an easy decision on my part, but I can't find words. My mouth is dry, my skull pounds, and my legs tremble. The gold group keeps staring at me, but I've got nothing.

I sense someone next to me, and I turn to my assistant coach, Gabe Diaz. He has avoided me the past few weeks, but I feel bolstered by his presence at my side. His dark eyes study me. Will he catch me if my shaking legs buckle and I crumple to the pool deck?

"How 'bout silver and bronze groups take over?" Gabe says.

I nod before clearing my throat. "Gold group, get out. Dryland starts in five minutes."

A cacophony of sound replaces the stunned silence that my belligerence created. Teenagers scoop fins, paddles, and snorkels into their mesh equipment bags, nine year olds snap on swim caps or bop each other with kickboards as they stream off the bleachers toward the pool, and parents gossip with each other, most likely complaining about my coaching.

Gabe shouts instructions for warmup as he leaves my side. I notice the same sixteen-year-old swimmer tiptoeing toward me. Lexi has pulled on gym shorts over her swimsuit and wears socks and running shoes. She blinks up at me with wary eyes. "Coach, is it okay if we eat a snack before dryland?"

The thought of food, on top of Lexi's irritating question, stirs up nausea. Her people-pleasing knows no bounds. If she doesn't take more risks in life, she'll get nowhere. "Lexi, do I always tell you to eat a snack before dryland?"

She licks her lower lip. "Yeah?"

"Then show some initiative and go do that." I try to smile at her, but my face feels so tight that I probably look constipated.

I watch her flit away, past Elena, and I know I should go talk to my wife. If only I had the energy to walk over there. The challenge of unlocking each unique swimmer's potential has always energized me, but now coaching adds to my unrelenting exhaustion. In the past, I shouted only rarely to motivate selected swimmers in need of tough love. Lately, though, my throat feels sore after screaming through these sessions.

Elena takes hold of the back end of Hailey's swim cap, while my daughter grips the front. Hailey pitches forward, and Elena stretches the turquoise latex over Hailey's mass of brown hair before helping her tuck the end of her ponytail beneath the rim of the cap. Brushing out my daughter's tangles is a nightmare ritual every morning. I've lobbied for a shorter haircut, but both Elena and Hailey have vetoed me. I must admit, I like the shine of my wife's long, dark hair, currently styled in a neat, straight look that complements her professional patterned dress and beige jacket. Of course our daughter wants to emulate her beautiful mother.

When Hailey rights herself, her ponytail creates a prominent lump that resembles a brain tumor. I stiffen. *What if one of my kids gets cancer?* My heart skips a beat as I picture a chemotherapy-bald head on my daughter, mimicking the hairless look of a newborn. Numbness seeps in, pushing down on my shoulders, spreading like the very cancer I fear. I resign myself to more tragedies around the corner, as nothing would surprise me now. God took away my sister and my father. He must hate me.

Elena bends over Hailey's swim bag on the bleacher, hunting through it. Something about her body position twists my insides. Hudson jogs up and thrusts his goggles in front of Elena's face. I hear her say something to him in an irritated tone as she gestures in my direction with her head. My ten-year-old son turns, and his deep brown eyes blink at me as he chomps on his goggle strap, seeming to assess my mood.

I bet Hudson needs help adjusting his goggles. How can I help him, though, when my hands won't stop shaking? As I try to compel my feet to step forward, he rushes off to the blocks. Hudson stops by Gabe, who finishes unscrewing a water bottle cap for one swimmer before assisting my son with his goggles.

My cheeks flame with embarrassment as I recall Hudson's tears this morning. In the chaos of rushing him and his sister off to school, I'd found his expensive gym shoes outside, drenched from a cold February rainstorm. The storm had awoken me at three a.m., and my inability to fall back asleep was maddening. But I shouldn't have yelled at Hudson like that. I shouldn't have called him a selfish disaster who's dragging down his family.

"Jordan." Elena's manicured hand rests on my wrist, and I wince. "You okay?"

Her light perfume settles over me — too bad the scent doesn't help loosen the tension in my muscles. I'm wound so tight that probably nothing can. "Just tired," I answer.

"Another rough night of sleep?" she asks. Her wedge sandals bring her closer to my height, but she still has to look up to talk to me.

I swallow and nod, jealous that she slept through the thunder.

"Have you eaten anything today?"

"Yeah." I feel my eyebrows pull together as the splashing of forty kids swimming behind us fills my ears. When *did* I last eat something? Elena blended smoothies for the kids and me before she left for work. "The smoothie—"

"No." Her lips press together. "Yours was on the counter, untouched, when I got home from working with my buyer."

We're lucky Elena's real estate business has taken off the past few years, given my paltry salary as swim coach. But her busy schedule has landed more of the childcare on me.

"You have to eat." She roots around in her large handbag and hands me a protein bar like I'm a child on a field trip. "And you need to get some sleep."

My jaw clenches as I pocket the bar. She's right, but it ticks me off, all the same.

"When're you going to call Wyatt back?"

The sickening thought of talking to anyone connected to Kim who might want to revisit Baja—*no way.* I already can't stop thinking about the scene from that hospital in La Paz, when Wyatt dashed up to me, frantic about Kim's condition. Once I told him she'd bled out before surgery, his eyes filled with tears. His guttural cries had stopped me from telling him the whole story. He lunged for me, clutching the thin scrubs I wore over my swimsuit, and I'd held him as his body racked with sobs.

But I didn't cry at all. There's something severely wrong with me.

"Jordan." My wife stares at me. "When will you call your doctor?"

This conversation squeezes my head. "I don't *need* a doctor!"

"You—" She stops herself, then forces out an exhale. We've had this discussion before, and I bet she's trying to think up a new strategy, based on the tic of her eyebrow. She's good at sales, but I don't want her to sell me. "Then what *do* you need, Jordan?"

Her question hits me in the solar plexus, blasting me like a piece of shrapnel. What the hell do I need? *To turn back the clock,* I think. *To convince my sister not to take that damn swim vacation, even though I'm the one who invited her.* I close my eyes and see blood pooling on the boat deck. *To stop being so selfish and egotistical.* If only I'd let Kim stay back and swim with me instead of demanding that she go on ahead... Revulsion crawls up my throat, but I force it down with a hard swallow.

Elena's hand rests on my wrist again, circling it like a handcuff. "You've lost a lot of weight."

My heart rate spikes as I fight the urge to shake her off. I know I'm not as muscular as I once was, but is she saying she finds me unattractive now?

"The house is a total mess. You don't help at all," she continues. "We've been out of milk for days, and the school keeps calling when you don't pack lunch for the kids." Her lips press into a line. "I don't want to be a single parent, Jordan." The pain in my chest intensifies.

"To top it all off, I was late to my meeting this morning because you didn't gas up the cars like you promised."

I cringe. More forgotten tasks, in addition to being late submitting the meet entries for the senior meet next month. I'm lucky a swim parent on the Lionfish board caught the missed deadline and begged to get our swimmers in. But that screw-up hardly endeared me to the board. The board president was one of the parents aiming disapproving stares from the bleachers earlier. We'll need Elena's income to carry us after I get fired.

"But the *worst* part?" She lets go of my wrist as her hands lift to her shoulders, spread out, and shake to emphasize her point. *Uh-oh.* I've activated her temper, inherited from her Czech father. She hates it when I don't respond to her in an argument. "You've become mean." Her eyes flare. "Cruel."

I swallow as I look around, hoping no one is witnessing this tongue-lashing. I deserve it, but I wish it didn't have to happen in front of my team.

"I heard about the awful things you said to Hudson this morning." The pressure in her voice reminds me of the hiss from our cat, Colby, when his brother takes their wrestling too far.

I want to fold into myself. I eye the pool exit and fight the urge to sprint out the door.

She reaches for my cheek and yanks my head back to face her. "I've given you leeway since October. I've given you time. But now it's February, and you're even worse!" Her last sentence echoes around us, and she looks to her left, seeming to realize how loud her voice has become. She removes her hand from my face and brushes it down her jacket. She's not done with me yet, though, and she steps closer while jabbing me in the chest. The blaze in her eyes stops me from backing up like I want to. "It's one thing if you treat me poorly. But I *won't* stand by and let you hurt our children."

What's she saying? My shoulders lock in place, my arms immobile at my sides. Will she leave me? Take away my kids? Fear closes my throat. "I worry about the kids every day," I say in a strangled voice. "I would *never* hurt them."

"Well, news flash, you just did." She huffs out a breath. "Hudson had a giant stomachache after school, and Hailey didn't want to go to practice, either. When I asked why, she confessed that you'd screamed at them this morning."

Even my sweet daughter no longer likes me. "If you think I'm such an awful parent, why'd you bring them to practice?"

"Because swimming is their happy place!" The lines around her mouth grow taut. "At least it used to be." She shakes her head. "I also thought you'd apologize to Hudson when you got the chance." Her phone dings, and she reaches for it in her purse. "But then you scream at your team, and when your son looks to you for help, you stand here frozen, like, like a mannequin."

A cold, unfeeling mannequin. She doesn't say those words, but I know she's thinking them. I'm either cruel or cold, evidently.

She stuffs her phone back into her purse. "Great. I'm late to another meeting."

Because of you, she must be thinking. "Then you should leave before you blame me for anything else in your life."

Her eyes narrow as she purses her lips. "Get some help, Jordan." She turns on her heel and stomps off across the pool deck.

I close my eyes and exhale a shaky breath as my headache enflames to a hotter intensity. I've berated myself all day for being the worst father in the world, and now I can add a second crown: world's worst husband. An added bonus is that my wife thinks I belong in a psych ward.

The back of my neck prickles with paranoia—maybe I *do* belong in the nuthouse. Once I spin around and look across the pool, I see gold-group swimmers gaping at me before snapping into action at their various workout stations. Mason laces his hands over the crown of his head as one leg bends forward into the perfect front lunge while Lexi crunches up for an ab workout on an exercise ball. Both of them sneak looks at me between reps. They should know the dryland routine well enough that they don't need me to lead them through it, but I wonder how much they witnessed of that marital spat. Elena yelling at me had better not undermine my authority with my team. They're all I have left.

The lulling sound of water lapping over the gutters redirects my focus to the younger swimmers. In the far lane, Hailey grins at a fellow eight-year-old teammate before she pushes off the wall at the deep end to swim the most uncoordinated butterfly I've seen. She dives so deep with each stroke that I fear she's drowning, but then she pops up again to take a huge breath. I don't know where the genetic lottery failed, but my kids are two of the slowest on the team. Hailey does look like she's having fun, though. When she finally makes it to the shallow end, she giggles at the teammate who submerges then jumps up with a little cheerleading hand motion. Hailey mimics her, bursting out of the water with both hands punching air, hollering, "Gggoooooo, Lionfish!"

Assistant Coach Suzy, a gray-haired woman whose children swam in college, tries to corral the jumping beans so she can introduce the next drill. But when Suzy can't calm them down, she doesn't yell. She does her own cheer, complete with choreography, which earns her claps, laughs, and rapt attention from the eight- and nine-year-old swimmers. I don't often envy Suzy for coaching swimmers with such low attention spans, but tonight, I long for the simplicity and freedom of childhood. A time before family members died and left me forever.

"Hudson, you okay?" Gabe's voice draws my attention to the deep end, where my assistant coach kneels by the block in a closer lane. My son clutches the gutter with one hand, his head mostly submerged and his face aimed at the ceiling as he gasps for air. I freeze. After a long moment, Hudson pulls himself up so his armpit hugs the gutter, and I can see the rapid rise and fall of his chest as he raises his goggles to his forehead. I don't see any blood on him, nor is there blood in the water.

"Good job, buddy!" Gabe extends his open hand, and it takes some effort for Hudson to lift his skinny arm for a high-five. My assistant coach rises to standing and claps. "Rest up before we try it again."

Try *what* again? It looks like my son barely survived the first swim. In a flash, I'm by Gabe's side. "What're you doing?" I demand, my breath as short as my son's.

Gabe's chin dips as he studies me. "Underwaters."

My mouth hangs open. He's making ten-year-olds swim without a breath the entire length of the pool? Is he insane? "No. That's too dangerous."

"Jordan." Gabe gestures to my son. "Hudson just made it all the way underwater, for the first time ever! It's a great accomplishment."

My heart pulses in my ears. "No," I pant as I clutch my pounding head, squeezing fistfuls of coarse hair. "What if he blacks out? What if he's too deep to get to the surface? You don't care at all about their safety!"

Gabe squints at me. "I *do* care about their safety. Also, their improvement." He points across the pool. "The gold group needs you, Coach. I got this."

He's trying to dismiss *me*, his boss? Complete lack of respect. Heat flushes up my neck, and my hands fly out to the side. *No!*

"Next one on the top!" Gabe hollers to the silver group.

I glance at the pace clock and see there's 10 seconds before the sendoff. I want to scream, put an end to the danger engulfing Hudson, but I can't move. It's hard to get air. My gaze darts to my son, who watches me with wide eyes. *I have to stop him!* But it feels like I'm floating, ungrounded, out of my body, out of my mind. I look down the length of my arm to my shaking hand. I wear a white glove covered in smears of blood, gripping Kim's hand as we bounce hard on the waves. Wind rushes past my ears, and salt stiffens my skin. Her hand feels limp in mine.

"No!" I roar. Looking up, I see Gabe walking toward the shallow end. A desperate scan of the lanes in front of me shows placid calm as twenty kids drown in the depths below from holding their breath till they're unconscious. "Stop!" I hustle to Gabe and lunge for him. "You have to stop them. They're drowning!"

He tries to shake off my grip on his arm. "Get off me, Jordan! They're fine—calm down!"

I'm so jacked from adrenaline that I can't see straight, but I have to rescue my son. I push away from Gabe. I'm about to dive in, shoes and all, when Hudson's head pops up near the halfway mark. He inhales a big breath and frowns at us. "Sorry," he calls.

"Finish up freestyle," Gabe tells him before turning to glare at me. "No wonder he didn't make it, with you freaking him out like that."

"I'm not the one putting his *life* in danger!"

Gabe plows a hand through his black hair. "What the hell are you talking about? Hudson's totally fine, just like all the silver-group swimmers."

"You're saying I don't know what's best for my son?" I step closer, glad I have the height advantage with this young punk. "That I don't know what's best for my team?" I stab a finger toward his face. "This is *my* team. Not yours. You got that, Gabe?"

"Coach Perry."

We both turn to Lexi's father, an attorney who serves as president of the team's board. Steve wears a white button-down shirt and navy slacks, far surpassing my T-shirt, shorts, and flip-flops in terms of professionalism. "You're not acting like yourself, Coach. Let's call it a night so you can head home."

I place my hands on my hips and try to slow my breath. "And why would I leave in the middle of practice?"

"Not much practice getting done tonight." Steve gives a rigid smile.

The cacophony of sound in my brain halts, forcing me to notice the dead silence in the pool. My eyes are the only part of my body that move as I take in the scene. Silver- and bronze-group swimmers stare at me slack-jawed from the shallow end, and my group no longer even pretends to be doing their dryland exercises. Motion from the end lane catches my attention, and I see Hailey brush the back of her hand under her eye. The telltale tremble of her lips confirms that she's crying. So now I've made both my kids cry today.

"Hey, Jordan." Suzy's comforting voice matches the warmth of her hand on my elbow. "How 'bout we talk in your office for a bit? I want to review the next set with you. I'm not sure how to explain it best."

I look down at her kind eyes and guileless smile, knowing full well she doesn't need my help with coaching. But in this little group intervention, it seems she's drawn the short straw as the nominee to get me out of here. She's a savvy mother and grandmother, and it's a wise move to help me save face, given I'm such an egomaniac.

I feel reverberations of adrenaline buzz down my spine. "Sure, Suzy." On numb legs, I follow her to the small coach's office near the locker rooms. Behind me, I hear Gabe shouting at the teenagers on deck to resume their strength training. Guilt presses up my throat as I realize I've left him coaching three groups at once.

A fifty-pound brick presses against my collarbone, and I collapse onto a squeaky chair behind my desk. I aim a weak smile at Suzy after she closes the door. "I see what you're doing here. Thank you."

She takes a seat in the chair across from my desk. "It's tough to lose control."

I deflate. "I'm turning into a rageaholic."

"Not just control over your emotions." Her eyes crease as she shakes her head. "Losing control over your children as they grow up." Her gentle voice reminds me why my daughter loves swimming for her. "Or losing control over life in general. Over bad things happening."

She doesn't mention Kim's name, but it hangs in the air between us. Suzy met Kim at one of Hudson's swim meets, and they bonded over their favorite musicians. Now I can't stand to hear a Shawn Mendes song. I swallow, fighting the nausea that creeps up my throat. "Want to talk about it?" Suzy asks.

Definitely not. "Look, I appreciate you trying to help. But before we came in here, I saw Hailey crying from my meltdown. Would you go talk to her? Let Gabe go back to coaching his group? That's what would really help."

She watches me for a long moment. "You got it."

"Thank you." Before she leaves, I add, "You're an excellent coach, Suzy." *Much better than me.* Maybe she can become the head coach after I'm fired. My team will be far better off without me.

Once I'm alone, I feel the full crush of my fatigue. But I don't want to go home to bed, since Elena might be there. I can't face her. And I don't think I'm allowed back on deck. The parents are probably holding an emergency meeting to boot me. I guess I'm stuck in my office, listening to thrumming water from a kicking set through the open door.

When I shift in my seat, I hear a crinkle in my pocket. Extracting the protein bar brings an ache to my chest. Elena is good at nurturing me, even when I reject her help. She deserves better. I unwrap the bar and take a bite, surprised it tastes so good. After wolfing it down, I find a can of sparkling water in my small fridge. Several bottles of orange juice, reserved for a young swimmer with diabetes, also catch my eye. I drain one of them, and the ice-cold juice soothes my throat.

I lean forward and cradle my face in my hands. How have I made such a complete disaster of my life? Kim would be mortified to call me her brother. But I can't seem to right myself. I can't get back to who I was—not for Kim, not for Elena, not for Hudson and Hailey or my swimmers. I can't get unstuck. I can't change the past, and I can't stop it from haunting me. When will that morning in Mexico stop drowning me?

A knock on the office door jolts me awake. Relief sweeps over me when I realize I fell asleep without even trying. And no nightmares this time.

"Coach?"

Furious blinks clear my bleary vision as I peer up from my bent-over position on my desk. A bare-chested, wet-haired Mason McCall stands in my office doorway. When did he get so tall? I watch a drop-let—sweat or leftover pool water—drip off his chin onto my floor.

"Uh, sorry." He shifts his weight from one big running shoe to another as he runs his thumbs along the waistband of his gym shorts. "What should I do for extra dryland?"

As I sit up, he scratches his pectoral muscle, and I gawk at the expanding definition of his chest and abs. When did his body transition from boy to man? He's only fifteen, but the indented groove above each hip is more reminiscent of my college teammates than a high schooler. His mother, Molly, must've found an Olympic wrestler for her sperm donor.

A yawn overtakes me, and I glance at my watch. "It's late, Mase. Don't worry about that now. You can go home."

He frowns and doesn't move.

"Hey." I clear my throat. "I shouldn't have yelled at you. That was about me, not you. Sorry for my meltdown."

"No, you were right! I was big yikes on those hundreds. I need to do better."

His effort to take responsibility for his actions impresses me, but I don't want him to shoulder the blame for my irritability. It's not his fault Kim died. That's mine alone.

"Can I…?" He points to the chair, and I nod. Once he's seated, he starts fiddling with the tie of his shorts. "I gots to confess, Coach." He looks at the wall, then back at me. "I was up late playing video games. That's why I sucked."

Wow. No doubt about it—he *is* becoming a man. "Now I gots to confess, Mase. I didn't get enough sleep either."

"Not a shocker," he replies. "You're looking extra faded."

Despite my exhaustion, I chuckle. *Faded* is the perfect word for how I feel.

His hazel eyes roam over me. "You okay, Coach?"

No. But I won't tell him the truth. I'm the adult. I shouldn't burden my swimmers with my troubles. "You're really impressing me, Mason. If my coach had yelled at me like that, I'd have hightailed it out of there and done my best to avoid him afterwards. No way would I approach him and ask for more work."

He shrugs like it's no big deal, but I do want to learn the secret behind his sudden maturity. I ask, "What made you decide to come to this office?"

"CBT," he says after a moment.

I squint at him. "What?"

"Cognitive behavioral therapy," he explains, "with Dr. Avery."

A memory of Gabe imploring me to get Mason into counseling rumbles at the back of my mind. But it's faint and fuzzy, probably because it happened before Mexico. My life changed the second Kim took her last breath, and I'll never be the same. When Mason keeps talking, I try to refocus.

"She's helping me change the stupid thoughts in my head. Like tonight, I was thinking, 'Coach hates me. He thinks I'm a giant waste of his time.' And I wanted to hide under the bleachers."

I recoil in horror.

Mason points at my open mouth. "I knew that was low-key sus. Dr. Avery helped me see all the times you've gone out of your way to help me, that you being tough on me is to make me better. That you're going through a hard time, not acting like yourself, but you'll pull out of it."

This kid giving me such grace when I've been an empty shell for four months? It's much more than I deserve. I keep showing up at practice, but I've been absent as his coach in all the ways it matters. My nose burns. For a second, I fear I'll start crying. My heart rate spikes, and I blink extra fast. I'm somehow able to suppress the emotion when Mason keeps talking.

"So, I told myself, 'Coachman's extra pissy tonight, but that's not on you. He needs a vibe check. The worst that can happen is he yells at you some more.'"

I nod, taking that in. "That sounds smart. I'm glad you didn't hide under the bleachers." I gesture to his muscles. "I don't think you'd fit."

He grins. "I'm slaying, right?" He flexes one arm, which is still a bit scrawny, but he's only in his first year of high school. "No cap, that's the first semi-joke you've told in forever. Can't believe I admitted to Dr. Avery that I kinda miss your dad jokes."

My shoulders drop. Posting a joke of the day on the whiteboard feels like another lifetime. "You talk about me in therapy?"

"Yeah, she's easy to talk to. Did you know she runs marathons? She was in the Navy? *Bussin'*. Anyway, I told her you're the best coach I've ever had, but I keep letting you down."

I'm an undeserving wretch. A lump rises in my throat, but I swallow it. *Don't cry. Don't cry.* My voice wobbles, but I'm able to get out, "I fear *I'm* the one letting you down, Mase."

He shakes his head. "Dr. Avery told me you might say something like that. She said, um, what happened, uh..." He looks down. After a beat, his eyes rise to meet mine. "She said your sister dying in a tragic accident would flatten anyone."

I flinch. Everyone has tiptoed around that word, *dying*. *"Kim passed away." "So sorry you lost your sister." "She's in a better place."* But this Avery woman is dead-on correct. I *am* flattened. Steamrolled. Ruined forever.

4. AVERY

As I sip strong coffee while rocking in the deck chair, I snuggle deeper into my soft hoodie and admire the lush greenery and lagoon. The curved, graceful neck of a white bird perched on the shore (maybe an egret?) mesmerizes me. In the misty chill of a February morning, the egret makes a dry, croaking squeal that sounds more reminiscent of a Jurassic jungle than the South Carolina coast.

I can't believe this is my house. Or rather, *our* house. The diamond sparkling from my ring finger still surprises me every time it catches my eye. I can't believe I'm married.

The rolling sound of our sliding glass door draws my gaze over my shoulder, and out walks my husband. A thrill zips through me when I use that word, *husband*. I'm married, actually married! Avery Clarkson — Miss Avoidant Attachment Style, Miss So Afraid of Commitment that She Can't Even Get One Tattoo, Miss Navy Officer Who Always Follows the Rules. But I'm sick of following the rules. I'm tired of being afraid.

Brandon comes up behind me and leans down to nuzzle his dark, stubbled cheek against mine. His bergamot scent, with an overlay of mint toothpaste, smells as yummy as he did that first night I met him at speed dating. Was that just four months ago? "Enjoying your morning, Mrs. Brown?"

I smile. "It's breathtaking here." I'm not just referring to the landscaping, but also the five-bedroom house behind us. I could never afford such a luxury home on Hilton Head Island, but Brandon insisted this second house we toured was the perfect place to start our lives together. He's an investment banker who didn't balk at the multimillion-dollar price tag. My longer commute to the office is negligible when I get to live in such paradise.

After he lowers himself into the wicker rocker next to me, I notice the muss of his thick black hair. I hide a smirk as I recall clutching his head with trembling hands as he ravaged me last night. I've read that women reach their sexual peak later than men, but I'd say our libidos are both kicking strong at ages forty-one and forty-five, respectively.

"No run this morning?" Brandon asks.

I hold up my coffee mug. "Need to energize first after that work-out last night."

We share a knowing smile. When the egret produces another staccato screech, Brandon shakes his head. "That thing sounds like a Dilophosaurus."

"*Right?*" I'm incredulous at our mind-meld. This man gets me.

Brandon shrugs down into the chair and curls his hands under his chin. I squint at him as he makes what sounds like a purr. What is up with him? In a flash, he jumps out of the chair as he circles his arms in a wide arc, flashing a vicious glare and a sneering hiss from his bared teeth. Damn, he's tall. So powerful. It takes a second to grasp that he's mimicking the dinosaur from the Stephen Spielberg movie. I realize I'm holding my breath, and I exhale with a laugh.

He retakes his seat. "How many miles today?"

I look at my watch. "Ooh, I have a new client at eleven." A challenging one, I anticipate. "Only time for three, four at most." I stand and collect my coffee mug.

"Hey."

I halt my departure and turn to him.

"I want to run with you."

I pause. "Oh." He has accompanied me a few times, his long legs pushing us to an uncomfortable pace the first bit, before he burns out and begs me to walk with him the rest of the way. Running is my chance to clear my mind and exorcise the ghosts of clients' emotional pain, and I don't want his incessant chatter interrupting my flow.

"You'd rather go alone?"

The downturn of his deep blue eyes tugs at my heart. I return to that October night when Nadia and I left the bar after speed dating. I shuffled to her car, despondent that the one man who'd sparked any interest had absconded before I even learned his name. The speed-dating organizer had identified him as Brandon, but she'd also delivered the blow that she couldn't share his email address because he hadn't stuck around till the end of the evening.

Noticing my hopelessness, Nadia had suggested we walk the beach in the twilight. I try to capitalize on the opportunity to feel grainy sand beneath my feet anytime I visit the island, so I'd agreed. As we walked, the ocean breeze had lifted my hair off my bare shoulders and swayed the sandals drooping from one of my hands. Nadia let the lulling waves soothe me while we walked in silence. After providing time for me to grieve another dating fail, she'd praised me for taking risks and tolerating discomfort. She'd just launched into a pep talk when we came upon a tall man sitting on the sand, staring at the ocean. *Brandon.*

There was just enough daylight left for me to see that he was crying. Once he spotted us, he dipped his head and scrubbed his hands over his face. With alarm, I looked at Nadia, and her hand covering her mouth echoed my sympathy. Seeing such a strong man in tears had set off a tender ache in my chest. He must have been embarrassed to have us to stumble upon him during an emotional moment, and I wondered if we should leave. But our psychologist sensibilities had kicked in, and we'd lowered to sit on either side of him.

"*Is this okay?*" I'd asked.

Brandon had glanced at Nadia, then over at me. He'd sniffed. "*Yeah.*" He'd swiped his cheek with the back of his hand and shook his head. "*Sorry about that.*"

"I'm *the sorry one,*" I'd said. "*Didn't mean to interrupt your moment.*"

He'd managed a faint smile. "*My moment just got better, believe me. Two beautiful ladies flanking me — the night's looking up.*"

Pleased he didn't view us as an intrusion, I'd leaned forward and gestured toward the attractive blonde on his left, hoping her wedding ring was obvious. *"This is my friend, Nadia. She's the one who forced me to come to speed dating."*

"Then I'm grateful to you, Nadia." He'd reached across his body to shake her hand. *"I'm Brandon Brown."*

Nadia had given a girlish giggle, one I'd never heard from her before. She'd seemed as charmed as I felt. *"So that's your name, Mystery Man. Avery was crushed you ran off with no way to find you."*

My mouth had dropped open as Brandon rotated toward me. I'd hoped he couldn't tell how much I was blushing after Nadia's overshare. In the encroaching dusk, I'd seen a twinkle in his eyes, still wet from tears. His eyes were so deep, so magnetic. But he'd broken our gaze and let out a long breath. *"That was rude of me. Sorry to rush out of there without a proper goodbye."*

"No need to explain." I'd thought about patting his knee, but hesitated.

"But I do need to explain." He'd pointed at his face. *"Crying after running off—it's not my usual behavior. Not my finest moment."* He'd sighed as he stared out at the darkening purple hues of the Atlantic Ocean. After long seconds ticked by, he'd said, *"This was my first time trying to date, since…"* His jaw had ticked. *"Since my wife died."*

The ache in my chest had intensified. I'd wanted to comfort him, but I couldn't find words.

Nadia had spoken for me. *"Tonight must've stirred up painful memories."*

"It did." He'd cleared his throat. Though Nadia had been the one to offer empathy, Brandon had swiveled to me. *"When that annoying organizer kept harping about finding a love match, I lost it. Turned and ran."* He'd pointed at the sea. *"Came here."*

I'd nodded. *"She was annoying—way too cheerful. I would've left, too, if Nadia hadn't threatened me and blocked my exit."*

My comment had earned a slow smile from Brandon, and what a stunning one it was. A slight parting of his lips, a gradual spread tugging up the corners of his mouth, finishing with a dazzle of straight, white teeth—I'd felt his smile deep inside of me. Though I didn't know the man, I'd found myself craving more of those smiles.

"Speaking of leaving," Nadia had interrupted.

Brandon's smile had vanished.

Noooo! I'd panicked a bit myself. I couldn't leave this hunky man so soon after we met.

"*I have to get home and put my daughter to bed,*" Nadia had explained as she gathered her beige heels in one hand. "*She hasn't been feeling well, and my husband always lets her stay up too late.*" She'd stood and brushed sand off her skirt. "*Ready, Avery?*"

Brandon had clasped my left wrist. "*Stay?*" His eyes had turned down, imploring me. "*I can drive you home.*"

I'd had no choice but to nod. Those eyes had held me in place.

Now on the backyard deck, holding a coffee mug with a banana peel shoved inside, I take in Brandon's identical expression when asking to join my run. I shiver from the cool breeze, just like I had that night before Brandon draped his sport coat over my shoulders. After Nadia left, we'd talked for hours. His goodbye kiss on the porch of my townhome had hit me down to my toes. That kiss, and all the ones that followed, had cured my fear of commitment. Turned out I just needed to find the right man.

"It would be *great* for you to run with me," I tell him, and he rewards me with his brilliant grin.

He rises to his impressive height. "Meet by the door in five, Cute Stuff."

Later that morning, still warm from my run and quick shower, I extend my hand to the man standing in the waiting room. He doesn't fill up the space as much as Brandon does, but he still has about five inches on me. "You must be Jordan Perry."

Beneath his black ballcap, his brown eyes dart right and left, and I'm glad the chairs are empty. No client for Nadia this hour. Jordan's faded, denim-blue T-shirt hangs off him, but his grip is strong.

Once we're seated in my office, I learn this is his first foray into counseling. I review confidentiality parameters, adding, "Though I won't share your private information with Mason McCall or anyone else, he has given me permission to speak to you about his therapy. He's told me such good things about you."

"Hmph." Jordan's head sags as he stares at my batik area rug. He rests his elbows on his spread knees, his hands clasped together.

When he doesn't elaborate, I ask, "That surprises you? Mason praising you?"

"He gives me far too much credit."

Is that a show of humility, or low self-worth?

Jordan looks up at me, and I see the creases of fatigue weighing down his eyes. *Haunted* eyes. "Mason's the reason I came in here." He makes a derisive sound in the back of his throat. "Well, that and my wife's threat to leave me if I don't get help." He points at my ring finger. "You know what it's like to be married, how your spouse zings you with the naked truth when you least want to hear it."

After two months, it still feels surreal when a client comments on my marital status. I almost tell Jordan how brave he is to start counseling, but his earlier deflection of my compliment holds me back. "How did Mason factor in to you scheduling the appointment?"

"I don't know what advice you're giving Mase, but he's swimming great, doing great—and not just in the pool. He's matured five years since he started seeing you." He grimaces. "He's probably more mature than I am at this point."

"What makes you question your maturity?" I angle my head.

He swallows. "Drinking too much. And my anger…it's out of control. I'm basically throwing temper tantrums."

"Temper tantrums?"

He huffs. "Freaking out. Yelling. At *children*."

There's a weighty feeling in the air, one I recognize in an instant: *shame.* "That sounds uncharacteristic for a man famous for his dad jokes."

"You heard about those, too." His mouth presses tight. "I, uh, haven't been in the mood to joke lately."

"Has it been difficult to feel positive emotions, like joy?"

His nod propels me to my next question.

"Hard to have loving feelings for people close to you?"

His eyes expand, and I read guilt in his expression. "I love my wife, my kids. I do. I just…" He lets out a long breath. "I just don't want to be around them. Anywhere near them, actually. They're not doing anything wrong; I'm the one who's super touchy all the time. It's my fault."

"How long has this been going on?" I ask. "The increased irritability, the decreased joy?"

"Since..." He looks out the window at the lagoon. "Since, you know."

I do know. Mason tried to hold back tears in our second session, but his eyes welled up when he told me about the freak accident that had killed Jordan's sister. *"How could this happen?"* Mason had sobbed. *"Coach is based! One of the good guys. It's so unfair."*

Jordan's hunched body position is similar to Mason's that day, minus the tears—minus the emotional processing of the trauma. My voice gentles. "Since your sister died in October."

Jordan doesn't move.

"How devastating," I say. "Such a tragedy. It must've been horrific for you." I imagine the engulfing heartache of losing a sibling. "When the waves of grief crash over you, it feels like you're drowning, like your heart breaks anew every time you think about her."

His head inches up, and he gives me a direct look for the first time. A moment passes between us, a moment of visceral connection. His eyes tell me, *Thank God you said the words I can't say. Thank God you understand.*

"What was her name?"

He jiggles his leg. "Kim."

"How old was she?"

"She'd just turned forty, two years older than me." His mouth crackles a bit, like he's dehydrated. "We were there, in Baja, for her birthday." His teeth clench. "I'm the one who planned the trip."

I bet he's using that to blame himself. "How close were you and Kim?"

"She's my best friend. Was my best friend." He pauses. "Well, except for Wyatt—he's one of our college teammates." He grimaces. "He was our teammate. *Is* our teammate. He's my college teammate, I guess."

His confusion with terminology tells me he hasn't had much practice talking about his sister since her death. Past tense, present tense—he's just *tense*.

"But Wyatt lives on the other coast, in Washington state," adds Jordan. "Too far."

I nod. "How have you been sleeping?"

"Sleep?" He gives a bitter laugh. "What's that?"

"Nightmares, then?"

He looks to the side and rasps, "Sometimes."

I take a bottled water from my mini fridge and offer it to him. "What do you dream about?"

He swigs water and presses his lips together. "Stuff from when we were young." After a sigh, he says, "A few times, I'm in that panga... with her." His body stills. He seems far away. "All the blood." Seconds tick by, and I watch the rise and fall of his chest. Quick shakes of his head bring him back, and he blinks at me. "A panga's a small boat—"

"I'm familiar with the term." I smile at him.

"Right." He lets out a breath. "What'd you do in the Navy?"

Now *I'm* the one who wants to avoid talking about the past. "Well, I didn't get into the Naval Academy." Much to my father's disappointment. "So, I did ROTC at my undergrad, served active duty, then the Reserves during grad school." Leaving the Navy and becoming a psychologist multiplied my father's disapproval.

"Mason told me you're a runner. You ran in college?"

I shake my head. I wasn't good enough to do that, either. "According to Mason, you were quite the swimmer yourself."

He scoffs. "Not like that kid. I didn't even qualify for the Olympic Trials, but if Mase swims like he's capable of in June, he could legit make the US team at age fifteen." A swallow bobs his Adam's apple. "All he needs is a good coach to lead him there."

I look at him. "That's not you?"

"They're going to fire me soon. Can't believe I haven't gotten the axe already."

"What would cause you to be fired?"

He tells me about panicking when his son swam underwater at practice, and my suspicion about his diagnosis solidifies. But I have more information to gather first. "Where'd you grow up?"

"Cincinnati, Ohio."

"Were your parents married?"

He nods.

"How well did they get along?"

After a beat, he says, "They were perfect together."

This time, the past tense is more practiced. The fairy tale also sounds rehearsed. No family is perfect—I should know. "What happened?"

Silence stretches on, and I let it. Jordan clenches his fist. "Dad passed away when I was twelve. It was...cancer."

More death. "How shattering."

"Kim got us through it."

But who will get him through *her* death? "And your mom?"

"She's a great mom, of course. She married my stepdad. They're still in Cincinnati."

"Any family history of mental-health disorders?"

That makes him frown. "No." He thinks for a moment. "No."

After further assessment of his past and current functioning, I take a screening questionnaire from my desk, attach it to a clipboard, and hand it to him. "I want you to answer these twenty questions about how you've been feeling the past month. Is that okay with you?"

He reads the title of the form. "PCL-five. What's this?"

"It will ask you how the accident in Baja has affected you—how much it has stuck with you. For example, the first question asks about disturbing memories of the event and how much they've bothered you."

As he fills in his answers, I edit what I've written so far on my iPad while taking peeks at his body language. If possible, his shoulders seem to hunch higher with each question. His grip on the pen is so tight that I'm surprised it hasn't broken in his hand.

"What does this one about taking too many risks mean?" he asks.

"You told me you've been drinking more since Kim died," I answer. "If you're drunk driving or getting into bar fights, that could be an example. Or gambling with money you don't have. Or not locking your doors because you say, 'Screw it, I'm too tired to care.'"

I once had a Marine client who had unprotected sex with men she'd just met after her trauma of being sexually assaulted.

Jordan nods, and a few minutes later, he hands me the completed form. Beads of sweat dot the dark circles beneath his eyes, and he wipes the back of his hand across his forehead, but doesn't remove his ballcap. It's a cool winter day, and I wonder why he's sweating. When I score his answers, I understand.

"Jordan, this is a screening questionnaire for PTSD—post-traumatic stress disorder."

His nose scrunches up, like he smells something bad, and he strokes his right thigh. "That's just for guys in combat, though."

I shake my head. "Common misperception. PTSD can occur after all sorts of trauma—severe car accidents, natural disasters, sexual abuse, sudden death..."

He swallows.

"You scored sixty-three."

His hand stops sanding the leg of his jeans.

I continue, "Scores above thirty-three suggest PTSD."

"So I almost doubled it." He huffs out a breath. "Quite the over-achiever."

At first, I think his attempt at humor is a good sign, but then, his sour laugh slices through the air. "My sister *bleeds out*, but I don't get one scratch on me. Men go and die for our country, but I'm the one crying in the corner."

I want to ask him, *Are* you crying, though? But he keeps ranting.

"I'm the one who can't get over it. How *pathetic*." He chops his arms through the air to emphasize his point. The self-hatred rolls off him in waves.

"You're angry at yourself."

His arms collapse to the sofa.

"You think you're weak."

He leans back against the cushions. "Yeah." He stares at me. "Don't you?"

I consider his question. "I don't think you're weak. But I'd probably judge myself for struggling, the same as you." I internalized my father's criticism like a champ. "Listen, there's a proposal to change the name of this diagnosis to post-traumatic stress *injury*. When that coral cut your sister, it cut you, too."

His tongue sweeps across his lower lip as his blinks gain speed.

"Of course this tragic accident affected you," I say. "Losing a family member—especially your best friend—would devastate anyone."

He averts his eyes as his chin quivers. *Let yourself process the emotion, Jordan.* But I can see his jaw clench as he fights off the feelings. After a few moments of silence, I hold the questionnaire aloft. "There are four symptoms of PTSD, of getting stuck in the trauma. The first one is called intrusions." I point to his responses to the first five questions. "You marked 'extremely' for feeling really upset when something reminds you of your sister's death. Same for heart pounding, trouble breathing, and sweating when the trauma intrudes on you in an unwanted way." I look up from the paper. "When have you experienced that adrenaline response?"

His eyebrows furrow. "Feels like all day long. Can't pick out one time."

"When Hudson swam underwater?"

He quails. A moment later, he cocks his head. "But that's different from what happened...in Baja. It was at the pool, not the ocean. And Huds was totally safe."

"Did you know that at the time?" I shrug. "You thought another family member was in danger, in the water, and you were determined to prevent a bad thing from happening again."

As he absorbs my words, his hand presses down the length of his thigh, stopping at his knee. A crease of his forehead seems to indicate he's thinking hard. "That heart-pounding thing—I've felt that every time I get a phone call from Wyatt. Or from my mom. But I let it go to voicemail." He grimaces. "Mom wants me to visit Cincinnati."

"Where Kim's funeral took place?" I guess.

He looks down and nods.

"Which brings us to the second symptom: avoidance." I wait for him to meet my eyes. "It's bad enough to experience the trauma the first time, but the breathtaking panic you experience when you think about it afterwards is almost worse."

"Yes," he agrees.

"So, you try to avoid thinking or talking about what happened. You don't take Wyatt's calls. You don't go to Ohio. You try to suppress your sadness and fear."

He watches me without moving.

"Have you gone swimming since this happened?"

He licks his lips. "If I didn't have to coach, I'd be nowhere near a pool."

I nod. "Have you been to the beach since October?"

He shakes his head.

"While it makes sense for you to try to avoid feeling so bad, the avoidance keeps you stuck in the past. We want to get you unstuck, Jordan."

"How?" He thinks a second, then he recoils. "By diving into the details of what happened?"

"No," I answer. "By examining what you've been telling yourself about what happened. If your conclusions aren't accurate, you can learn to talk to yourself in a more balanced way, so you feel better. Which brings us to the third symptom: negative thoughts and feelings about yourself, others, and the world." I point to the questionnaire again. "You've had thoughts like, *There's something seriously wrong with me?*"

"That's a fact."

Now is not the time to explore the truthfulness of that belief—that will come later. "Earlier you told me you planned the Baja trip for your sister's birthday. In your mind, does that make it your fault she died?"

He curls into himself into a ball of shame. "Also a fact," he chokes out.

I wish I could get him to see how wrong he is, but I'll have to help him uncover that truth himself. "Blaming yourself like that leads to feelings of guilt, shame, and self-directed anger, for which you also marked 'extremely.'" I can tell he's running out of steam, so I move on. "The fourth symptom is called hypervigilance. It's feeling on edge, on guard all the time, like you can't relax or sleep."

"That's definitely me," he says. "I thought I was just a control freak."

"You probably are." I smile. "Trauma survivors often worry about control."

He harrumphs and tugs up and down on the bill of his ballcap. His shaggy brown hair would never fly in the Navy, and I wonder about the last time he got a haircut. Personal grooming often takes a hit during mental-health crises.

"Let's talk about how to recover from this traumatic injury you've experienced," I suggest.

His squint conveys his skepticism.

"You may not believe me, Jordan, but you *can* get better. I want to start an evidence-based treatment called cognitive processing therapy." Though he reported difficulty with concentration on the PTSD screener, his body language tells me he's listening. "CPT utilizes cognitive behavioral therapy, which teaches skills for you to coach yourself more effectively. I've had clients start with even higher scores than you and finish much lower. They cured themselves of PTSD. Here, I want to show you a short video."

I pull up a whiteboard video about cognitive processing therapy on my tablet, and we watch it together. A male client experiences fear and rage, then sees a female therapist to help him change. The video ends as the male narrator promises, "You *can* get better."

"Does anything in that video resonate with you?" I ask.

Jordan looks up at the ceiling. "That dude *is* me." He shakes his head. "Avoiding the grocery store, worrying all the time, blowing up at other drivers..."

"The therapy could help change all that. It's about twelve weekly visits, with practice assignments in between. Are you ready to start next week?"

He draws in a breath. "We're entering championship season. Taper meets. I'll be even busier than normal—I don't know about this."

I nod. "I want to respect your schedule while not enabling your avoidance. You said you're close to getting fired?"

His eyes narrow.

"If you don't take time to address your symptoms, will you get to coach at those taper meets? Is your hesitation possibly more about avoidance than your busy schedule?"

Though his expression remains hostile, a hint of a smirk tugs a corner of his mouth. "I see why Mase called you tough." He sighs. "Truth is, I don't want to delve into this crap."

"That's a normal stance, a symptom of avoidance. But something brought you in today, Jordan. Something inside of you wants to heal, to get back to yourself—get back to the compassionate and light-hearted husband, father, and coach you are. The *brother* you are. Sick and tired of being sick and tired. Maybe there's another way."

He twists his mouth to one side. "Or maybe I'll just get better on my own."

Spoken like the self-reliant man he is. Swimming or his family, or both, have likely taught him to be independent. "It's possible," I say. No matter what I want or think, the hallmark of cognitive behavioral therapy is Socratic questioning, helping the client arrive at his own answers. "How about you read more about cognitive processing therapy and think it over? Maybe talk to your wife about it. I'll send you some links to a website and podcast."

He still seems noncommittal, but after I send a message through the electronic chart portal, I ask, "Would you like to schedule another appointment? I recommend we meet again, even if we don't start CPT."

He pauses. "Okay."

I give a silent cheer and schedule him for next week.

At the door of my office, Jordan turns to me before leaving. "Hey, Dr. Avery. Why are therapists good at basketball?"

I lower my chin as I try to figure out the punchline. I suck at basketball.

"They always anticipate the defense."

He's out the door before I have a chance to respond.

5. JORDAN

A tremor vibrates down my arm as I glance at my watch. It's five minutes past ten, and Dr. Avery hasn't shown up yet. That's a sign, right? A sign this therapy thing isn't for me. A sign I should book it out of here.

"Jordan!" She sweeps into the waiting room with flushed cheeks and damp hair. "So sorry I'm late." She gestures down the hall. "Ready?"

No. I stand and follow her into her tidy office. I was too anxious last week to notice my surroundings, but today I take in the taupe leather sofa with soft blue throw pillows, an area rug in shades of gray and navy, and a clock with a seaside design. Standard coastal décor for Bluffton, South Carolina.

Elena brought similar pillows as a housewarming gift after she sold a condo to me thirteen years ago. When I accepted a coaching position for a youth swim team down here, I had no idea I would marry my realtor and start a family and swim club in the Lowcountry. I hadn't planned to live so far from my sister and mother.

Dr. Avery smiles at me as we sit. I like how she doesn't hide behind her desk. Instead, she sits in a chair next to her desk that faces the sofa. Her eyes are an interesting color—so light brown they almost look green. "I apologize again for my tardiness," she says.

"Did you run into the obligatory accident on two-seventy-eight?" The road that runs through Bluffton, connecting the interstate to Hilton Head Island, is notorious for crashes because of all the vacationers and retirees.

"Ha, no. Brandon—uh, my husband—he just had to show me the new weightlifting equipment he bought before I left the house."

There's a hint of lean muscle beneath her form-fitting black yoga jacket and army-green hiking pants, and I'm not surprised she works out. I'm jealous she has the energy to exercise. "You lift weights?"

"About twice a week. You?"

I scowl. "I used to. My college coach was all about strength training. He would geek out over exercise physiology—created a new lifting routine for us each season. He was always studying ways to build power in the water." I remember Coach Stevens hugging me at Kim's funeral. I've let *his* calls go to voicemail, too.

"My husband makes fun of me. He says a runner like me should be able to lift heavier weights—"

"He's wrong," I interrupt. When her eyebrows rise, I worry I've overstepped. I add, "Marathoners need more reps with lighter weight. At least, that's how I train my distance swimmers."

Her face softens. "Thanks, Coach. I love learning from my clients."

I doubt I have anything further to offer her.

"So." She holds aloft a manual that reads, *Cognitive Processing Therapy for PTSD*. "What do you think? Let's start this today?"

My heartbeat kicks up, followed by a squeezing sensation in my chest.

She lowers the book. "You look *thrilled* about this." Her slight smirk quashes my worry that I'm disappointing her. "Have you talked it over with Elena?"

The fact that Dr. Avery remembers my wife's name earns her some points. For some reason, I don't want to talk about this stuff with Elena. It feels too…raw or something. Also, Elena hopped up and down in a giddy frenzy when I told her I'd scheduled my first counseling appointment. I can't drag her into this more, only to disappoint her when I fail.

Dr. Avery maintains a neutral expression as she waits for me to continue. Her short hair has lightened a bit as it dries, the chestnut-brown bob curling at an angle toward her jawline. My thrumming heartbeat reminds me of another time I balked at trying something new. "Before NCAAs my senior year of college, our coach wanted us to do a newfangled relay start."

Her eyelids close partway in a look of intrigue. "Go on."

"We had to stand at the back of the block, hop over the wedge, and take off right as the incoming swimmer finished." I cringe thinking about practice that day. "I worried about slipping or DQing, uh, disqualifying, our whole relay if I timed it wrong. So I told Coach I wasn't going to do it."

"What'd he say?"

"He said if I didn't do the start, I wouldn't be in the relay. Not in a threatening way, just a matter of fact. I *really* wanted to be on that four-hundred free relay." I huff a breath from the back of my throat. "Good thing Coach pushed me through my nervousness, because we set a national record that year."

She stares at me for a long moment, and it's almost like I can see her psychologist brain whirling. "Jordan, it's normal to feel anxious about treatment." She leans forward. "But if you don't start this therapy, you won't get better." She sits back in her chair and shrugs. "Not a threat, just a matter of fact."

Well, I walked right into that one. I have to admit, the information on the Veterans Administration PTSD website seems solid. My college biology major taught me how to understand conclusions from scientific research, and the studies on cognitive processing therapy showed significant improvements in negative thoughts, sleep, and even the brain. As I read about trauma survivors who felt much better after CPT, I felt a glimmer of hope. And hope has been hard to come by since Baja.

"Okay." I let out a breath. "Let's do it."

Her full smile lights up her face.

"Just don't get your hopes up when it comes to me," I warn. "You'll soon figure out I'm cuckoo for Cocoa Puffs."

She chuckles as she opens a desk drawer next to her chair. "I think we just identified your first stuck point." As she hands me a clipboard, she must notice my confusion, because she adds, "We'll get to that." She glances at her watch. "Is it okay if we go a bit past the top of the hour? I want to have enough time for our first session, and you waffling about whether to start has put us behind."

From the crease of a dimple on one cheek, I can tell she's ribbing me, so I dish it right back. "*You're* the one who was late." I narrow my eyes. "I almost left."

Her grin fades. "I'm grateful you stayed."

I don't feel so grateful. It's a big mistake to agree to this.

She points to the questionnaire on the clipboard. "We'll start off every session with the PCL-five to check in on your PTSD symptoms." After handing me a pen, she nods. "Just like the last time, answer the questions based on how you've felt the past month."

I answer "extremely" for the first five questions. When I get to the item about avoiding people, places, and conversations related to the trauma, I have to mark that one high as well. Though I arrived early at Dr. Avery's office, I sat in my car for twenty minutes before forcing myself to come inside.

After I hand over the completed form, she gives me another piece of paper. "Here's a cognitive processing therapy contract for you to read while I score this."

A *contract?* That sounds extreme. But as I scan over the information, I realize she's already told me most of this stuff. It appears my main responsibility is committing to the therapy and practice assignments. I suppress a scoff. That's true—I need to be committed.

I give her the signed contract, and she adds her signature below mine. She asks, "Any questions?"

"Nope." My casual response contrasts with the tension strumming through me. My spinal cord feels like a piano wire stretched tight.

She holds up a graph on her tablet. With her stylus, she has drawn a dot high on the left side and labeled it with today's date. "Your PTSD symptom score today is sixty-five."

I blanch. "I got *worse?*"

"I don't think so." The warmth in her eyes is kinder than I deserve. "I think you were more honest on the checklist today. Clients often minimize their distress early on with therapists."

I wish I could minimize my distress. Between nightmares and worrying about today's counseling session, I hardly got any sleep last night. I slump back against the sofa.

"You may feel hopeless right now, but your score will come down, Jordan." She points at the graph. "The way your score lowers can vary—some scores stay high and then dip big-time, and some steadily decrease with small spikes here and there. I had one survivor of childhood sexual abuse lower her score from seventy-two to five." When my eyes bug, she holds up her hand. "Not a typical result, but many clients end up under twenty or so by the twelfth session." She taps low on the right side of the graph. "A much better quality of life."

Where will my score end up? A flicker of that old competitive fire ignites in my gut. I want to outscore them all.

Dr. Avery turns a page in the manual on her lap. "Here's our agenda for the rest of our time today: we'll review PTSD, including what happens in the brain. I'll introduce cognitive behavioral therapy as a way to heal and change beliefs that keep you stuck in the trauma. Then we'll identify the index trauma, provide an overview of CPT, and give you your first practice assignment."

A knot tightens in my stomach. *Here we go.* She takes a paper from a thick manila folder and passes it to me. I look at circles on the page as she continues.

"PTSD is a disorder of non-recovery. Some people who experience trauma don't develop PTSD. Those individuals take a more active approach. They're able to process the natural emotions of the event, including fear, anger, horror, and sadness, so they can draw accurate conclusions. And they don't get stuck in the past."

I try to untangle that. It sounds like another screw-up on my part. I should've figured out how to be unaffected instead of wallowing in grief.

"But with PTSD, the memory of the traumatic event activates intrusive flashbacks that then lead to the fight, flight, or freeze response. The memory, something called intrusions, and hyper-arousal trigger each other and get stuck together."

Sounds about right.

"A key symptom of PTSD is intrusions. These include sounds, smells, or visions that impose on you in an unwanted way. They may come at you when something reminds you of the event, or maybe when you're sick. One example you mentioned was your son swimming underwater, and you panicked. Can you give me other examples of intrusions you've experienced?"

I blink at her as I recall thrashing in the sheets, sweaty and scared, last night. "I keep waking up in terror." I swallow. "I think I've been dreaming about Kim."

"Does it feel like a nightmare?"

I nod.

"You've said before that you were dreaming about the panga?"

My lips press together. "Sometimes, but last night, it was when we were younger." I clench my teeth. "My dad's funeral."

"Painful memories." She writes on her tablet. "Remind me, how old were you when he died?"

"Twelve. Only two years older than Hudson." *I'll die and leave them fatherless.*

"Is your son in your nightmares, too?"

My chest jolts on a sharp inhale, and I realize I've been holding my breath. "Sometimes." Scraps of recollection come to me. In many nightmares, I try to save Kim or one of my kids, but they disappear before I can get to them. Sometimes, Hudson or Hailey is in the coffin, not my dad.

Soon after my father's funeral, Kim and I agreed we wanted to be cremated when our time came. Maybe it was strange for kids to go to such a morbid place, but I worried about dying young back then. Thank God I don't have another image of a waxy, gaunt face painted with too much makeup swirling in my mind after Kim's funeral. However, the urn filled with her ashes taunts me from the shelf of our walk-in closet. It seems wrong to hide the urn like that, but I don't want to display it and trigger more of Hailey's tears from missing her aunt.

"Any other triggers for re-experiencing traumatic memories?" Dr. Avery's question reorients me to her office.

I wince as I pull my ballcap lower over my face. "Elena cut her finger on the new paring knife." My elbows press into my sides. "I yelled at her for being careless." I shake my head as I breathe out through my nose, trying to shake off the memory. "I had another temper tantrum—like the ones I told you about. She ended up being fine, and I wasn't really mad at *her*. I was mad at myself. I should've warned her that knife was sharp."

"It must've been frightening to see your wife's blood."

She's right. I was *terrified*. Over a little cut. I'm so ridiculous.

"How do you feel when you think about Kim's death?"

I look at her. *How do I feel?* Words escape me. There's a faint gushing sound from the fountain in the nearby lagoon. As I stare out the window at the water, the sound morphs into the drone of a motorboat, and I'm back in the Sea of Cortez. The docks of La Paz approach — at last — and I compress my grip on Kim's hand. But she doesn't squeeze back. Her suntan is gone, replaced by pallid skin. A scream traps itself in my throat. I can feel her slipping away.

"Frightened?" Dr. Avery prompts.

I turn back to her as chills bloom up my back.

"Angry?"

I swallow and give a quick nod.

"You said you were angry at yourself after the knife thing. And when you think, 'I should've warned my wife,' maybe you feel guilty or ashamed?"

I consider that question. "Yes. I should feel guilty when Elena gets hurt."

"Should you?" She gazes at me for a moment. "Those are some tough emotions: fear, horror, anger at yourself, sadness, and shame. It makes sense that you try to avoid the trauma so you don't experience those. And we humans have countless ways to avoid. See the types of avoidance listed on the handout? Which ones resonate with you?"

I read over the list. "Aggression, check. Social withdrawal, check. Substance abuse?" I shrug. "After we returned from the funeral in Cincinnati, I started drinking more to help me sleep. I don't think it's abuse, though. Does that count?"

"Are you still using alcohol to help you sleep?"

I squirm as I recall an argument with Elena that woke up both the kids in December. "My wife shut that down pretty fast."

"Smart woman," says Dr. Avery. "Alcohol helps you fall asleep faster, but it interferes with REM sleep — it makes your sleep worse." She points at the handout. "Cognitive avoidance is when you try not to think about the trauma. Is that the case for you?"

"Absolutely yes. And…somatic complaints — are those like headaches?"

She nods.

I read farther down the list. "I don't think I'm bingeing on food. If anything, Elena gets on my case for not eating."

Dr. Avery takes more notes. "That could explain the headaches and the hangry outbursts. Food restriction is also an avoidance strategy. When you restrict food, you restrict feelings."

I'm not missing food on purpose—I'm just not hungry. But I'm too tired to argue.

"As I said, it's understandable that you try to avoid painful memories and feelings." She waits for me to look at her before she continues. "That avoidance, though? It prevents you from recovering."

I feel my eyebrows pull together.

"Okay. Let's talk about what goes awry in the brain with PTSD, and how we'll correct it." She opens a new window, a blank screen, on her tablet. "This'll be a horrible drawing of a brain, so prepare yourself." With her stylus, she creates an image that looks more like a blob than a brain—she's not joking about her awful art skills. "Our bodies are wired for survival. When there's a threat in the environment, that information goes straight to the emotional brain, the amygdala. We don't waste time analyzing in the thinking brain, the prefrontal cortex." She points at the front of the image. "We want a fast, automatic response from the emotional, reptilian brain. Have you seen that movie, *Inside Out*?"

"Yeah." Hailey made us watch it over and over when she was five.

She smiles. "I love that movie—it teaches us that all emotions are important; they all have a purpose. Anyway, that control center where the emotions live? That's the amygdala. So, back to the threat. Say a little boy lifts his hand toward a hot burner on a stove."

I shift in my seat. That sounds like something Hudson might've tried when he was little. Even though we did everything to childproof the house, he still ended up in the ER twice for surgical glue to close gashes on his head. A frantic car ride to the hospital replays in my mind and sends my heart rate soaring.

"When the boy's hand approaches the hot burner, that sensation goes to the amygdala, which sends signals to the brainstem." She draws an arrow from the amygdala over to the back of the brain. "The brainstem awakens the sympathetic nervous system. The little boy's heart pounds, blood rushes to the limbs, and he yanks his hand back. Then the brainstem sends signals to the thinking brain." She draws another arrow from the brainstem to the PFC. "Finally, the thinking brain calms the emotional brain. The PFC tells the amygdala, 'Phew, that was close. Don't do that again.'" The arrow she draws from the front down to the middle of the brain closes the loop. "The brain returns to baseline. That whole process might take about ten seconds. You with me so far?"

I study the picture and give a slight nod. *My* brain has not returned to baseline, as evidenced by the pressure in my throat and the unrelenting image of blood dribbling down my son's cherub face after falling off our bed. As I recall, Elena sobbed on the way to the hospital, whereas I was the calm one that day. Now, I don't feel so calm.

"It's a different process in PTSD." Avery marks an X over the word *THREAT* and writes CS instead. "A conditioned stimulus becomes the threat—something that's not inherently threatening but has been paired with the traumatic memory. Your son swimming underwater, for example."

I tense as an image replays in my mind like a video glitch. *He's drowning!*

"Same start to the brain pathway, beginning with the emotional brain." She draws an arrow from the conditioned stimulus to the amygdala, then another one from the amygdala to the brainstem. "The emotional brain sends signals to the brainstem, which initiates the body's fight, flight, or freeze response."

Freeze response? Check. I'm a block of ice at the moment—if the block of ice were left in the sun, that is, given the sweat sliding down my back.

She continues, "Signals travel from the brainstem over to the thinking brain. But in PTSD, the pathway from the thinking brain back to the emotional brain disappears." She erases the arrow from the PFC to the amygdala. "If you look at brain scans during intrusions, the amygdala is on fire, but the prefrontal cortex is offline, totally quiet. The amygdala hijacks the rest of the brain, and logical thought goes out the window."

Yes. This has been my brain since October. I thought I was going crazy. But this happens to other people with PTSD as well?

"The emotional brain keeps firing with nothing to calm it down. For the average person with PTSD, this emotional fire rages for up to two hours at a time, three or four times a *day*."

My jaw lowers.

"Yep. So disruptive to your life. But we can heal your brain. How? Cognitive behavioral therapy. When you practice more balanced thinking, you reestablish the path from your thinking to emotional brain." She draws an arrow again, darkening the line with repeated stylus strokes. "If you practice your CBT worksheets, your brain will heal. When you remember the trauma, it'll probably be sad and unpleasant, but it won't steal your breath. You won't feel panic or shame when you think about Kim."

I nod. I want that arrow back. I want to stop freaking out all the time. But these worksheets sound bad.

"Let's discuss CBT theory," Dr. Avery says. "It's not what happens to us that determines how we react, but rather, the way we interpret events. Our thoughts lead to feelings and behavior."

I look up at her. Is she saying my thoughts are wrong?

"From the time we're born, we try to make sense of the world," she continues. "We create narratives to organize all the information that bombards us. For example, my friend has a daughter, Charlotte. When Char was two, she met her older cousin, Nick. Nick was a tall teenager who gave Char all kinds of attention, playing with her and tossing her in the air. Char worshipped Nick. Then, when Char went to the beach and saw another tall teenage boy, she pointed at him and said, 'Nick.' To her, all teenage boys were Nicks."

Charlotte sounds almost as cute as Hailey was at that age. *Almost.*

"One narrative we learn is the just-world belief: *Good things happen to good people, and bad things happen to bad people.* Did you learn that?"

I ponder her question. "I think so."

"When an awful thing happens to us, the just-world belief makes us wonder if *we* are bad. We wonder if we're being punished for something we did."

But I *did* do something bad. I should've let Kim stay back and swim with me. If I hadn't been such a grumpy child, my sister would still be alive.

"It's attractive for us to blame ourselves when bad things happen," says Dr. Avery. "If it was my fault, then I'll just change what I did, and I won't experience the trauma again. Self-blame helps us feel more control." Her honey brown eyes study me. "Unfortunately, blaming ourselves brings on self-directed anger, guilt, and shame."

I grimace. It's not like I'm *choosing* to blame myself. It's just a fact: it's my fault.

"In addition to assigning blame, our beliefs can become more extreme. For example, 'I must be on guard all the time.' Or, 'You can't trust anyone.' Or, 'If I let someone get close to me, I'll get hurt.' Does that sound familiar?"

I nod, but it's not quite right. If I let someone get close to me, *they* will get hurt. They'll die.

"The more we say something to ourselves, the more we think it's true, and the less we pay attention to evidence that negates it. Your beliefs become ingrained over time, and some of them keep your PTSD symptoms going. These beliefs that prevent you from recovering are called *stuck points*." She hands me another paper. "They may be all-or-nothing beliefs, like a dieter saying, 'Either I'm good and eat zero cookies, or I'm bad and eat the whole bag.'" She smirks. "I think members of the military — athletes, too — tend to be extreme people with all-or-nothing thinking. Like, 'If I'm not perfect, I'm a failure.' As a runner, I've had that thought many times."

I can relate to that belief as well.

"And stuck points are thoughts, not feelings," she explains. "For example, 'I'm terrified my kids will die young,' is a fact, whereas, 'If I'm not on guard, my kids will die young,' is a thought, a stuck point. Also, stuck points might be moral statements like the golden rule — 'Treat others the way you want to be treated.' While that's a nice concept, different people have different expectations and behaviors, and there's no way we could all treat each other the same."

I frown. "But shouldn't I treat others the way I want to be treated?"

She shrugs. "Should you? They're different from you. How do you know what they want?"

I feel the crease on my forehead deepen, and she moves forward.

"In this therapy, we'll focus on your thoughts or stuck points, and we'll also focus on your emotions. When a trauma happens, it's a huge ordeal that brings on natural, hard-wired emotions like fear, sadness, and anger. The emotions can fade after you feel them. But in PTSD, you avoid the emotions and don't process them, similar to bottling up your feelings."

I shift uncomfortably in my seat. Elena has accused me of that multiple times.

Dr. Avery says, "Think of a carbonated beverage that gets shaken up. If you unscrew the lid, it spews all over the place. But then the bubbles die down. Same thing with natural emotions—they'll soon die down if you let them out. Emotions are temporary. They don't keep gushing forever."

Maybe that's true for others, but not me. If I think about what happened, I'll never get it out of my mind. If I let myself get angry, I'll do some serious damage.

"*Manufactured* emotions are different than natural ones," Dr. Avery continues. "They come from our thoughts. For instance, instead of telling ourselves that bad things can happen to good people, which brings on sadness, we blame ourselves for mistakes we made, which elicits self-hatred or shame."

I swallow as she looks up from her manual. It's like she can see through me. I don't want her to know how much I screwed up on the day Kim died.

Dr. Avery chews on her lip. "Imagine you're swimming in the ocean, near the shore. The waves hold a lot of energy, just like emotions do. If you let yourself float in the waves, what will likely happen?"

Is this a trick question? I tense. But she keeps waiting, so I say, "The waves will push me back to shore."

"Exactly. You'll return to shore if you just float through the waves. Just like you'll return to baseline if you let yourself float through your emotions. But what if something unexpected occurs, like a riptide, and you try to fight the waves? What happens if you try to swim straight back to shore?"

"That's dangerous," I say. "The riptide pushes you out to sea no matter how hard you swim. You have to relax and swim parallel to shore to get around it."

She nods. "Yes. A riptide is like a trauma—an unexpected event that propels you out to sea. If you try to fight the waves, you work against yourself. You won't process the natural emotions of the event. And what if you add 'thought currents' to the riptide—things like, 'I should've known better' or 'I'm totally to blame'? Those thoughts produce manufactured emotions like shame and guilt. The tide can't bring you back to shore because extreme thoughts keep pushing you away from your goal.

"In cognitive processing therapy, we process the natural emotions by floating through them, experiencing them until the energy drains out. We also want to remove the energy that has kept the manufactured emotions pushing us farther from land by changing any extreme or inaccurate thoughts. How much sense does that make?"

Imagining the relief of returning to shore after being caught in a riptide, I lean back against the sofa. *Is it possible for me to feel better?* "Interesting," is all I say.

Dr. Avery turns a page in her manual. "Let's identify the index trauma, or the one we'll focus on for your worksheets." She looks up at me, her gaze steady. "I'm aware of your sister's tragic death four months ago—obviously a trauma." She blinks. "Have you experienced any other events that felt like life or death, or any kind of physical or sexual abuse?"

"No," I blurt.

Her head tilts. "Your father's death when you were twelve…what a horrible, sad event. Do you think you blamed yourself for that?"

I tuck in my chin as I press my body against the sofa cushion. "Why would I blame myself? I was just a kid."

"Good point." She gives a half-smile. "Did you have nightmares about his death?"

Heaviness weighs down my heart. "At first." I remember crying, alone on my bed, in the darkness of night.

"What helped stop the nightmares?" she asks. "Did your mom comfort you?"

A shaft of light spreads in an arc across the carpet as my bedroom door opens. I sit up in bed and see a feminine form approaching me. The tracks of tears on her cheeks glisten in the low light. *"I miss him, too, Jords,"* she says. Despite being almost the same size, she somehow gathers me in her arms.

I clear my throat. "No. My mom's bedroom was on the other side of the house." Not to mention, Mom was a ghost of herself from the tranquilizers her doctor had prescribed. "It was Kim. She helped me."

My psychologist stills and asks in a quiet voice, "How'd Kim help you?"

"She told me Dad would want us to keep swimming, to keep working hard." I tug on my ballcap. "Dad was a star swimmer for Ohio State, so we threw ourselves into swimming, lost ourselves in the sport. Kim said we could honor his memory that way."

When I look up, Dr. Avery's eyes seem glassy—*is she about to cry?* She looks away as she twists her wedding ring. After a moment, she says, "Okay, let's identify Kim's death as the index trauma for now." She looks at her manual and takes a deep breath. "Learning new skills takes a lot of practice. Take that relay start you talked about—how many reps did you need to get the timing right?"

"Way too many."

She nods. "We also know that it takes effort and energy to get results. Practice, effort, and energy are the complete opposite of your desire to avoid the trauma." Her eyes meet mine. "But avoiding hasn't been working for you, Jordan."

I sigh. Now she sounds exactly like my wife. I hate it when Elena's right.

"We'll start by exploring what you've been saying to yourself about why the trauma happened. If your beliefs aren't based in evidence, we'll practice considering more effective beliefs. Later, we'll cover aspects of your life that can be affected by trauma: safety, trust, power and control, esteem, and intimacy."

She turns a page. "We'll use worksheets to re-establish the pathway from the thinking brain to the emotional brain. I encourage you to practice with your worksheets every day."

Ugh. I suppress an eye roll. *What am I signing up for?* I finished school a long time ago.

"If you don't practice with your worksheets outside of session, it's tough to make progress."

In other words, you won't improve if you don't put in the work. I harp on this truth with my swimmers all the time. *Better buck up. Don't want to be a hypocrite.*

"Which brings us to our first practice assignment." She hands me a paper. "You'll write a statement on why the traumatic event occurred. I don't want you to write details of what happened. Focus instead of what *caused* Kim's death."

A wave of nausea rolls in my gut. *This sounds terrible.* All my shameful secrets exposed.

"Also, you'll write out your beliefs about yourself, others, and the world related to those five aspects of life I mentioned earlier. They're on the sheet. Bring your statement with you next Wednesday, and please read over the handouts we reviewed. You'll likely feel a strong urge to avoid this, but I encourage you not to wait till Tuesday night or Wednesday morning." She waits for eye contact. "We're off to a great start. Any reactions to session one, Jordan?"

After I take a shaky breath, I give her my best sarcastic jazz hands. "This is gonna be *so* awesome. Can't wait."

6. AVERY

Just as my client, Janet, starts crying, my cellphone vibrates against my desk for the third time this hour. For some reason, my mother pops into my mind as the possible caller. I haven't talked to either of my parents in months, just the way I like it, so why would they infiltrate my thoughts now?

"My dad, he...he never came back for me after the divorce." Janet sobs. "Not once."

Her father sounds like a first-class jerk, and now I know why my mind has drifted to my parents. Healthcare professionals struggle most when patients present issues that echo their own struggles. "He didn't visit you after he left?" I ask.

She sniffs and shakes her head. "I haven't seen him since I was four."

Whoa. Janet didn't tell me this during our trauma therapy, but it makes sense that it's coming out now when she's working on her current marriage. My parents divorced when I was eighteen and my brother sixteen. How would we have fared if Dad had left Nate and me before the age of five? I don't have to ponder that long to know we would've been much better off. Maybe Nate would actually talk to me now instead of resenting me for being Dad's favorite—not that I wanted that overwhelming pressure from our military father. Without Dad's constant criticism and unfair comparisons, Nate and I might've learned to support each other. Maybe we could've been close, like Jordan and Kim Perry. It's been a week since Jordan and I last met, and I've thought more than once about the loving way Kim soothed him after their father's death.

"He abandoned me." Janet's voice shakes with each word.

My phone buzzes again, and I give it the side-eye. Soon after my parents divorced, my mother remarried. Her new husband had three younger children, who replaced my brother and me as her family. I know all about abandonment.

I refocus on Janet. "No wonder it's been tough for you to stand up to men." I watch her take a shuddering breath and consider her ex-husband's physical and emotional abuse. Like many battered women, Janet regrets staying so long with him, but he convinced her she couldn't do any better. "You told yourself your dad left because you weren't perfect. Your father's abandonment likely led to your stuck point, 'I'm not good enough.'"

Janet smiles through her tears. "But Ian isn't like that," she says, referring to her current husband. "He's seen me at my worst—like when I snapped at my father-in-law—and he still loves me."

"Way to challenge overgeneralizations with evidence." I smile back at her. She's learned so much through cognitive processing therapy. *I'm* trying to learn to challenge destructive childhood narratives as well. Maybe all men aren't like my alcoholic father. Every time Brandon stops after one or two drinks, I let my guard down a little more. And Brandon is kind and supportive, unlike my critical father.

After Janet's session, I look at my phone, surprised to find the missed texts are from Brandon. I hustle toward the waiting room and hear his deep baritone, followed by Nadia's buttery voice.

As I walk out, Nadia smirks. "I wish *my* husband would surprise me with a lunch date."

Brandon grins broadly, seeming proud of himself. "You ready?" he asks.

"I'm sorry, but I can't." Guilt clenches my chest. "I have my next client in thirty minutes."

His face falls as he glances at his Tag Heuer watch.

"Oh, too bad," Nadia says. "I was just telling this one—" She gestures toward Brandon. "—that I'm still waiting to hear from you about rescheduling our dinner date."

I shift from one foot to another. I've floated multiple dates Brandon's way, but he's evaded me each time.

The outer office door opens, and a tanned gentleman in his fifties strides in. He halts when he sees our little group gathered in the waiting area, which is usually not this crowded. Nadia gives me a knowing look before she turns to him and asks, "Ready?"

I watch the client we've nicknamed Silver Fox follow her toward her office. He's met with Nadia for years, and though she hasn't shared details of their therapy, I know she doesn't *hate* his suave hotness.

Brandon studies me. "You don't have male patients who look like *him*, right?"

I contemplate teasing him by asking if he's jealous, but I read the tense set of his jaw. "No," I assure him.

If Jordan arrives early, though, Brandon might think I'm lying. Jordan isn't as handsome or debonair as Silver Fox, but he does rock a brown-eyed Jake Gyllenhaal vibe. No matter how attractive our clients are, though, Nadia and I would never be involved with them outside the parameters of therapy. Our shared professional ethics are one of many sources of trust between us.

I reach for my husband's hand. "Sorry I can't go to lunch. Want to share a sandwich in my office?"

"Hmm..." He pauses. After a moment, he lets me lead him down the hall.

He aims a dejected look at the turkey sandwich half I give him, but he does take a bite. I may need to raid my snack drawer this afternoon after sharing part of the lunch I packed.

"Maybe next time you'll check my schedule first?" I suggest.

He swallows a bite. "I wanted to surprise you."

That tracks. He dreams up grandiose gestures to impress me—which I should be grateful for—but I wish he would ask what *I* want.

"To celebrate," he adds.

I stop chewing. *Celebrate what?* But then I remember our conversation during our run this morning. Brandon told me one of his investments had hit paydirt, shoring up our finances for the rest of our lives. Though it should've been wonderful news, I felt uneasy. I've never seen my husband do any actual work, so how is he killing it on the stock market? "Of course," I tell him. "You must be riding high from your investments. How about dinner tonight instead?"

He scowls. "I'm golfing later, and you'll be too tired to talk by the time I get home."

He makes fun of me for going to bed at nine, but my father made us all wake up early, and the Navy drummed that habit deeper into me.

After staring at me for a beat, he says, "I have a proposal for you."

"Yes?" I wonder why my grip on whole-wheat bread tightens.

"Wouldn't it be great to go out to lunch on a weekday? Enjoy fine dining instead of this sad sandwich?"

I nod. "Sure. Just let me know ahead of time, and I'll reschedule clients."

He shakes his head like I didn't understand him. "That's too stressful. Wouldn't you like to travel the world with me? Take that trip to Iceland we talked about?" Scooting forward, he takes my free hand. "Now that we're set financially, you can stop working."

What? I gape at him as I fight the instinct to snatch my hand away. As if I would ever give up my career! I clawed my way through six years of graduate training to earn my doctorate, including serving long, hard weekends as a Navy Reservist to make ends meet. Psychology is in my blood, and I feel blessed to have found a career that feels like a calling. I'm not perfect, but I pour everything into helping my clients.

"Think about it, Avery. Think about the long hours you work. You don't have time for me now, so how will you have time for our kids? How will you give them everything they need?"

He's bringing up the reason we married after only two months of dating. Once I fell in love with Brandon, I was finally honest with myself about how much I wanted to have children. I've always been a nurturer, as evidenced by my love for helping therapy clients, though I had buried my craving for motherhood deeper with each year that passed. Each dating fail shoveled more dirt onto my buried dream.

Brandon unearthed my maternal longing on our fourth date, when he confessed that his wife died just after she had started fertility treatments. His quiet tears broke my heart in two. I knew in an instant I wanted to have his children to help him overcome his grief.

74

And offspring will help me, too. I'll do whatever it takes to parent more effectively than my mom and dad did.

My doctor was less excited by the idea, given that I'm forty-one. But she did say I was healthy for my age, and Brandon told me medical tests had revealed that his swimmers were strong. Though it's unrealistic to expect that I'll get pregnant soon due to my "advanced maternal age," Brandon and I have sure enjoyed trying.

I look into his deep blue eyes. "I know you want the best for our family. I want a strong family as well. But this is what happens after we decided to marry so soon. If you think I could just walk away from my career — one I've built for almost twenty years — you don't know me very well."

He leans back like I've stung him. "I thought you said I get you on a deep level."

"You do!" I squeeze his hand as I remember confessing some of the appalling things my dad had yelled at me over the years. Brandon hugged me and promised he would never criticize me like that. "How deeply can we know each other, though, after four months? There's so much I still don't know about you." He hasn't shared any details of his wife's death, for example, and I've hesitated to bring up such a painful topic.

"Stuff we could discuss over a nice meal," he replies. "Look, I see how much you give to your clients. And after work, you don't have anything left for me."

My lungs deflate as a crater of culpability lands on my chest. He's right — sometimes I'm too spent to say one word once I get home. To emphasize his point, the blue light on my desk clicks on and signals that Jordan has arrived for his critical session two of CPT. A moment of truth approaches: has Jordan written his impact statement?

Brandon lets go of my hand. His gaze flits from the blue light back to me, a silent recrimination. "Looks like my time is up, Dr. Clarkson."

I wince at his wounded tone, reminding me of yet another disagreement. He wants me to change my name to Brown, but I can't get on board with the idea.

"Just think about it," he says as he rises to his feet.

I stand and circle my arms around him. Looking up, I muster a smile. "Thank you so much for stopping by, my hot husband. Let's talk more tonight, okay?" *Maybe I can cut back my practice.*

His cloudy eyes clear a bit as he gathers me close and leans down to kiss me. His sexy scent and supple mouth melt away my tension. His hands slide down my hips and cup my bottom, zinging a spark of excitement up my spine. I wish I had time to follow him out of here, maybe not to a restaurant, but to our bed.

He pauses at the open door and grins at me. "Catch you later, Cute Stuff."

"Have fun on the golf course. Remember to use your swing thought for every shot."

His grin widens. "What other golfer has a psychologist in their back pocket? My playing partners don't stand a chance."

I brush crumbs off my sofa and take out a folder of handouts and worksheets. As I enter the waiting room, Jordan doesn't seem to notice. Motionless, he keeps his back to me as he watches the exit.

"Hi, Jordan."

He flinches as he spins to face me, his eyes flared beneath the bill of his black ballcap.

"Everything okay?" I ask.

He blinks. "Yeah, this…" As he stands, he shakes his head. "It's fine." He picks up the clipboard from a side table, along with the manila folder I gave him last time, and trails me to my office.

Once we've sat, I take the clipboard with the filled-out symptom checklist. "Thanks for completing this in the waiting room." I hold my breath as I nod at his folder. "Did you write your statement too?"

"Yes." His voice is clipped.

Yay! I score the PCL-5. "Great. Your score is sixty-seven."

"*Great?*" He glowers at me. "I got worse again."

"Very normal," I say. "Good processing of the trauma—I expect your score to come down soon. What has your brain been getting you to think about?"

He angles his head with a sulky purse of his lips. "What do *you* think?"

Ah. Here's the temper tantrum he's warned me about. "Let's take out your assignment."

With a sigh, he removes a piece of lined paper, filled front and back with neat, black scrawl. The frayed edges indicate he likely tore it out of one of his kids' school notebooks.

"Way to confront your avoidance and complete your impact statement." I smile at him. "Now, I want you to read it aloud."

His eyes magnify like he's just encountered an alligator on the sidewalk. "You want me to read it?"

I nod.

"Out *loud?*"

Another nod. It's not unusual for clients to balk at this instruction. Avoidance is powerful. I wait out the silence for him to begin. His head stays down, and I study the sky blue writing on his black ballcap, *Lowcountry Lionfish.*

"Why did my sister die?" His low voice cracks on the last word, and he shudders. "I've asked this question over and over in my head, but it feels strange to write it down. I don't want to write about it. I don't want to think about it. If I let myself think about it, I'll never get it out of my mind. But I guess I have to write this." He looks up from the paper his grip has puckered. "What's the *point* of reading this aloud?"

The rationale is to decrease avoidance and increase emotional processing, but I don't want to facilitate his avoidance by pausing to explain it. He's already too much in his head. "Good start, keep going." I'll ask him later about his statement, *If I let myself think about it, I'll never get it out of my mind.* It could be a stuck point.

He gives a suffering sigh, but after a beat, he resumes. "Why did the smartest, most competent, most caring person I've ever known have to die? How is that fair? How is it fair, especially after our dad died so young? How could God let this happen twice? All I know is the common denominator between my dad and my sister. *Me.*"

It's interesting that Jordan mentions his father's death again, especially so early in his statement. Though he insisted he doesn't blame himself for his father's cancer, I wonder if his father's death — not his sister's — might be his most distressing trauma. Did he witness something horrific, like his father fighting for breath, drowning from fluid in his lungs? But Jordan didn't seem to have PTSD symptoms till recently. I'll have to keep a pulse on his index trauma to make sure our focus is correct. I add the stuck point, *I'm the common denominator when people die*, to my tablet.

He clears his throat. "Kim helped me all the time. She single-handedly pulled Mom and me through our grief. She got on my case when I slacked at high school practice. I was so nervous about college swimming, but she introduced me to her friends at Kenyon. She liked Elena from the start, and she didn't let me screw it up like I did with my college girlfriend. She was the best aunt..."

The increasing waver in his voice piques my attention. We're getting to something important here. I wish he would take off his hat so I could see his face better.

He gulps. "She was the best aunt to Hudson and Hailey. She loved those kids, almost like they were...her own." His breath seems labored. "I robbed her..." When his eyes close, a tear slides down his cheek. He sniffs and swipes the back of his hand across his face, but then a tear leaks from his other eye. "I robbed..." Then his voice is too thick from crying to continue. He looks down, and the paper trembles in his grasp.

Oh, Jordan. I wish I could soothe his suffering. But he has run from these feelings for too long, and I know he has to experience them to get unstuck from this trauma. I practice a few diaphragmatic breaths to keep myself in check. Nadia has told me that growing up in an alcoholic family turned me into an emotional sponge, and I don't want to absorb so much of his pain that I'm too overwhelmed to help him.

After a few more moments, I say, "You're doing great. Keep reading when you're ready."

"I robbed her of..." His throat bobs with another swallow, and his exhale vibrates his chest. After another sniff, he says, "...having children of her own." *Sniff.* "She helped me so much, but did I help *her?* Where was I when she needed me? Nowhere to be found." His voice grows stronger as an edge of anger creeps in. "I never should've booked that swim trip for her birthday. When Wyatt almost had to cancel, I knew we shouldn't go — I felt it in my gut. The dates didn't jibe with her teaching schedule, but I insisted on the Baja trip because it fit *my* schedule. I'm so self-absorbed."

I'm relieved his statement is a minefield of possible stuck points, which will facilitate the treatment. Sometimes I have to keep digging to find what clients have been saying to themselves. When trauma survivors insist they didn't play any role in the trauma, it's tougher to help them heal.

"Why did Kim die? Look no further than her selfish brother. I'm an idiot for choosing a trip on a remote island with no cellular service. I showed zero regard for others' safety. If I had kept up with Kim — if I'd been in better shape — she never would've hit that coral. If only

I'd brought fins on the panga. If only I'd stopped the swim when my shoulder hurt. I did so many things wrong that day. I should've just gotten on the boat. Instead, I insisted on finishing the swim to protect my fragile ego. I'm such a petulant child. My last words to her were so cruel—I'm a horrible brother." His voice catches. "It's all my fault she died."

On my tablet, I jot down a few follow-up questions to ask after he finishes reading.

He turns the page. "My sister would've been a much better parent than I am. It should've been me."

I look up from my iPad to see if he's finished, but there's more writing down the page. He seems to be fighting an internal battle with the urge to cry again. After a pause, he soldiers on.

"How has the trauma affected my sense of safety? I worry about my kids all the time. If they don't die at swim practice, cancer will get them. I imagine them dying from a horrible accident. If I don't watch them every second, they'll get hurt. They'll die. Or *I'll* be the one to die in two or four years, leaving my kids fatherless. They shouldn't trust me to be there for them. And if something happens to me, their lives will be ruined. I have to protect people from getting too close to me, or they'll end up dead, too."

Whoa, overgeneralization city. He's made himself the grim reaper.

"I don't trust the Lionfish board of directors. I started that team, and I've given everything to my swimmers, but they'll fire me any day now. And I don't trust Gabe at all. He's gunning for my position behind my back. Suzy, on the other hand—I trust her completely. At least I know she'll guide the team in a positive direction after I'm gone." His smile is bitter.

"I have no control over my family or my swimmers," he seethes. "Mason should get a better coach, because I sure as hell can't take him to the level he deserves. I'll just drag him down with me. If he doesn't become an Olympic champion, it'll be my fault. My whole team should steer clear of me, actually. I used to think that if you want something done right, you should do it yourself. But now I don't trust myself to do anything right." He looks up at me, his eyes tight. "Almost done reading this nightmare."

I nod. As I continue writing down possible stuck points, I marvel at how well Jordan has done with his statement. Sometimes clients barely write a paragraph, but he gave us a lot to work with.

The statement also conveys raw emotion, especially guilt and self-directed anger. He did mention that his college was known for its English department.

"I don't know how Elena stands to stay with me," he continues. "I'm not even the breadwinner of the family. And I should be more patient with my kids. I shouldn't let people annoy me so much. If I let myself get angry, I'll do some serious damage. I already throw temper tantrums like a three year old. I should love my family more. They deserve better."

With that, he heaves a breath. The paper dangles from his grasp as he shrinks into the sofa. He sets it on the cushion next to him, then shoves it to the other end of the sofa like it's toxic.

"Excellent work," I say, concentrating for a moment on a long exhale. "How did writing and reading that statement affect you?"

"I'm fried." He tugs the bill of his ballcap up and down. "I avoided it for days, like you predicted." It seems to take a massive effort for him to look up at me. "Once I forced myself to start, though, it flowed out of me."

"That's effective emotional processing." I wait for him to meet my gaze. "There may be other ways to interpret the trauma."

He squints at me for a moment. Then he accepts a lined piece of paper and pen that I hand to him.

"This is your stuck point log. We'll use your writing to identify stuck points. Will you give me your statement?" I gesture at the offending piece of paper.

He stretches for it and hands it to me.

"Okay. I want to ask some questions about what you've been saying to yourself since Kim's death. If your beliefs keep you stuck in the past, we'll add them to the log. First, let's look at your beliefs about why the trauma happened. When you think, *It's all my fault because I'm selfish*, how do you feel?"

The slant of his eyebrows and tuck of his chin seem to indicate guilt, but he says, "Mad, I guess."

"Maybe guilty, too?"

He doesn't move as he weighs my question. "Yes."

"Let's add that to your stuck point log." I wait for him to finish writing before I ask, "Do you believe it's all your fault because you have a huge ego?"

His jaw muscle ticks as he nods.

"Write that one, too." After a moment, I add, "Also, *It's all my fault because I abandoned her.*"

He huffs a breath through his nose as he writes.

"You wrote, *If I had kept up with Kim, she never would've hit the coral.* Another stuck point." I gesture to the log.

"Why is that a stuck point? That's a fact."

"Possibly." I shrug. "We'll explore the evidence later."

After a long stare, he writes the belief.

His log fills in as I continue to ask questions. "What makes you think you'll die in two or four years?"

"Because I'm thirty-eight."

I cock my head.

He adds, "Kim was only forty. My dad was forty-two."

"Ah." Now is not the time to question how he jumps to conclusions.

Once he has filled up the page with stuck points, I ask him to star the ones that blame himself or non-guilty others for the trauma. "I want you to explore them first with your worksheets. These stuck points offer more bang for your buck in terms of feeling better faster."

After I've helped him identify which beliefs to star, we move to the accommodated beliefs. "Your stuck point, *If I let someone get close to me, they'll die*, is more about the future, or how you've changed your beliefs as a result of trauma," I point out. "We'll get to that later."

With my tablet, I take photos of his impact statement and stuck point log. "Okay." I smile at him. "Next step. Remember that pathway from your thinking brain to your emotional brain that stopped working with PTSD?"

He gives a weary nod, and I hope he has enough energy to finish the session.

"We're about to rebuild that path so you start feeling better. Let's review our first worksheet…"

7. JORDAN

Dr. Avery is still going strong like a distance runner, but my eyelids droop with the aftermath of crying. After admitting *aloud* the countless ways I let Kim down, I feel drained and exposed.

But as I exhale, I do feel a bit lighter. There's a decrease in the bone-crushing weight that's tightened my shoulders since Baja. And the buzzing sensation that has filled my ears seems quieter, replaced by the low gush of the lagoon fountain outside Dr. Avery's office. All I want right now is my bed. I think I could finally get some quality sleep.

"You still with me, Jordan?"

I give her a drowsy nod. This therapy is like swimming a mile, and the sixty-six laps ahead of me feel daunting.

"Not too much left in today's session," she assures me. "Before we get to the ABC worksheet, let's review this handout." She hands me a paper.

There's a graphic of arrows pointing outwards from a middle circle.

"Author Brené Brown has found that most adults can only name three emotions: anger, sadness, and happiness. But there are many more. This handout helps you identify different emotions at varying levels of intensity." She points at the same graphic in her manual. "Take the *afraid* arrow, for example. A mild feeling is *apprehensive*, but as you move down the arrow, *panicked* is more intense."

I nod. I know both degrees of that feeling well.

She hands me another paper. "This is the ABC worksheet. It helps you talk to yourself in a more balanced way, so that you feel better. Column A is an activating event, column B is your belief or stuck point, and column C is the consequence or feelings. For example, let's say I'm running the two-mile event at a track meet, and I trip and fall. That's my activating event."

"That would suck," I say.

Her eyes roll. "It *did* suck. Happened to me in high school. What would be the equivalent in swimming?"

"Your goggles fill up with water or slide down over your mouth when you dive off the blocks."

"Rough." She nods. "When I fell, my belief in column B was, *Bad stuff always happens to me.* Also, *This race is over.* After I said that to myself, I felt ashamed, furious, and hopeless in column C."

I survey the three columns on the worksheet as she continues.

"In the big picture, we often can't control the activating event. That's life — good stuff and bad stuff happens. We don't have total control over our feelings, either. We're hardwired to experience emotion, and we can't just stop. However, we *can* control the intensity of feelings by homing in on our beliefs in the B column. We can change what we say to ourselves and then feel better. It's difficult, though. We may not be aware of our thoughts. Also, the more we say something to ourselves, the more we come to believe it as fact, and the less we pay attention to evidence that contradicts it."

Her voice has picked up speed and conviction. She's passionate about this CBT crap.

"We want to be curious about our beliefs, to ask questions about them. Below those columns are questions you'll ask yourself. Things like, how *useful* and *factual* are my beliefs? And if they aren't useful and factual, *what's an alternative thought I could offer myself?*"

I nod for her to continue.

"Back to my example. When I tell myself, *Bad stuff always happens to me,* and *This race is over,* how useful are those beliefs?"

I shake my head. "Not at all."

"Exactly. The beliefs made me so disheartened that I gave up. Now, how *factual* are my beliefs? When we talk about evidence in CBT, we mean evidence that could stand up in a court of law or be published by a reputable news source. So, how factual is the belief, *Bad stuff always happens to me?*"

I've said the same thing to myself many times. "Very factual."

She pauses, like she didn't expect my answer. "Is that a belief you have?"

"Yes."

"Okay. Please add *Bad stuff always happens to me* to your stuck point log." She gestures to the lined paper next to me on the sofa.

I'm not sure why she wants to label a fact as a stuck point, but I don't want to prolong this, so I get it done.

Once I'm finished writing, she says, "Tell me about your morning."

I tense, wondering where she's going with this. "I gave up on sleep around four and watched TV while I wrote tonight's practice. One of my cats kept me company. Hailey woke up after a bad dream, so I let her fall back asleep on the sofa next to me. Once Elena got up and made breakfast, it was a mad dash to get the kids ready. Then I drove them to school."

"You said you planned practice. That means you still have your coaching job?"

I scowl at her. She knows this already. "Uh-huh."

"You comforted your daughter after a bad dream, and you watched her fall asleep?"

I nod. Colby, my orange cat who's more of a cuddler than his brother, Jack, had hopped off the sofa as Hailey rushed up to me. Through tears, Hailey told me about her nightmare, a frantic search for her mother and me. She'd cried harder when she explained the part of the dream where Coach Suzy told her we had died. As she'd sobbed, I held her and wondered if we should stop letting her watch that Lemony Snicket TV show about orphans. Her mussed brown hair fell like a curtain over my elbow as she'd snuggled into me, and I'd drawn the throw blanket up over her pink pajamas. Her warmth at my side and trust in me had felt like gifts I didn't deserve.

Dr. Avery interrupts the memory when she asks, "Elena made you breakfast?"

"Yeah, eggs and bacon." Though it tasted like cardboard, I was able to get some down.

"Would you say having a job, your daughter turning to you for comfort, and your wife making you breakfast are good things?"

"Definitely."

"So how factual is the belief, *Bad things always happen to me,* when you've had several good things happen today?"

I stare at her, opening my mouth and then closing it. *She does have a point.*

"Back to my example," says Dr. Avery. "It's not a factual belief for me, either, because just today, I've already experienced a mix of good and bad. My husband showing up to take me out to lunch was a good thing. But I felt irritated that he didn't check with me first, and I was unavailable—kind of a bad thing." Her mouth tightens.

"Sorry I interfered with your lunch."

She starts. "Oh! I wasn't blaming you—I'm the one who scheduled a twelve-thirty session. Which reminds me of another good event today: you wrote a beautiful impact statement."

Her smile makes my cheeks burn, and I find myself wanting to please her. Too bad she'll be another person I let down when I fail at this therapy.

"My other belief, *This race is over,* isn't factual, either," she adds after a moment. "Have you ever seen that video of the University of Minnesota runner who fell at the Big Ten indoor championships?"

I sit up. "I did! Heather Dorniden. Coach Stevens sent the video to me years ago, and I show it to my swimmers all the time. So inspiring."

"I agree—what a feel-good video. My race didn't have to end when I fell. If I'd told myself, *It'll be tough to catch up,* that's a fact. But a more extreme belief like, *My race is over,* isn't factual."

She taps on the second question at the bottom of the worksheet. "If my beliefs aren't useful or factual, I want to talk to myself differently. I might say, *That was embarrassing. Try to finish the race.* I'd still feel angry, but I probably wouldn't feel ashamed or hopeless. Maybe I'd feel a new emotion, like determination. Do you see how this ABC skill works?"

I let out a breath. "I think so."

"You said it's okay if we run long today. How much time do you have left?"

I look at my watch. "About fifteen minutes." I don't tell her I have a meeting after this with the president of the Lionfish board, Lexi's father. That good thing about me still having a job is about to move over to the bad column.

"Okay, let's practice an ABC example for you. Tell me about a recent time when you felt strong emotion."

I grit my teeth, wishing I could leave. But I'm about to get fired and lose our health insurance, so I better practice this crap now. "I'm stressed about Mason's big meet coming up."

"Write *Mason's meet* in column A. What have you been saying to yourself about the meet?"

My shoulders sag. "He deserves a better coach."

She tells me to add that belief and my resulting feelings of anxiety and insecurity to the worksheet. "How useful is that belief?" she asks.

"Not useful," I admit. "It makes me dread going to the meet."

"Right. What evidence supports your belief? How factual is it?"

"Oh, it's a fact."

She twirls her wedding ring. "What leads you to conclude that Mason deserves a better coach?"

"It's only three weeks till the pro swim series. He'll bomb on a national stage." Pressure hits my chest.

"What makes you think he'll bomb?" she asks.

"A feeling in my gut."

She hesitates. "I see. And has your gut ever been wrong in predicting meet performance?"

I consider that. "Freshman year of college. I had a bad feeling about my conference meet. I thought I was too rested, thought I missed my taper. And sure enough, my two-hundred IM, uh, individual medley, sucked." I frown. "But then Coach Stevens got on me, told me my taper was fine, told me to get my head out of my butt. He made me time-trial my event after finals, and when I didn't improve much, he made me swim it again." I huff out a breath. "That's when I dropped three seconds off my best. Went on to have a great meet. We won our twenty-fourth NCAA title in a row that year."

"Wow," she says. "Seems like an exception to your belief. Feelings don't equal facts."

After a beat, I nod.

"I explained before that Mason gave me permission to talk about his therapy with you. He tells me he's 'slaying' at practice. Does that jibe with what you see?"

I feel the ghost of a smile spread. "The kid's putting up amazing times, it's true."

"And you're the one coaching him. Maybe it's not so factual that he deserves a better coach?"

I think for a moment, then I write a different belief, *I worry I won't be there for Mason the way he needs me.* The new belief helps me feel a little better, I guess.

"Great work. It might be tough to buy in to the alternative belief because it's unfamiliar, unpracticed. Which brings us to your practice assignment." She hands me a paper. "I want you to complete one ABC worksheet each day until we meet again. At least one of those worksheets should be on the traumatic event, and the others can focus on everyday things or stuck points. Make sure to use your emotions handout to help you with column C."

I glance at my watch and see I need to go. *Time to face the firing squad.*

"Any reactions to session two?" she asks.

"I'm exhausted."

"Sounds about right." She stands, and I follow suit. "Excellent progress today, and I'll see you next week."

Lowcountry Lionfish Board President Steve Redfield sets a cardboard carton of four coffees on the table before he unbuttons his suit jacket and sits across from me in Old Town Bluffton. Corner Perk's rich aroma of coffee beans typically soothes me during weekly planning meetings with my assistant coaches after Saturday morning practices. But nothing can calm my nerves at the moment. As I entered, three sets of eyes turned to me, and I knew my career was toast. The only reason Steve would invite my assistants is to replace me.

To my right, Gabe takes a to-go cup and hands it to Suzy across from him. He does the same for Steve, for himself, and then for me.

Though Steve called the meeting, Gabe's power play with the coffee tells me he's about to be named the new head coach. *Punk.*

I try to quell the tremble of my hand as I raise the cup to my mouth. It's a sunny yet crisp day in late February, and I welcome the scalding, bitter brew on my tongue. I need to snap out of my therapy haze.

Suzy cringes after a sip, and I suppress a smirk. Figures Steve ordered our coffees black. The attorney is all business. He used to be my biggest fan after I helped his daughter, Lexi, drop five seconds in the hundred breaststroke. If Lexi continues to improve, she could earn a college scholarship. She doesn't need one to afford college, but her dad would be ecstatic—probably brag about it to all his friends. He piles way too much pressure on his daughter. I've tried to balance his intensity by joking around like a goofball before Lexi's races, but I haven't had the energy this season, and she choked at her last meet.

"Oh dear, I need cream and sugar," says Suzy. "Anyone else want some?"

At first I shake my head, along with the other two, as if we're gunslingers in the masculine Olympics. *Real men take it black, ma'am.* But then I sense an opportunity to strategize, and I pop out of my chair to follow Suzy to the counter.

I accept the silver pitcher of cream from her and murmur, "Steve-o is about to give my job to traitor Gabe."

Her mouth pulls down at the corners. "Yes."

My heart gallops. I was hoping my read on the situation was wrong.

"I'm sorry, Jordan. They're idiots." She shakes a packet of sugar. "I tried to convince them to give you another chance."

I close my eyes. After one of my worst nightmares ever, I blew up at the gold group a few days ago, yet again. I'm sure Lexi told her father all about it. I pour cream and look at Suzy. "I would've picked *you* as the head coach. You don't want the job?"

She leans away from me. "Hell no. I'm sixty-three—way too old to deal with parents like *Steve.*"

Despite the dire situation, I almost grin at her disdainful tone.

"But I wasn't asked, anyway," she adds as she stirs her coffee.

I gawk at her. She has *decades* more experience than Gabe. She and I coached together for a different team when I first moved to

South Carolina, and I was so impressed by her compassion and acumen that I poached her as my first assistant coach when I started the Lionfish five years later. But she seems unbothered by the sexism, or whatever this is. "Any advice for me?"

She turns toward me, her warm blue eyes angled up to meet mine. "You started this team, Perry. It's your team. *Fight* for it."

Her words hit me hard. How do I fight when they've already decided to boot me? I slump. How do I fight when I'm so tired and faded?

"Fight for these kids," she adds in a fierce, low tone.

I close my fingers into a fist. My back is to the table, and I feel their eyes on my spine. "Are they watching us?"

"Yep." She tucks a strand of gray hair behind her ear and picks up her coffee. "Ready?"

After a long exhale, I follow her back to the table, slurping caffeine on my way. How would my college coach have handled a situation like this? Taking a seat, my jaw ticks. He never would have faced a shameful firing. He's such a legend that the college revered him.

From the sudden silence as I sit, it's obvious Gabe and Steve were talking about me. Gabe shifts in his chair, and Steve runs a hand over his short, black hair. I'm startled to see a salting of gray hair near his temples. As a successful attorney, Steve was my first financial backer when I started the Lionfish eight years ago, right after Hailey was born. His daughter, Lexi, was a tiny eight year old who could barely swim the length of the pool. Now, in addition to his graying hair, I notice smudges under his eyes indicating strain and fatigue. It strikes me that he doesn't want this meeting, either. But I've forced his hand with my appalling temper.

"Coach Perry," Steve begins. "The board met yesterday."

I tense. *They're all out to get me.*

"We've been concerned about your behavior at practice."

Concerned? What a fake word. If they were concerned about me, they would've come to me first, let me explain things. They wouldn't force me off a team that I myself created.

Steve leans toward me. "Frankly, some board members pushed for this meeting a month ago. But I held them off because of the..." He looks down at his coffee, then back up at me. "Stress you're under."

I swallow. I have to admit, Steve is one of the only parents who approached me directly to offer condolences after I returned from Baja. Most of the swimmers and parents have avoided bringing up any mention of my sister.

Steve opens a leather notebook and extracts a stapled document—a contract I signed years ago. Given the success of the team, we haven't bothered to update it other than yearly signatures each fall. I've earned a raise or two along the way, though my salary is nowhere close to Elena's realtor income. But the health insurance for my whole family has been essential.

"You signed this in September," Steve says. It's not surprising that he's getting all official with the employment contract. "I'd like to bring your attention to section two, job responsibilities. You're an excellent coach, Jordan. But you haven't met an important stipulation of the contract this season." He points at a bullet point and reads, "Provide a positive, encouraging environment that fosters skill improvement for all swimmers, regardless of ability."

My face flames. He's one-hundred-percent right. I sneak looks at my assistant coaches, but both of them stare at the table, one sympathetic and one for sure gloating.

"Because of this breach of contract, we're placing you on leave till March thirtieth, at which time you'll meet with the board to reassess."

I stop breathing. Despite Suzy giving me the heads up, I still can't believe it has come to this. At least I'm not fired, though it sounds like I will be come April. Then the timing of this decision hits me. "But we're in taper—our big meets start in two weeks."

Steve grimaces. "It's not ideal timing, you're right. But it needs to happen. You've been through a lot, Coach. We want you to take a breather, collect yourself." He hesitates. "We've named Gabe as the interim head coach."

Gabe lifts his head and nods at Steve. The coward won't look at me, though. I turn to Suzy and find her watching me with careful eyes. Is it worth arguing for her to take the position when she doesn't even want it? I decide against it. What's the point? I've lost the only career I've ever cared about. I'll never be the man my college coach mentored me to become.

As I sag against my chair, a hush descends over the table. I want to get this disciplinary hearing over with.

Suzy breaks the awkward silence. "Is Jordan's leave paid or unpaid?" "Paid, with full benefits." Steve scoops the contract back into his notebook.

I close my eyes. Even with that small grace, Elena will be furious with me. I feel a light touch on my wrist and look up to find Suzy clasping it. "Anything you'd like to say for yourself?" Her tone implores me to stop my pity party.

I blow out a breath. *Does the accused wish to defend himself?* My mouth jams shut as a memory intrudes my mind. I'm back in my Ohio bedroom, age nine or ten, with my dad's weight on the mattress next to me. I had hidden Kim's diary and played dumb when she screeched that it was gone. My dad was furious when he found it behind my headboard.

"I can't believe you did this!" Dad had yelled. *"Did you read it? Violate her privacy?"*

"I didn't, I swear!" My voice had been shaking with the effort to hold back tears. I wasn't telling the whole truth, though. The only reason I hadn't read Kim's secrets was because I couldn't figure out the lock. *"Everyone hates me now."* My nose had burned. *"Everyone likes Kim better than me!"*

Dad had let out a long sigh. But after a beat, he'd wrapped his thick arm around my shoulders. *"Does this have anything to do with the swim meet?"*

I'd sniffed but didn't answer.

"Listen, I get it. It's tough when your sister swims faster than you. But you don't retaliate by stealing her stuff."

I remember staring at my shoes. He could see right through me.

"And then to lie about what you did? Unacceptable. In this family, we take responsibility for our actions. After you apologize to Kim, you're grounded to your room."

My tears had come then. I hated disappointing him.

He'd squeezed my shoulder. *"Buddy, in a few years, you'll crush the girls at meets—just wait. And there's no way I like Kim better than you. I need you, Jords. You're my wingman when your mom and sister gang up on me."*

The slap of Steve's palms on his thighs, like he's getting ready to leave, brings me back to the coffee shop. I can't let this meeting end before I say something. I force myself to look up at them, meet their eyes. "I understand why you're doing this." My voice wavers, and I clear my throat. "You're trying to protect the kids from me, from my temper. I've been a horrible coach. I'd probably do the same thing if I were you."

Steve holds my gaze, unblinking.

"I know you, Jordan," Suzy says. "You're not an aggressive person. This is just grief."

"It's not—" I cut myself off. I was about to tell them it's PTSD, not "just grief," but how can I admit that? If I tell them I'm in therapy, they'll think I've lost the plot. They'll think I'm weak.

But then a voice in my head asks, *"Will they?"* It takes a moment to realize it's Dr. Avery invading my brain. She keeps going. *"How do you know for sure what they'll think?"* I shake my head to dislodge her annoying questions.

"What were you gonna say?" Gabe asks.

I expect to see hostility in his eyes, but Gabe's curious, open expression reminds me of the first time we met. After graduating from college three years ago, Gabe moved from Florida to South Carolina for a position as a Spanish teacher. As a former high school swimmer, he used to swim laps after work in an open lane next to my club. Once Gabe learned I'd swum for a national-champion team, he'd seemed to revere me, bombarding me with questions about my coach and stroke-technique advancements. I invited him to swim with the team, and I admired how he helped his younger lane-mates with their strokes and attitudes. When another assistant coach left the Lionfish for a head coaching position, Suzy and I agreed we wanted Gabe to join us.

Both leaning toward me, Steve and Suzy seem to echo Gabe's anticipation of my response. My tongue traces the groove of one tooth. "It's not just grief." I clench my fists. "I have post-traumatic stress disorder."

Gabe's eyes widen. "I thought… Don't only soldiers get that?"

"No," Steve responds. "Victims of crime, natural disasters, car accidents, uh, people who've experienced sudden death even…" He avoids my gaze. "They can all develop PTSD." He specializes in contract law, but he's probably been around the block a time or two with all sorts of clients.

Suzy cups my shoulder. "Kim's death was sudden…and traumatic."
I nod. *And my fault.*

"Dude, I'm sorry," Gabe says. "I had no idea."

From the tilt of his eyebrows, he seems almost contrite. *Huh.* I must concede that Gabe never gave me a reason to doubt him before Baja. Maybe the problem isn't with him. It's with me.

"No, *I'm* the one who's sorry." My eyes plead for Gabe's forgiveness. "I'm so sorry I yelled at you at that practice—that day a month ago, when the kids were swimming underwater." I rub the heel of my palm against my forehead as I feel a headache coming on. "Not that it's an excuse, but I was flashing back to the day my sister died—at least that's what my psychologist says." I wince. "I thought Hudson was about to drown, and I took my fear out on you. Crazy, right?"

Gabe's dark eyes seem to spark with understanding.

"Cuckoo for Cocoa Puffs," I add, but no one laughs.

Steve asks, "You're seeing a therapist?"

Whoops, didn't mean to let that slip. But I nod. "Dr. Avery Clarkson."

A low chuckle comes from Steve. When my brows furrow, he sits up. "Oh. I was just thinking about the board. One of them proposed anger-management counseling for you. But I questioned our legal footing to mandate therapy. And I didn't think you'd go for it."

Me neither, brother.

Steve assesses me. "What's your prognosis?"

Now it's my turn to scoff. "Don't know. She's got me doing some trauma therapy, and she says I'll get better. But I can't see it." *I don't deserve it, either. I don't deserve to live a good life when Kim is dead because of me.*

"Hmm…" Steve scratches his chin. "The board considered keeping you in your position as long as you went to therapy. Maybe we should think about this…"

8. AVERY

A week later, I enter Jordan's PTSD score on the digital form and hide my disappointment as I turn the tablet toward him. "Holding steady at sixty-seven today."

He gusts air out his nose and turns to stare at the lagoon. "Figures."

"What figures?"

His gaze stays on my window. His black ballcap shades his eyes, but sunshine highlights the scruff of whiskers on his chin. "Told you not to get your hopes up."

"It's only session three. Too early to throw in the towel." Though I wish his score came down, I have faith he will improve at his own pace. One reason I love my career is people's unpredictability. My job is never boring. I just wish I weren't so sleepy today.

I look at the unopened folder on his lap. I bet he didn't do his practice assignment, which would explain his symptom score. "How many ABC worksheets did you complete?"

With a sigh, he opens his folder and hands me a stack of papers.

"Thanks." After I shuffle through them, I feel more confused. "Wow, all seven, just as I asked."

"I didn't know what I was doing, though. I screwed them up."

As I read through the worksheets, I can see that's not true at all. He attempted one worksheet on a stuck point and the others on everyday events. "These look good, Jordan." I hand the stack back to him. "Let's review them. How about you take me through the one exploring your belief, *Everyone pities me?*" I didn't get a chance to see what he wrote in column A. "What activating event preceded that belief?"

"When the Lionfish fired me," he says.

I blanch. "They *fired* you?"

"Well, they wanted to. They were going to suspend me." A quick shake of his head. "But they took pity on me."

I need to clear my brain fog and catch up. "What exactly happened?"

He shifts on the sofa. "Last week, right after our session, I had a meeting with the board president. I knew I'd won an all-expense-paid trip to the job market when I saw Gabe and Suzy there."

"Your assistant coaches?"

He nods. "I knew it—I knew my temper tantrums had gotten me the boot. But Steve saw how pathetic I am, and for some dumb reason, he kept me on."

Something's off here. I want to dig into it, but I need to stay with the protocol. "Which emotions did you write in column C?"

"Uh…" He glances at the paper. "Embarrassed. Mad."

"Mad at yourself?"

"Yeah."

"And how useful was telling yourself that everyone pities you?"

"Not useful. But it *is* factual."

I angle my head to one side. "What leads you to conclude that everyone pities you?"

"The way they look at me."

"And what way is that?"

"That simpering, fake-sympathy look." His eyebrows slant and lips press together in an exaggerated pout. "They're looking down on me, judging me. They think I'm a loser."

"You believe the board president thinks you're a loser?"

"Definitely. He said they wanted to fire me a month ago but held off because of my…" He air-quotes. "Stress." He leans against the sofa.

"How do you know what Steve was thinking?" When Jordan doesn't answer, I add, "Is it possible he was acknowledging the impact of your sister's tragic death rather than looking down on you?"

He scowls. "No."

I twirl my wedding ring around my finger and try a new tack. "Even if Steve did pity you, does that mean everyone does? I'm part of 'everyone,'" I add after a moment. "Do you think I pity you?"

"Don't you?"

I dip my chin. "I feel compassion for what you're going through, but I don't look down on you." His smirk implies disbelief, which annoys me. "Actually, I'm offended that you think I'm judging you as a loser." I feel a flash of heat across my cheekbones. "Don't you *dare* try to tell me what I'm thinking."

His eyes widen at my sharp tone.

"I'm sorry." I backtrack. "That came out too harsh. I'm crabby when I'm tired."

Those wary brown eyes study me. "Why're you tired?"

My heart rate soars. It's way too early to disclose the reason, and I haven't thought about the best way to tell my clients about this, anyway. I need to consult with Nadia. "Just didn't sleep great last night," I lie.

"I'm overwhelming you. I'm too far gone to help."

I shake my head. "Also not what I'm thinking." His personalization and hopelessness are intense. "In session five, we'll explore thinking styles that make us feel worse. One of them is called mindreading, and I'm guessing that's one of your go-to patterns."

He grunts.

When I continue asking questions about the meeting with the board president, I learn the real reasons the board didn't suspend him: he apologized for his behavior and outlined a plan for improvement (therapy). After a grudging concession that his belief about being pitied isn't factual, he comes up with an alternative belief: *My reputation as a good coach likely outweighs the last few months.*

After he finishes writing his new belief on his worksheet, I ask, "How do you feel when you say that to yourself? Still embarrassed?"

"Not really."

"Angry at yourself?"

"A little." He considers my question and exhales. "Maybe sad."

I perk up. Sadness is a natural emotion from losing his sister that he hasn't been able to process. "Sounds like a small change in thinking produced a big change in feeling. I wonder...what makes you feel sad?"

He grimaces. "That my reputation as a coach—which took years to build—is now a dumpster fire."

"Ah." Despite his PTSD, he still has a sense of humor in there. I gesture to the paper on his lap. "Please add that to your stuck points: *My reputation as a coach is a dumpster fire.*"

I give him time to write. "Okay, let's review your worksheet on the stuck point, *It's all my fault because I was out of shape.* For emotions, you wrote mad."

"Yeah. At myself."

"Anything else?" I prompt.

He shifts on the sofa. "Guilty, I suppose."

I nod as he writes. "Ashamed?"

He sucks air through his teeth. "Yes."

"Okay." I wait for his shaky hand to add to column C. "Let's look at that first question. You said the stuck point is useful and factual. How is it useful to tell yourself, *It's all my fault because I was out of shape?*"

He squints at the paper. "It's useful to get my butt back into gear, back into shape."

"*Has* that thought helped you get back into shape?"

He gestures toward his body. "Obviously not."

"How has that thought affected you?"

"It's made me feel awful about myself." He grimaces.

I give him a gentle smile. "So, the stuck point isn't useful, then?"

"Guess not."

"Good job. Next, how factual is that thought? What leads you to conclude that you were out of shape?"

"Easy. I couldn't keep up with everyone else on the trip."

"Everyone else swam faster than you?" I ask.

"Well, no. There was a slower group of swimmers, but most of my group—my former teammates—trained more than I did before the trip."

"Would you call someone who can swim four miles a day out of shape?"

His lips press together. "Probably not."

"What leads you to conclude that Kim's death is all your fault?"

He closes his eyes as pain flits across his face. "It's simple." He seems to choke on the words. "If I were fitter, I could've kept up with her, and she wouldn't have hit the coral."

Another stuck point. As I search my tired brain for an effective follow-up question, his expression darkens.

"Men are faster than women," he says. "Kim should've had trouble keeping up with *me*, not the other way around."

"I see." I nod. "If you had trained more prior to the trip, Kim would've had trouble keeping up with you?"

"Yeah."

Now we're getting somewhere. "So, she might have hit coral if she were swimming behind you, instead of in front of you?"

He jolts. After a pause, he says, "That's the point—we should've been swimming together!" He pounds his right hand into his open left palm. "Peter. Told. Us. To. Stay. Together."

"If you were swimming together, how do you know she wouldn't have hit coral?"

He stills. "I…" He licks his lips. "I could've seen the coral, warned her to be careful."

"Could you? I thought you said visibility was poor that day."

His forehead creases.

"I'm not sure how it works on these trips," I say. "If you're swimming in a group, how easy is it to stick together? Did you ever drift apart?"

"Sometimes. It was tough to swim in a tight group no matter how hard we tried."

"Even if you were together, is it possible you couldn't have stopped Kim from swimming into coral?"

He's motionless for a long moment. "Um…yeah." He blinks. "It's possible, I guess."

I dip my head in an emphatic nod. "So, you didn't train as much as you'd hoped, and that made it hard to keep up with Kim. Then you concluded it's your fault she died because you weren't next to her. But you're telling me it's possible she could've swum into coral whether you were behind, ahead of, or right next to her. Does that sound correct?"

A vein in his neck pulses as he stares at me.

"If you can find exceptions to your belief, it's not a fact," I say. "Now that we've examined the evidence behind this belief that your fitness level caused Kim to die, how fair is it to say this stuck point is not factual?"

"But you're backing me into a corner. It's still my fault."

"Okay." I shrug. "I don't expect you to stop blaming yourself in session three. I'm just asking about this specific stuck point—how factual is it that your fitness level led to Kim's death, given that you said she could've hit coral regardless of your swimming speed and location?"

He sighs. "It's hard to debate the logic you're throwing at me." He taps his thigh. "Not factual."

"You can answer no to that question then." I point to the worksheet and wait for him to write. "If your stuck point isn't useful or factual, we want to practice an alternative belief." I point at the bottom question. "There's no right answer here, and it doesn't have to be a positive thought. In my ABC example last time, my new thought was, *How embarrassing. Try to finish the race.* What else could you say to yourself about this situation?"

He slumps as he looks at the paper.

I break the silence. "This is difficult, huh? We never learned these CBT skills in school."

"Maybe…" He taps the pen on the paper. "I should've stayed up with her?"

After a beat, I cross my legs. "Interesting. How similar is that to your original stuck point?"

He seems to deflate. He thumps his fist against his forehead like he's trying to activate his prefrontal cortex. "How about…If I'd been in better shape, I would've been ahead of her, and she still might've hit coral."

"That sounds quite effective." I smile at him. After he writes, I ask, "When you say that to yourself, how do you feel?"

"Better," he says.

"Do you still feel…?" I glance at my tablet. "Mad at yourself?"

"Less so."

"Guilty and ashamed?" I add.

"Yes, but not as bad."

"Okay. Any new feelings emerge when you tell yourself, *If I'd been in better shape, I would've been ahead of her, and she still might've hit coral?*"

"Hmm," he says. "Not sure how to describe it. Kind of like the feeling you get when you're floating in a pool. I read somewhere that we only feel about fifteen percent of our body weight in water."

I imagine that weightless sensation. "Relieved, perhaps?"

"Maybe."

"Okay. Great job on your worksheet. You see how a small change in thinking can produce a big change in feeling."

His eyebrows crawl together. "Maybe I'm relieved, but I also feel…" He glances at the emotions handout. "Uneasy. I don't really believe the alternative thought."

"Totally normal." I gesture to his written statement. "You've told yourself that being out of shape makes it your fault Kim died for how long? Almost five months? You've said it so much that it's become routine."

As we continue to review his worksheets, I'm frustrated by the heaviness weighing down my eyelids. I find myself arguing with Jordan's answers—never a solid therapeutic technique. I need to get back to Socratic questioning and let him find his own way instead of forcing him to see reason with impatient rebuttals. I try to unclench my jaw and breathe through it, but then the tension in my chest morphs from irritation to worry.

How will I be a good therapist for the next eight months if I'm too tired to think straight now?

"This sunshine feels exquisite," says Nadia the next day on one of our frequent workday walks. "And not too hot yet."

I lift my face to the cloudless blue sky and soak in the perfection of springtime in Bluffton. But then I notice Nadia has stopped walking as she waits for me. I'm typically the one to push the pace on our walks, especially when she wears heels. But today she remembered her walking shoes, and I'm not feeling like myself.

"You sure you're not too tired to walk between clients?" she asks.

"Sorry." I force myself to jog a few steps to catch up, which is harder than it should be. I haven't gone for a run the past few days. *Pathetic.* "Thanks for walking with me," I pant. "I need to energize—I've got five clients in a row after this."

She falls into stride next to me. "That's a long day, even if you *weren't* pregnant."

I groan. "How'd you keep working through your first trimester?"

"Well…" She grins as she bumps my elbow. "I was thirty-five, not forty-one."

I'm feeling every one of those years at the moment.

"But for me, morning sickness was worse than the fatigue," she adds. "I hope you don't have to deal with that."

Amen. I was able to eat lunch before our walk with no problem.

She chuckles. "I remember I was seeing this married couple, and I was *so* nauseated. But I tried to hide my pregnancy because the main source of their conflict was years of unsuccessful fertility treatments."

"Uh-oh."

"You can see where this is going. I held off running to the bathroom so long that I didn't even make it out of the office. I ended up vomiting in the trash can, right in front of them." Her gold bracelets clank as she brings her hand to her forehead. "So embarrassing."

I shake my head. "You must've felt guilty when you told them you were pregnant."

"Indeed. Once I cleaned up and returned to the session, I had to give them my news. The wife started crying."

"Oh, no." My worries multiply. I had hoped talking to Nadia would help me with this situation, not make it worse.

"Actually, it turned into a breakthrough for them. Picture this— the wife's sobbing into her hands, and the husband gives me this angry, helpless look. I motion to him to hug his wife, and finally, he does. She just melts into his arms. That was one of their issues. He grew up in a cold family that didn't know how to comfort each other, and I could tell it meant a lot to his wife when he held her.

Anyway, I started empathizing with them about the devastation of not being able to conceive when even their *therapist* is pregnant, and the husband jumps in and says, 'I wish you could barf from morning sickness too, honey.'"

I snicker at that.

"We all laughed, even his wife. And that was the perfect prompt to discuss how they could support each other better."

I think about Brandon, who has become way too involved in my menstrual cycle. When I was just two days late last week, he rushed out to buy five pregnancy tests. As the little plus sign materialized, I froze from shock, but he lit up like a Christmas tree. He twirled me around the great room, pausing only to pull up "the perfect playlist" on his phone. While we danced to "Small Bump" by Ed Sheeran, Brandon's giddy grin transformed my stupor to excitement. I'm a clumsy, inexperienced dancer, but once I learned to surrender to his lead, we moved together as one. Two parents for one child. I've never felt so close to a man before.

"How is Brandon supporting *you?*" asks Nadia, like she can read my mind.

I pinch a miniscule of air between my thumb and forefinger. "He's just a little excited."

She smiles, and we walk a bit more. "And how're you feeling?"

Such a psychologist question. "I'm excited, too."

"Nervous? I was."

She knows me well. "For sure. Any advice for how to tell clients once I start showing?"

"I don't think there's a right answer, and you're such a competent therapist. I'm sure you'll handle it well."

I wish I felt as confident in myself. I imagine waddling into the waiting room with a massive belly, and a tendril of unease curls my insides. I'm uncomfortable with my clients knowing something personal about me when I haven't chosen to share it.

"Just follow your instincts," Nadia says. "Like with my couple, everything's grist for the mill. Maybe your bump will start a discussion about their relationship with their mother. Explore what your pregnancy means to them, how it may change their view of you. For example, I think some clients might envy your unborn child."

"*Envy?*" I scrunch my forehead.

"They may worry your baby will take all of your attention, that you won't be there for them when they need you."

Or there might be envy about my career consuming all my attention. Brandon's increasing complaints about my long work hours intrude on my mind. I've learned he played basketball in high school, and he's started a full-court press on my priorities since the pregnancy test.

"How long do you plan to take for maternity leave?" Nadia asks. "I could see a couple of your clients for a few months."

"Thank you." There's a quiver in my voice that draws my friend's prying gaze, but I look straight ahead as I keep putting one foot in front of the other. "It'll be longer than that, though. Brandon thinks I should stay home with the baby full-time."

Nadia halts, her melodic voice turning shrill behind me. "What?"

I swivel and meet her eyes, which have doubled in size.

"You're going to stop seeing clients?"

"I…" I lick my lower lip. "I'm giving full-time motherhood a try after I give birth." *If* the baby survives till then — anything could happen, especially at my age. "If I miss my career too much, I'll come back."

Nadia flips her long, blond hair over her shoulder, and her bracelets jangle again as she perches her fist on her hip. "But you can't leave your clients just hanging around, waiting for you to decide. You'll have to refer them all out."

"I know that," I snap. I cringe at my defensive tone. Worry about terminating my clients hasn't helped my sleep.

"Avery." She steps toward me. "You told me being a psychologist is your *calling*. I — I can't believe you'd just walk away. Is that what you want?"

Is it what I want? What *do* I want? I want peace in my house — Brandon's house, I mean. He paid for it. I'm just so tired. This baby is already zapping my physical and mental energy. My caffeine-withdrawal headaches have subsided, but I still crave coffee. From what I've read, once I get through the first trimester, I'll start feeling more vivacious. It can't come soon enough.

Nadia clasps my wrist. "Hey, Aves. I'm sorry. I don't want to push too hard. I'm just stunned. This doesn't sound like you." She's a good five inches shorter than me without her heels, and her blue eyes look up, beseeching me. "I was so happy when you and Brandon found each other. But are *you* happy? You can say no to him, right?"

"Of course!" Maybe I answered too quickly. I let out a breath. "It just makes sense for me to stop working. We don't need the money."

"Who cares about *money?*" She shakes my arm. "This is about your fulfillment, your gifts. You've been working since you were a teen. You love being a psychologist, and your clients think the world of you."

I can't keep listening to this. I dislodge her hand from my wrist to look at my smartwatch. "I need to go. Don't want to be late for my next client."

She traces a finger below her bottom lip as she studies me. "Go on ahead." She shakes her head. "I'm going to stay out here a bit longer, try to make sense of this bomb you've dropped on me."

Our role reversal continues, as I'm usually the one to cajole her into more walking. I don't want to worry or disappoint her. "It'll be a good thing," I say as I walk backwards toward our office. "You'll see." From the crease between her brows, I can tell she's unconvinced.

Back in my office, I pull up my notes for my next client. For a moment, I cradle my belly. The outer shape feels the same as last month — mostly flat — but within blooms a beautiful package. Despite my fatigue, I grin from the thrill of a little human growing inside of me. I pat my belly. "I'll take good care of you, sweetheart." The blue light on my desk clicks on. "But first, I'll take good care of five clients." My grin fades. "In a row."

Brandon's right. I do deserve a break from my insane schedule.

9. AVERY

As Jordan takes a seat to begin our session six days later, I worry about the mushrooming scruff on his face and lengthening shag of coffee brown hair beneath his black baseball cap. Lack of grooming is not a good sign for his state of mind.

But maybe I'm reading into his appearance. I've been on edge all morning, with an anxious sensation in my gut and pressure pushing up my throat. It started when Brandon nuzzled my neck at the breakfast table. His pricey aftershave used to turn me on, but now one whiff roils my stomach. I haven't had the heart to ask him to stop using it. Instead, once he left for a meeting, I scrubbed my neck with soap and water to get rid of the stench. Even so, I had to toss my English muffin down the garbage disposal. Now I can't tell if I'm nauseated or hungry, but I do know I need to focus for Jordan's important session four.

When he hands me his PCL-5, I notice shadowy bruises beneath his eyes. "How'd you sleep last night?" I ask.

"Awful." He rubs his temples. "Nightmares about Mason's meet."

I start to score his PTSD symptoms. "The meet is soon?"

"Yep. We leave for Knoxville in a week."

After a couple of minutes, I tell him his score is sixty-five.

He shrugs like it doesn't matter, but then he looks down. It's a cloudy, gloomy day, and the vibe in the room gets even heavier as he tells my area rug, "I didn't do my worksheets."

He continues to stare at the floor, but I try to hide my concern anyway. I'm confused by his backsliding, given the strength of his impact statement and first round of worksheets. "That happens," I say. "What do you recall from our first session about the role of avoidance?"

He's quiet for a moment. "You said it's a symptom of PTSD."

"Right." I feel a surge of nausea and swallow it down. "Anything else?"

He looks up at me. "Trauma memories make you panic, so you try to avoid them, but avoidance makes the trauma stick."

My eyebrows elevate. That was the perfect answer. "Exactly. What led to your avoidance this week?"

"I was going to do them. I was. But then I got a phone call." The tiny muscles around his eyes grow taut. "From my sister's teammate."

"Who?" I ask.

"Danielle. She's the head women's swim coach at University of Tennessee."

He stares at me like that should mean something, and I take a deep breath, pushing down the churning in my stomach. "Oh." I sit straighter. "She called because you'll be in Knoxville for the meet?"

"Uh-huh."

"You said she's Kim's friend, not yours?" When he nods, I add, "But don't you have a lot in common with a fellow coach like Danielle?"

He rolls his eyes. "You'd think. But Danielle hates me. Or, she did...I guess." He must read my intrigue, because he continues. "Kim and Danielle were friends with another girl on the team, who ended up being my girlfriend in college." He rubs his hand across his mouth, and a faint blush colors his cheeks. "I worshipped Anna. She was such a great butterflier. And totally hot. But I was a cocky, immature loser, and I broke up with her."

I try to picture Jordan twenty years ago. "That sounds rough."

"I thought Anna was flirting with another guy, so I ended it. When I found out she wasn't into him, it was too late. She wouldn't take me back."

The patter of raindrops pulls my attention to the window. Thinking about his father's death, I wonder if Jordan dumped Anna before she could abandon him.

"Danielle never let it go. Kim yelled at me, too, but then..." He lowers his head. "She forgave me."

I understand better why he dodged his worksheets. "Danielle's call triggered memories of Kim's death."

The bill of his ballcap moves up and down as he nods. "There are triggers everywhere."

"Oh yeah?"

His chin trembles as he looks up at me. "It was Wyatt's birthday yesterday. He turned forty."

"Ah." My gut clenches. "You and Wyatt planned the Baja trip for Kim's fortieth birthday."

His lips form a bitter smile.

I hope he can get back on track. "You'll continue to encounter reminders of Kim, but if you give in to the avoidance, your score won't come down."

"I *need* it to come down." He looks up at the ceiling. "Don't know how I'll get through this meet if I can't get some sleep."

"Okay. Since you did all seven ABC worksheets last week, let's move on. I'll introduce a new exercise today. How confident do you feel that you'll complete the assignment this week?"

His lips protrude as he exhales. "I'll do it. I have to." There's a ripple in his jaw muscle. "It's the only way to keep my job."

I hand him a sheet of paper. "This next handout explores your role in the trauma, focusing on your intent." I hope this exercise will lower his self-blame. "There are different levels of responsibility we may hold. We are least responsible in the case of an unexpected event. For example, a driver rear-ends my car as I'm sitting at a red light, which has nothing to do with me. I will likely feel grief when that happens."

"Okay."

"We bear partial responsibility when we play a role in the event, but we don't *intend* the outcome. Maybe I'm speeding down a dark road, and I hit a pedestrian who darted out from the side of the road. I certainly didn't intend for the pedestrian to die, but I did play a role due to breaking the speed limit. An emotion like regret fits the facts of this situation."

He yawns, which makes me yawn, too. "Sorry," he says.

I nod and go on. "The most responsibility we hold is when we intend the outcome. Let's say I got a divorce and want revenge on my ex-husband. I drive to his workplace and gun him down as he walks in."

Jordan leans away from me. "Yikes."

I grin at his feigned fear. "Hypothetical, of course." My smile fades. I came up with these driving examples to explain the worksheet long before I met Brandon, and I probably need to revise them. "*Guilt* fits this scenario. Our legal system also differentiates levels of responsibility. Hitting the pedestrian would be involuntary manslaughter, but killing my ex-husband would be murder since my intent was harm."

He studies the worksheet. "Makes sense."

"Think about your role in Kim's death, Jordan. How much responsibility do you hold?"

He stills.

After a bit, I prod, "Did you intend for Kim to die?"

"Of course not." He frowns. "So not total responsibility. But I did play a role. I planned the trip. She would've been completely safe if she'd stayed in Ohio."

"Sounds like another stuck point. Will you add that one?"

He pauses, then he shuffles through the papers in his folder and writes on his log.

"You want to go with partial responsibility, then?" I ask. "Or was it an unexpected event?"

"Maybe it *was* unexpected, but like I said, I had a part in it. I planned the whole trip. I didn't train hard enough. I should've gotten into the boat. I should've been there for her." He shakes the paper, and his volume increases. "I made all these mistakes. Can't you see? She should've been able to pursue her dreams, not die because I wasn't there for her. I robbed her of ever having children!"

As his last statement echoes, nausea gurgles in my stomach. *Why does he have to talk about having children? What does that have to do with the trauma?* I steady my breath. "It sounds like it was an unforeseeable event, and you didn't intend for her to die. But you still feel guilt, which doesn't fit the facts of your role."

A line creases his forehead. "You're saying I shouldn't feel guilty?"

"Guilt is an effective response to *intending* harm. But you didn't want her to die. You just wanted to celebrate her birthday."

He squints at me. Despite the turmoil in my GI tract, I can see he's starting to question his intense culpability. If I can get through this nausea, our next exercise has the potential to blow up the self-blame.

"Let's explore this a bit more." I draw a circle on my iPad. "This is a responsibility pie. We're going to break down the factors that led to Kim's death." Below the circle, I write *Jordan*. "You told me you played a role in the trauma." I point at his stuck point log. "This includes your beliefs that you should've trained more, shouldn't have chosen a remote island, et cetera." I jot down a few of his stuck points next to his name. "Now, what else caused the trauma?"

He stares at the circle for a long moment. "Just me. I'm the only one responsible."

He's digging in his heels. I listen to raindrops splash into the lagoon outside, competing with the hum of the fountain. "What about the conditions that day? You said it was wavy? That the clouds caused poor visibility?"

"Yeah." His eyebrows push together. "I guess that's a cause, too."

"How about the coral?" It seems I'm stating the obvious, but it's tough to break through long-held beliefs. "It played a role in her death, true?"

"Okay, true."

I add weather conditions and coral to the factors responsible for Kim's death.

"Do you ascribe any responsibility to the company who ran the trip? The guide or other staff?"

"No!" His back straightens. "Peter did everything he could. He feels just as guilty as me. When he found out..." His voice trails off, and he ducks his head.

"When he found out what?"

"Just drop it," he tells the floor.

A lightheaded sensation lifts my brain, and my face grows hot. *Please don't throw up.* I need to chase down Jordan's evasiveness, but all

I can focus on is fighting my stomach. *Get yourself together, Avery. We're close to something here.* I puff out my cheeks and force a steady exhale.

He's still looking down. I need to take a soft approach with my next question. "What about Kim?"

His eyes flare with shock as his head snaps up.

"Is there anything about Kim that contributed to her death?"

After a long moment, he shuts his open mouth. "Peter told me she kept saying she was careless. But it's not her fault. She was probably just tired at the end of a long swim."

"Just like you were tired?"

He doesn't answer. The paper in his grasp trembles.

I tremble too, but I continue to ignore my quaking insides.

"What about the medical care in Mexico?" I ask. "They couldn't stop the bleeding? What'd the doctors tell you?"

Color drains from his face. His eyes glass over with tears that his rapid blinks can't clear. I watch the quick rise and fall of his chest as he begins to hyperventilate. His hands cover his face, and he starts to rock back and forth on the sofa.

At the same moment, a flush of heat and pressure pulses up my throat. *No. No.* But I have no choice—I'm on my feet before I can think. "Be right back," I manage to blurt before I rush out of the office and make it to the bathroom just in time.

10. JORDAN

The whoosh of Dr. Avery's departure snaps me back to her office. I no longer see the scrub-green tile of hospital walls or hear the accented English of the Mexican surgeon as he delivers devastating news. Instead, the gushing hum of the lagoon fountain draws my gaze to the window. The rain has stopped, but dark clouds remain. Just like the day of Kim's death.

I pivot my head to stare at the closed door. Where did my psychologist go? I lift a shaking hand to my face and yank it away when I feel wetness. I've been *crying?* Revulsion crawls up my throat. Dr. Avery must be repulsed by me, by my weakness. She's decided I'm too messed up to help, and she's not coming back. I don't blame her. I wouldn't want me for a client, either.

Get it together, Perry. I can't leave the office a snotty mess. I snatch some tissues, wipe my face, and blow my nose. But how will I tell Elena my psychologist fired me? I still haven't confessed my close call with the Lionfish board. I'll have to pretend to keep going to therapy so my wife doesn't worry about me. I won't have to maintain the charade for long, though, because Elena *will* leave once she sees I'm not any better. She'll take the kids, and I'll be alone. It's what I deserve.

As I stand on wobbly legs, I notice a bruised banana peel on Dr. Avery's desk with half a banana inside, along with a package of saltine crackers and some scattered papers. I squint at the atypical mess. There's also a mostly empty bottle of Sprite.

I jump when the door opens. My right hand covers my racing heart as Dr. Avery takes a step inside.

"I'm so sorr—" She cocks her head when she sees me standing with my folder in my left hand. "Are you about to leave?"

"Um, yeah."

She wipes the back of her hand across her mouth and closes the door behind her. "Why?"

"Because you don't want to see me anymore."

She gapes at me like I'm a patch of fungus on the pool deck. "I have no idea what you're talking about." Her outstretched hand points at the sofa. "Would you sit back down and tell me what's going on?"

So, she wants to let me down easy, tell me to my face that she can't keep seeing me for therapy. Why do psychologists always have to process everything?

I lower myself to the cushions. She seems unsteady on her feet as she crosses to her desk, unscrews the cap on the Sprite, and drains it. When she tosses the empty plastic bottle to the garbage can, it bonks off the rim onto the floor. "Whoops." She starts toward the can, but I beat her to it.

"I got it." I place the bottle in the trash, but I don't retake my seat. There's something weird about her, a vulnerable vibe I've never sensed before. I feel like I need to stay on my feet to catch her if she falls. The sensation reminds me of pudgy little Hudson's first tentative steps, when Elena told me to stop hovering so much.

"Oh, uh, thank you." She opens her desk drawer, and I hear the crinkle of a wrapper before she pops something in her mouth. After reaching into her desk again, she turns to me and holds out a white mint. "Want a Life Saver?"

I bristle. "No thanks." The medicinal scent of peppermint wafts my way. Kim had a bag of those in Baja. And just like that, my heart starts to thunder again.

Dr. Avery looks at me after she takes her seat. "Jordan, what's happening?" When I don't answer, she asks, "Will you sit?"

A tremor knocks my knees as I return to the sofa.

She's still looking at me. "What makes you think I don't want to meet with you anymore?"

"Because I disgust you."

Her head draws back like I've slapped her, but I keep going.

"Because I'm too far gone to help. I'm making you feel bad about yourself since you can't help me. But it's not your fault. No one can help me. I'm a mess." A burning sensation flares in my nostrils, but I can't cry in front of her again. I also can't keep looking at the pity in her expression, so I duck my head. "My breakdown made you run out of here." My voice cracks on the last word as my chest spasms.

"Jordan."

Don't cry. Don't cry.

"Jordan, will you look at me?"

I force myself to meet her eyes.

She says, "Me running out of here had nothing to do with you."

My blinks come rapid-fire. She *has* to say something like that, but she doesn't really mean it. I shake my head as I bite the inside of my lip.

"Jordan." She sighs. "I ran out of here because I was about to throw up."

I scrunch my nose as she confirms my fears. "I disgust you that much, huh?"

Her mouth drops open. "This isn't about you. I'm *pregnant*! I have morning sickness."

Now I'm the one who feels slapped. I stop breathing as my vision swims with sharp, vivid images…the Mexican doctor's apologetic eyes…blood pooling on the boat deck…Kim's small smile, her face illuminated by birthday cake candles before she blows them out…

A sob rips through me, opening a cavern of pain in my chest. I can't breathe. The waves crash onto the shore, mere feet from where Kim and I sit. As my bare feet make circles in the cool, grainy sand, I hear my words echo through the darkness of night, *"What'd you wish for, birthday girl?"*

"Hey."

A woman's voice sounds a mile away.

"Jordan."

I'm underwater, and Dr. Avery's muffled voice calls to me from the boat. Brownish coral juts out from the ocean floor all around me, its cutting edges inches from my legs. But I can't pull myself up to the surface. Surging waves force me down, closer to the coral, sending my heart rate into orbit.

"Open your eyes, Jordan."

At once, I feel my body: the squeeze of my chest on my thighs, the pressure of my palms on my face. I realize I'm a tight ball curled onto myself, a frozen block of tension. With an involuntary gulp of air, I bolt up and press my spine against the back of the sofa. The gushing of the fountain fills my ears. My gaze darts around the therapy office and lands on Dr. Avery's face. Her wide eyes seem full of concern.

"What do you notice about your breath?"

Her question puzzles me at first, then my chest bounces with quick inhales. "Hyper...ventilating," I get out.

She nods and hands me a box of tissues.

I accept them with one shaky hand while the other flies up to my face. Horror floods me when I feel the dampness of tears.

"Before you try to sprint out of here, I want you to know I'm not disgusted by you crying," she says. "Quite the opposite—crying is the most effective thing you can do right now. You're processing your emotions instead of bottling them up. Excellent work."

Yeah, I'm doing really great. I don't deserve her kindness. I pluck about ten tissues from the box.

"I wonder..." She waits for me to wipe under my eyes. "Which emotions are you processing?"

The rapid up-and-down of my chest feels similar to finishing a one-hundred freestyle race. I consider her question. Panic? But why would I be scared? Sadness, I decide. And ever-present guilt.

"You seemed to have a strong reaction to my abrupt departure," she adds. "I'm sorry about that. Would you share it with me?"

I swallow. "It's *why* you left—that's what I reacted to." I huff out a breath, angry with myself. I've revealed too much.

She nibbles her lip. "You have a phobia about vomiting?"

"No." I close my eyes. I can't tell her. It's too shameful. Nobody knows this, except for Peter, the swim guide in Baja. When I open my eyes, I notice her hands cradling her belly.

Following my gaze, she looks down, and she moves her palms away in an instant. "Oh! You're reacting to me being pregnant."

Bingo.

"What...?" She hesitates. "What does my pregnancy mean to you?" I can't tell her. My lungs constrict, and it's hard to get a full breath. She studies me. "Have you and Elena had any fertility issues?"

I shake my head.

"Did your mother have difficult pregnancies?"

More head shakes. *What are these strange questions?*

"Um, some clients may worry about me being here for them, uh, after I have my baby?" She seems to cringe. "You know, this therapy is only about three months long, so we'll be done before I give birth."

Her intellect and intuition have been first rate, but she doesn't understand me at all right now. "That pie thing," I blurt as I point at her iPad.

"The responsibility pie?" She picks up the tablet and shows me the circle.

Dr. Avery wrote one word beneath the circle that captures my full attention: *Kim.* My muscles tingle. *Oh, God.* I'm going to tell her. The compression squeezing my chest leaves me no choice. "You asked..." I force the pressure down with a swallow. "You asked about Kim and factors...that contributed to her death." I try to quell the shakes ripping through me as I hear the Mexican doctor's explanation echo in my mind. "She was pregnant when she died."

A gasp parts Dr. Avery's lips, and she doesn't move for several seconds. "How shattering." Her face fills with sadness, which brings tears to my eyes again. I can't stop crying, no matter how hard I try. "But I'm a bit confused," she says. "Her pregnancy contributed to her death?"

"That's what the doctor told me. Told...us. Peter was there, too." My breath hitches. "She bled out because her platelets were low. It, it happens with some pregnant women, the doctor said. Gestational..." I force air into my trembling chest to get the word out. "Thrombocytopenia." It's the first time I've spoken the word aloud, though I've read countless web pages from Dr. Google.

Dr. Avery leans back in her chair. "Whoa. Did she know she was pregnant?"

I sniff. "Don't think so. We thought she was seasick." I think of the big, bearded man who approached me in the parlor of my mom's Methodist church. "The guy Kim was seeing—another teacher—*he* didn't know she was pregnant." A lump forms in my throat. "I didn't tell him, either." My sob brings on a sharp inhale. "I couldn't tell him. Couldn't tell anyone." Not my mom, my wife, or my best friend. Tears flood my eyes, stream down my cheeks. "She wanted kids...so bad." I swipe a tissue beneath my nose. "She dreamed about it, wished for it. She never had the chance."

Crying engulfs me again, turning my breath ragged. The veil of tears blinds me. "She...would've been...an amazing mom."

Dr. Avery lets me cry. After a few moments, she says, "Kim took such great care of you after your dad died."

I sob harder. Kim's death on top of my dad's—it's too much. I can't handle it. Rivers of grief pour out of me, emanating from a deep hollow of my chest, pushing up my throat, wrenching through me. I thought the ache of my despair after Dad died was bad, but it's doubled now, deeper than I thought possible, like I'm about to break in half. My body rocks to the frantic rhythm of each staccato breath. I have to stop this breathtaking pain, but I can't. It keeps flowing out of me. I'm terrified it'll never end.

At some point, though, minutes or hours later, my grief starts to fade. As I exhale, I notice the spasms in my chest subsiding. I'm able, at last, to take my first steady breath. My eyes have stopped generating tears, though my eyelids droop from the effort of sobbing. I feel a clump of wet tissues in my fist and realize I've used nearly the whole box next to me.

"How're you feeling?"

I look up at the sound of my psychologist's voice. "Sorry I used all your tissues." I push to my feet, marveling that I can stand, and walk to the wastebasket.

She gives me a gentle smile after I retake my seat. "I've got more."

Of course she does. She's probably bought stock in Kleenex.

"How're you feeling?" she asks again.

I consider her question. "Tired."

"I bet. That was quite a secret you've been carrying around." When heat blooms in my face, she adds, "I'm so grateful you shared it with me. I think your bottled-up devastation over the pregnancy has prevented you from healing."

I pause. She's saying I can start healing now? But I'm still the one who caused Kim's death. I don't deserve to heal.

"Let's revisit this responsibility pie, now that we've filled in all the pieces." She taps the circle drawn on her tablet. "Out of one-hundred-percent responsibility for Kim's death, how much did the pregnancy/blood-platelet issue contribute?"

I feel my lungs inflate and deflate. "The doctor said it was a big factor. But he also said they could've stopped the bleeding if we'd been closer. It took over an hour to get to the hospital."

"So, the remote location also contributed to her death."

I wince. *A location I chose for us.*

She writes, *Pregnancy + Remote Location* under the circle. "How much did those factors contribute to her death?" When I don't respond, she prompts, "Ten percent? Ninety percent?"

"Gotta be over fifty percent."

"Are you saying...fifty-five percent? Sixty?"

I shrug. How can I parse out the exact factors leading to this horror? "Sixty."

"Okay." She writes *60%* next to those factors. "Leaving forty-percent responsibility to divvy up. How much would you give the coral? Or the poor weather and visibility conditions that day?"

I rub my tongue along the roof of my mouth. Both had a role in my sister dying, I have to admit. "Probably fifteen each."

"Leaving you about ten-percent responsibility?"

I flinch. *What?* That doesn't sound right.

She draws lines inside the circle that create a pie chart, with *Pregnancy + Remote Location* taking up a little over half the circle, *Coral* and *Weather* each consuming another sizable chunk, and finishing with *Jordan* as a small sliver.

"Does this look about right?"

How can that be? I *have* to shoulder the blame for more than ten percent. But it's math. I can't deny that a confluence of events — factors outside my control — contributed to my sister's death. As I stare at the circle, my jaw falls open. A bizarre sensation tugs up the corners of my mouth. A smile? *I want to smile?* But it's wrong to smile when we're talking about Kim leaving this earth. I clamp my mouth shut.

"Any changes you'd make to this responsibility pie?" Dr. Avery asks.

I shake my head. "It's right, I guess."

"This is quite different from what you've been telling yourself. You've imagined this circle filled completely by you." She moves her stylus around the circle. "But now you can see you own only a small part of it."

I absorb this plot twist. *Has my narrative been way off?*

"The next time self-blame stuck points bombard you, I want you to visualize this pie." She taps the tablet. "Want to take a picture to help you remember?"

I take out my phone and snap a photo.

"Good work." She places her tablet on the side table and hands me a piece of paper. "Ready for our next worksheet?"

A steamroller of emotions has flattened me, but hey, let's keep diving into the pain. I manage a nod.

"This worksheet is one of my favorites. We'll write a stuck point at the top of the page then ask some questions about the belief." She gestures at my folder. "Let's choose a stuck point to practice with."

I fumble through the looseleaf pages for my log.

"How would you feel about choosing a stuck point based on our earlier discussion?"

My fingers freeze on the papers.

"How about *I robbed my sister of becoming a mother?*"

I narrow my eyes. "Going for the jugular, huh?"

One corner of her mouth quirks. "You're a tough athlete. You can take it."

That's debatable, but I write the stuck point at the top of the page. I have to trust Dr. Avery. She's gotten me this far, and I can't deny the lighter feeling in my body at the moment.

She says, "Look at the first question. What evidence supports or refutes the belief? So, if you went before a judge and said, 'I robbed my sister of becoming a mother,' what evidence would you present?"

My chest clenches, and the tightness in my throat returns. "If I hadn't planned the trip, she'd still be alive."

"Hold on." She reaches out to stop me from writing that answer. "We don't want another stuck point as evidence for *this* stuck point."

"But that's a fact. She wouldn't be dead if not for me."

"Is it a fact? How could you know for certain — how could you prove in court — that Kim wouldn't have died if she'd stayed in Ohio? How do you know she wouldn't have died in a car accident, for example?"

I frown. That's absurd, but I can't think of an argument she'll accept.

"What other evidence do you have?"

I force my brain to work. "I should've known she was pregnant when she kept getting sick. I should've stopped her from swimming that day."

From the look on her face, I know what she's going to say before she has the chance. I exhale. "More stuck points, huh?"

She smiles. "Yep. Add them to your log, please." After I write them, she says, "*Robbing* someone sounds like an intentional action. What *was* your intent?"

"To give her an awesome birthday with her friends, doing something she loved. She worshipped…" My jaw clenches. "Swimming."

"Okay, that's a solid challenge to your stuck point: your intent was to celebrate her birthday doing something she loved."

I write it down. It's true that all I wanted was to celebrate Kim.

"At this point, is there any supportive evidence that you intentionally robbed your sister of having children?"

After a beat, I grunt, "No."

"Then please write *None* for that question. But if something comes to you later, you can add it. Next question: is your stuck point repetitive or factual? Here's a hint — if you can't come up with any evidence to support the stuck point, it's probably not a fact. How many times have you said this stuck point to yourself?"

I click my tongue. "I've tried to shove it out of my mind, but it keeps coming back."

"Intrusions and avoidance, no fun." She shakes her head. "Is it possible you've said it so many times that it feels true?"

"I think so."

"Then it's more repetitive than factual?"

I roll my eyes and write, *Repetitive.*

"Let's move on. What important information does your stuck point leave out?"

After a moment, I say, "I didn't know she was pregnant?"

"That's a great one! This is about context—what you knew at the time, what your options were. That nugget of information isn't included in your stuck point."

This time, I can't stop myself from smiling. Who doesn't love to be praised?

"Here's more information your stuck point fails to include: You told me Kim loved to hang out with her nephew and niece, right?"

I nod.

"Though Kim didn't have children of her own, you folded her into your family. Instead of robbing her of children, you *gave* her children. You helped her spend quality time in a parental role."

Wowzers. That's right. I often tried to sell her—hell, *give* her—my children. But she always laughed and called me a horrible father. When I look up, Dr. Avery has a wistful grin. "What?"

"I think this is the first time I've seen you smile." She pauses. "Okay, next question: are there black-or-white concepts in your stuck point? Beliefs like *It's all my fault* or *I have zero self-confidence* could fit the pattern of one extreme or the other. Other times, the extreme concept is more implied, like…" She picks up the tablet on her lap and scrolls down. "*If something bad happens to me, my kids' lives will be ruined.*"

I recognize one of my stuck points.

"It's all or nothing," she notes. "Either something good or something bad will happen to you, and either your kids' lives will be perfect or ruined. Neither extreme is probably true. So, does *I robbed my sister of becoming a mother* include black-or-white terms?"

My mouth twists to one side. "I don't think so?"

She nods. "Not all of these questions are relevant for each stuck point. You could write N/A, or you could challenge the idea that either she was a mother or she wasn't. She *was* maternal in many ways, with your kids and her students." She waits for me to write my answer, then moves on to ask about exaggerated language in my stuck points.

I tap the pen to my forehead. "I guess *robbed* is kind of a dramatic word."

"I agree. Excellent. Next question: Does your stuck point focus on only one aspect of the story, ignoring other aspects?"

I gnaw on my bottom lip.

"There's not one correct response," she says. "Does this stuck point focus only on *your* role in the trauma?"

I blink. "Yeah."

She holds up the responsibility pie. "Your role only contributed ten percent, though. What about the other ninety-percent responsibility? Does this stuck point neglect those factors?"

My slow nods pick up pace. This bit about me robbing Kim of being a mother is ridiculous. I write, *Only focuses on my part, but I didn't even know she was pregnant.*

"Moving on. Where did this belief come from? Is this something you've told yourself, or did another person say this?"

"Me."

"And how reliable are you as a source of information on this stuck point?"

I angle my head to one side.

"Had you ever heard of gestational thrombocytopenia before? How much expertise do you have with emergency medicine? Marine ecosystems?"

I retract my chin. "I'm pretty clueless about all of that."

"Then you can write that you're not a reliable source on this topic."

"Almost done," she continues when I've finished. "How do you feel when you tell yourself, *I robbed my sister of becoming a mother?*"

That familiar squeeze grips my throat, though its hold over me doesn't seem quite as intense. "Guilt. Anger."

"Anger at yourself, I bet. Do you think this stuck point is more about your guilt and self-directed anger than about facts?"

I let out a disgusted chuckle. "Probably."

"Well done. On to the last question, maybe the toughest. Does this stuck point zoom in on irrelevant parts of the story? Here's an example. Let's say I'm driving, and a driver in a yellow car hits mine, injuring me..." She stops and seems to think for a moment. "Let's change that to a *red* car. If I then think, *All red cars are dangerous,* that's incorrect, because the color of the car is irrelevant to the story. Does your stuck point focus on any irrelevant aspects?"

I sit still for a second, but I can't come up with an answer.

"How did you feel about having a wife and kids while Kim was single?"

"Awful." I swallow. "Kim stopped me from screwing it up with Elena, but I couldn't help her find a good man. She had bad luck with guys. Also, I wanted cousins for my kids. Maybe that's selfish."

"Nothing selfish about that." Dr. Avery nods as her hand moves toward her waistband. She doesn't seem to notice she's rubbing her belly. "Could this stuck point be more about your guilt over having a loving family, and wishing Kim had that as well, than it is about robbing her of having children?"

"Huh. Never thought of it that way." I let that idea sink in. "I think so." I write my answer.

"And…we're done for today!" She looks at her watch. "Just in time, too." She hands me the practice assignment. "The goal is to practice with this worksheet each day of the week. How confident do you feel about completing your assignment?"

"I'll do it." I'm surprised to feel the stir of determination inside of me. I'm going to crush these worksheets.

"Good to hear. Any reactions to session four?"

I look her up and down. Can she take some teasing? Though she's sick from her pregnancy, she *was* in the Navy. "Mason told me you're a great psychologist. I gotta admit, I haven't agreed with him."

She holds still, seeming to brace herself for criticism.

"But you did good today, kid."

A smirk spreads across her mouth. "Glad I proved myself, Coach. Our next session's right before you leave for Mason's meet, right?"

That fire in my belly burns hotter. "Yep. See you then."

11. AVERY

Four days after my mid-session vomit episode, I hear our doorbell ring. At first, the sound loosens the strain in my neck. *My brother found our island home without getting lost.* I want Nate's unexpected visit to end before Brandon returns from a Sunday-morning round of golf. But my heart starts thumping as I walk toward the front door. Despite Nate living a mere ninety miles north of me in Charleston, I haven't talked to him in over a year. He called me about thirty minutes ago after showing up at my former home, only to find new owners.

My brother's brown eyes, a shade darker than mine, widen after I open the door. He swivels and sweeps his arm across the lush landscape of our front yard. "You win the lottery or something?"

"Haha." My chuckle is more nervous than amused. Just wait till he sees our deck and private lagoon. Our father's military salary could never afford a place like this. "A step up from my townhouse in Bluffton, huh?"

He steps in and continues to gawk at the architecture. Though he's not quite as tall as our father or Brandon, he's got several inches on me. However, his presence diminishes inside our cavernous foyer. I peek at our driveway before I close the door. No sign of my husband.

We stare at each other for a moment. Nate, or his wife, has let his golden-brown hair grow out longer than I like, almost touching the collar of his blue polo shirt, and his gray cargo pants look rumpled. I also can't miss his ruddy cheeks, nor the telltale rosy bulb of his nose. He's drinking again.

He meets my eyes before averting his gaze, and my shoulders stiffen. Should I hug him? We aren't huggers in our family, though he did take the time to drive down here to see me. "C'mere, little brother." I step toward him, and he folds me into an embrace. Surprising tears spring to my eyes. I'm sure he's here to ask for something, probably money, but seeing him still stirs tenderness in my heart.

We both look away after stepping out of the hug. I clear my throat and gesture to the great room. "Can I get you something to drink?"

"You're *married?*" He gapes at the ring on my extended left hand, which I clap back to my side.

Before Christmas, when Brandon and I leaped at the chance to jet off to Aruba for a destination wedding, it seemed like a good decision not to tell my family. I try to avoid them, especially around the holidays. My alcoholic father has no part in my life, and my mother would have meddled, with too many questions and unsolicited advice. I also knew my brother and his wife couldn't afford the airfare, and I didn't want to make it awkward by offering to pay. But seeing the hurt in his eyes, I regret it now.

"Yes." *And pregnant.* "Sorry I didn't tell you. It all happened so fast." I turn and walk into the kitchen, pressing my laptop shut and grabbing my breakfast plate from the table on the way to the sink. "Want a club soda and lime?"

His eyes roam over the oven's ornate hood and the kitchen island's breadth before landing on the refrigerators. I think it's ostentatious to have an entire fridge dedicated to chilling wine, but Brandon says he can't live without it. "Sure." Nate sounds distracted.

I take out a tall, green bottle from the main refrigerator, and the hiss when I unscrew the cap reminds me to exhale. He's just my brother, my lone sibling. Only we know what it was like to grow up with our father. Despite our differences, I love Nate.

As I hand him the sparkling beverage, I ask, "How's Morgan?"

"Good, good." He averts his eyes again as he takes a sip.

His wife is *drama.* I'll bet he's lying. "Let's sit on the sectional." As I head to the great room, I hear him draw in a breath behind me.

"Dude," he says.

The view out the floor-to-ceiling windows *is* breathtaking. Beyond the expansive deck is a lagoon with a fountain — my favorite part of the house, especially when various birds visit, like today's cormorants.

He settles onto a leather cushion at an angle from me. "What does your husband do?"

Good question. "Manages investments or something." I set my drink on the coffee table and wave my hand to the side. "It's all over my head."

"Huh." He glances at the giant TV on the wall between built-in white bookshelves. "I guess he's good at it."

Your guess is as good as mine.

"How'd you meet him?"

A flush climbs up my cheeks. "Speed dating?"

His laugh lights up his face and spins me back to our childhood. We moved to Beaufort, South Carolina, our sixth state, when I was thirteen and Nate eleven. Whenever a Navy jet rockets through the sky, Beaufort residents point up and exclaim, "The sound of freedom!" The best times were when Dad worked long hours at the Marine base on Parris Island. I still remember Nate's mischievous grin every time we heard the rumble of my dad's Jeep as he backed out of the driveway on his way to work. My little brother would grin as we shouted together, "The sound of freedom!"

Nate shakes his head. "Speed dating. You must've been desperate."

His comment stings. "I didn't go willingly. My friend Nadia dragged me there." I need to redirect the conversation from my marriage to his. "At least we didn't meet drunk at a bar." Once the words leave my mouth, I want to steal them back.

Nate's smile vanishes.

"So…" I feel a clamping in my stomach and pray my toast stays put. "You said Morgan's good?"

He blows out a breath. "Well, not really." His hand trembles as he lowers his glass to the coffee table. "Her jerk boss at the spa fired her."

"Oh, that's rough." Morgan is an aesthetician who has trouble holding a job. Based on her horror when I admitted I don't have a skincare regimen — "*You don't own even one facial cream???*" — my guess is her blunt approach offended customers. But I still ask, "What happened?"

"Eh, she was late a couple times, called off a few days, no big deal. If you want your employees at work as early as ten a.m., you gotta give them more leeway."

I nod as I edit the reason she was fired in my mind. I bet she and Nate had been out drinking late with his fellow servers from the seafood restaurant. Not only do I have nothing in common with my girly sister-in-law, I also don't care for her negative influence on my brother. He has enough risk factors for addiction without her egging him on to do shots. The helpless weight on my chest reminds me why I haven't reached out to him in months.

"Don't tell Mom, okay?"

His plea breaks me out of my gloom. I don't even have to consider before I say, "Okay." Keeping secrets, giving the silent treatment, and criticizing each other are all on the list of our family's greatest hits. Also, I've been avoiding our mother, so it's not like Morgan's firing will slip out in conversation.

"I don't want Mom coming up here from Florida," he continues. "She's already on my case about us not giving her grandbabies. I don't need another reason for her to dislike Morgan."

Nate has never told me why they don't have kids, but having children would certainly put a crimp in their boozy lifestyle. "I'm surprised Mom even cares." Bitterness laces my voice. "She has all the grandchildren she needs." *Step-grandchildren.*

"Truth." Nate looks out the windows again at the lagoon.

The only reason Mom finally got the courage to leave Dad was meeting a widower with three children who wooed her away from our family. Though I was already eighteen and at the University of South Carolina, I'm still angry at her for leaving Nate with our father. Nate won't talk about the details of their divorce, but I bet it was horrific. When I told Nadia I didn't plan to share my pregnancy with my mother, she said she felt sad for me. But I don't think Mom deserves to know.

I study my brother's profile as he stares at the water. From his vacant gaze, it seems like he's far away, reminding me of Jordan Perry. I close my eyes as I feel a tug on my heart—a deep hope that Jordan's symptoms decrease. He was so tortured in our last session, but I also think there was a bit of a breakthrough. A fresh thought enters my mind: *Does Nate have PTSD, too?* His alcohol misuse would certainly fit as an avoidance symptom. Another clue is him marrying an emotionally unavailable woman who seems to drift through life, just like he does.

I should ask him about his drinking. At minimum, I shouldn't enable his substance problem. But I'm too tired, and I don't want to start an argument. Who knows the next time I'll get to see my brother? "Nate?"

He flinches as he turns his attention my way.

"I'm guessing money's tight for you and Morgan now."

His eyes flare, and his cheeks bloom a darker red. He looks at his feet. "Yeah."

I slide my cellphone from the pocket of my yoga pants and open my banking app. "How much do you need?"

"Who's our guest, Avery?"

I'm not sure who jumps higher — my brother or me — when Brandon sweeps into the room. *Where did he come from?* I didn't hear the sound of his car or the front door opening.

I pop to my feet, and Nate also stands. There are beads of sweat beneath Brandon's hairline and grass along the hem of his pants, like he just stepped off the golf course. I'm alarmed to see he's still wearing his golf cleats because he'll be angry with himself if he marks up the expensive wood floors. He's agitated, with fidgeting hands and darting, icy blue eyes.

What's going on here? "Hey, Brandon." I take slow steps toward him and fold his left hand into my right. "This is my brother, Nate."

Nate approaches and extends his hand. "Good to meet ya, man."

It's a long few seconds before Brandon accepts the handshake. "Wow, an actual brother, in the flesh. I've wondered if she was lying to me about her family."

My brow furrows. It's not like Brandon has been forthcoming about his family, either. His parents are deceased, and I haven't met his estranged older brother, who lives in California. Our shared outcast status in our families is one reason we've bonded.

"Yeah." My brother shuffles his feet. "I should've called or something."

I frown. "No, it's my fault. I should've at least told you I was married."

Brandon chuckles as he reaches across his body for my left hand, lifting it so the diamond captures the streaming sunlight. "You must've spotted her big rock, huh?"

"Can't miss it," Nate says.

Brandon might not catch the sarcasm in his voice, but I hear it.

"Sounds like we made the right call not inviting you to our wedding in Aruba," Brandon says. "You definitely couldn't have afforded the trip if you're asking us for money now."

My head whips toward my husband, but he keeps his gaze forward. What a cruel thing to say. And now I know why I didn't hear Brandon arrive. He snuck in so he could eavesdrop.

I turn back to Nate. Instead of looking wounded, the way I feel, one corner of his mouth winks up, right near his small scar. At once, I tense. It's the same bring-it-on smirk Nate would give our dad during one of his rants. Dad didn't like insolence, and given the clench of Brandon's hand in mine, he doesn't, either.

"I regret not inviting you," I tell Nate. "You could've met Brandon when he was in a better mood." I squeeze my husband's hand as I look up at him. "Rough day on the golf course, honey?"

"A great day, actually." He looks down his nose at me. "Till I got interrupted."

I tilt my head. It's not like I *asked* him to rush off the course. How did he even know Nate was visiting? And why would he care?

"What's your handicap?" Nate asks.

Both of us look at my brother. To my knowledge, Nate's never picked up a golf club in his life.

"Seven," Brandon answers. "Though I'd just birdied when the app notified me that our doorbell rang."

Mystery solved. *Stupid smart home.*

"What's *your* handicap?" Brandon asks.

The lines around Nate's eyes tighten. "No idea. Don't have time to chase a ball around the grass all day long. Some of us have to work for a living—you know, earn a paycheck."

"Hmm." Brandon's head angles to one side. "Sounds like you're failing at that, my man."

Once again, I'm appalled by his callous remark.

"I think it's time for you to leave," Brandon says. "Avery and I need to talk over financial decisions in private. She has to run this by *me* first."

I blanch at the sexism of that statement, but Brandon's next words shock me even more.

"We have to be careful with money now that a baby's on the way."

Nate gasps as he steps back, his big eyes full of betrayal.

My hand covers my open mouth. "Nate! I, I was going to tell you—"

He's gone before I finish my thought. The front door slams.

Brandon drops my hand and walks into the kitchen. I hear the rumble of the icemaker followed by clinks of cubes into a glass as I try to make sense of that standoff between my husband and brother.

"My five iron was on fire today," he calls from the kitchen. "You should've been there to see it."

He keeps acting like I'm his personal sport psychologist, but I couldn't care less about golf at the moment. He just treated my brother like trash. I take a few steps toward him. "You didn't need to rush off the course."

"You're lucky I got home when I did."

"*Lucky?*" Ooh, hot fury floods my veins. I stomp toward the island, where he pours himself a scotch and soda. "How could you be so cruel to my brother?"

His neck retracts, and his eyes flare. "Cruel? Have you forgotten everything you've told me?" He picks up the glass tumbler and swirls it in his hand. "You worry nonstop about Nate's drinking, but you were about to completely *bankroll* his habit before I stepped in." He takes a sip. "I just did the most loving thing a brother-in-law could for an addict, stop enabling him."

I watch him take a long pull of his drink. It seems hypocritical to consume hard alcohol before noon while patting himself on the back as a paragon of virtue. But as I absorb his words, my heart rate starts to decline. I have to admit, I have been hesitant to give my brother money in the past. "That makes sense, but you didn't have to be so cold. It's not Nate's fault his wife lost her job."

He snickers as he shakes his head. "I didn't know she got fired, but honestly, is that a surprise? They're both such losers."

My stomach coils. Nate and Morgan could make better choices, but it doesn't mean they're deadbeats. My brother is the only family member I still want in my life—not that he'll visit me again after today's debacle. His abrupt departure replays in my mind, stirring outrage in my body.

"And how could you just drop the pregnancy bomb on him?" I demand. "I wasn't ready to tell him yet!"

Brandon circles the island. "How is our little one?" He reaches for my belly, but I don't want him to touch me. When I shy away, he straightens. "Hey, what's wrong?"

"You don't know?" I gawk at him. "I'll probably never see my brother again because of you!"

His eyes bulge. "Dramatic much? I think those pregnancy hormones are getting to you."

My jaw lowers. "How dare you use our baby to minimize my feelings?"

"I was trying to *help* you!" he shouts. "Forgive me for looking out for your interests, for not allowing your family to take advantage of you. Of us." He reaches for his drink and takes another swig. "Once your brother sees this house, you think he won't keep coming back for more? I worked hard for my money. I'm not throwing it away on him."

"But this is *my* family, *my* money!" My heart pounds once more as a knot twists in my gut. "You don't get to dictate how I spend my money."

"Oh, you're wrong there, sweetheart." Venom drips from his words. "Who paid for this house? Your precious lagoon?" He swings his arm toward the great room, and his drink sloshes to the floor. He curses. "Look what you made me do."

Despite my anger, I grab a kitchen towel and hand it to him. He seizes it and bends to wipe the floor with the hand not holding his drink. More swear words flow as he cleans the mess. From his crouched position, he glares at me. "How could you let me wear golf cleats in the house?"

I retract my chin. How is that *my* fault?

He bursts to his feet and slams the tumbler on the island, just like he did when the speed-dating organizer irritated him. Only this time, the glass shatters in his hand. The crack of glass breaking freezes both of us in place. I hold my breath as the electricity of fear lifts the fine hair on the back of my neck. What's his next move, and how will I protect myself? But when I see a sickening streak of blood on the island, I spring into action. I unroll a fistful of paper towels and rush to him. "Don't!"

He removes a sizable shard of glass from the outside pad of his palm before I can stop him, and the trickle of blood turns into a stream. I swallow a surge of nausea.

"Press these against the cut," I order. He winces as I place the towels under his hand, but he follows my instructions and lifts his other hand to apply pressure to the wound. A bizarre sense of relief strikes me as the thick paper towels absorb the blood. Growing up, we could only afford the bargain brand. I remember using almost an entire roll of the cheap towels to stem the tide of blood from my brother's mouth after Dad had backhanded him. Then our dad screamed at us for being wasteful.

"I think it's stopping."

Brandon's voice brings me back to the present, and I watch him lower the bloodied, bunched-up towels. Contrary to his assertion, the flow of blood has *not* stopped. "Keep applying pressure," I command as I pull out a stool and ease him onto it. I squat and untie the laces of his golf cleats. I smell grass and sweat once I've removed his shoes.

His cut seems less severe than the one I've imagined on Kim Perry's leg, and our hospital is nearby. I stand. "I'll take you to the emergency department."

"No!" He slides off the chair onto socked feet.

"It's a big cut. You'll likely need stitches. At minimum, you should have a doctor look at it, see if there's nerve damage. Your hands are important."

He huffs as he shakes his head. Then he growls, "This will *ruin* my golf game!"

I try to keep my face neutral, but I want to throw his words back at him: *Dramatic much?* His hand will heal, no doubt. At once, a wave of fatigue rolls over me, the aftermath of adrenaline from our argument and the scare of blood. My stomach is still unsettled, but at least I don't feel the urge to run to the bathroom. I rub his shoulder as I look up at him. "I'm sorry for yelling." I sigh. "My family makes me crazy."

He peers down at me. "Let's get this hospital trip over with."

I stare at his back as he strides toward the garage. *Thanks for apologizing.*

12. AVERY

"Wow." Back in my therapy office two days later, I raise my eyebrows at Jordan. We're meeting on a Tuesday morning instead of our typical Wednesday sessions so he can drive Mason to Tennessee today for the big meet. "Your score went down to forty-four!" I'm so relieved. After that awful argument with Brandon, I need good news in my life.

Jordan rewards me with an easy smile that stretches his mouth and crinkles his eyes. The smile enhances his good looks. Once I entered the waiting room and noticed he wasn't wearing his ballcap, revealing the neat contours of a recent haircut and shave, I expected his score to be lower. But dropping over twenty points is a massive improvement.

"I *knew* I'd ace this," he says.

It's the first time I've seen mirth in his eyes. "You knew all along, huh?" I set my tablet on the side table. "How many worksheets did you complete?"

"Six. One for each day, just like you told me."

"Excellent. I want to take a look at them." He hands me a stack of papers, and I read through his challenges to stuck points.

"You feeling okay, Doc?"

His question lifts my head. I'm still exhausted from the weekend, and I hope it doesn't show. I haven't slept well since spending hours in the Hilton Head Hospital emergency waiting room on Sunday. Brandon's cut had stopped bleeding by the time we arrived, and the staff's rush to treat two kids who'd almost drowned bumped us to triage. Brandon didn't say a word to me the whole time we waited, and he's been a grouch since then without his precious golf. But it's inappropriate for me to share any of this with Jordan. "Yeah, what makes you ask?"

Jordan studies me. "Any vomitous urges in sight? Want me to drag the trash can closer?"

His concern for me is sweet, and I manage a small smile. "I promise I won't barf on you today. Just a bit tired." I return the papers to him. "But your awesome worksheets have energized me. Your hard work decreased your symptoms big time. How was it to answer the questions?"

"Better than I thought. I kept thinking about that pie thing, how I'm responsible for only ten percent. The stuck points putting all the blame on me couldn't be factual if that's true."

"Nice." I nod. "And you did much better with finishing your practice assignment this week. What helped with that?"

"I made myself start a worksheet every morning. Elena—" He reaches for his forehead, like he wants to tug down his ballcap, but it's not there. He ducks his head.

"What is it?" I ask.

After a beat, he says, "Elena caught me filling out a worksheet, and she asked what it was. I had to show her."

"You hadn't told her about cognitive processing therapy?"

He looks away. "I didn't want her to get her hopes up."

Jordan seems similar to my husband in terms of withholding information from his wife. *Hmm…* Does Brandon have PTSD, too? Despite my questions, he still hasn't told me how his first wife died. I wonder if her death was traumatic.

"She saw…" Jordan clears his throat. "The one you and I did together."

About him robbing Kim of the chance to be a mother. "Elena now knows Kim was pregnant?"

Jordan nods.

"How'd she take it?"

"She cried." He blows a breath out his nose. "I did, too."

I let him sit in the emotion for a bit as I twist my wedding ring. "How'd you feel when you told her about the pregnancy?"

As he blinks, the glisten of his eyes makes my throat burn, but I don't let myself cry. I don't want to interfere with his moment. It appears I am indeed more emotional when pregnant. Not that I'll admit that to Brandon.

"Sad," he says.

"I'm sad as well," I tell him. "It's such a sad thing that happened." I hope he doesn't hear the quiver in my voice.

His eyes meet mine. "Take good care of your baby, okay?"

His soft plea squeezes my heart. Trying to keep up with my clients and marriage in the midst of unrelenting fatigue has consumed me to the point that I haven't thought much about the viability of my pregnancy. But I can't deny my fierce desire—an iron fortress in my core—to protect my baby. I'll do anything to guard the little peanut. Did my mother feel the same way when she was pregnant? And how in the world did she tolerate her husband's despicable treatment of her babies after they were born?

"I'll do my best," I promise Jordan. After what he's been through, it would be awful if I had to tell him something happened to my baby. That's one reason I don't want to share my pregnancy with my clients, especially in the first trimester. But I couldn't have Jordan blame himself for me running out of the office. "How about you take me through one of your worksheets? Maybe the one about choosing a remote location?"

He shifts on the cushion and shuffles through the papers. *"I'm an idiot for choosing a vacation in a remote location without cell service.* That one?"

"Yes. You came up with some effective challenges to that stuck point."

"Thanks." He sits up a little taller. "Okay, that belief is not factual. I mean, I *am* an idiot, most of the time, but not because I chose that trip."

I can tell he's joking, so I just arch an eyebrow.

"Evidence against?" he continues. "I remembered Kim told me she *wanted* a remote location."

I bring my hand to my collarbone. "Really?"

"She was sick of telling her students to put away their cellphones. She wanted a break from all that."

I recall that Kim taught at an elementary school. "Kids that young have cellphones?"

"Some of them—fifth graders, at least. Hudson's all up in our grill for a phone, but that's a big no from me and his mom, dawg."

I pat my belly. No way will I allow my child to have a phone that young. And I hope Brandon won't, either. But how will we parent as a team if he won't talk to me when he's irritated?

Jordan says, "Next answer. It's repetitive, not factual. I've chided myself for the remote location countless times."

"Right," I say. *Focus, Clarkson.*

"Is my stuck point missing important information? I couldn't think of something for this one, or at least not a different answer from what I said about Kim liking the Baja trip best." He pauses. "Come to think of it, everyone in our group was excited about detoxing from technology."

"That fits," I say. "And there's something else you're leaving out about the context. What did you know at the time?"

He considers my question. "I knew we all needed a break, and an island in the middle of nowhere sounded awesome." He scratches his hairline with the pen cap. "It *was* awesome—the most picturesque place to swim. The perfect chance to reconnect with my college teammates. We saw sea turtles, eels, dolphins…"

His gaze is distant, but his flashback doesn't seem to bring him pain this time.

"Those happy memories of the trip aren't included in your stuck point," I point out. "Do you want to add them to your answer?" As he writes, I marvel at his brain's healing. By processing, he's now able to remember positive things he'd stuffed down.

Jordan shares his responses for the other questions, but his answer is blank for the last one. "I'm not sure how the stuck point focuses on irrelevant aspects of the story."

"Mmm…" I nod. "If you knew Kim would have a medical emergency, would you have chosen this remote Mexican island?"

"No way!"

"Exactly. But you didn't know that when you booked the trip. This belief is about second-guessing your decisions before the trauma. How common is it for trauma survivors to second-guess their decisions?"

He shrugs. "Not sure—you're the expert. But I do remember you saying we blame ourselves when bad things happen to feel more in control."

"Good memory. Is it possible this belief is about the normal tendency to blame or second-guess ourselves after a tragedy occurs, instead of about the story itself?"

He nods and writes on the worksheet.

"Great job on the questions, and we'll return to these later. For our next worksheet, instead of examining one stuck point, we'll explore tendencies in your thoughts." I hand him a paper. "We all have thinking styles that cause distress from time to time. These are styles more typical for trauma survivors. I'll describe the style, and we'll look for a stuck point that fits. Any one stuck point may fit multiple styles. You ready?"

"Let's do it."

I smile at his enthusiasm. "Catastrophic thinking is about predicting the worst-case scenario." I remember what I said to myself getting in the car this morning. *If I'm running late, there'll be a crash on two-seventy-eight.*

He smirks. "That one sounds like a fact. But I get the concept."

"Which one of your stuck points exemplifies catastrophic thinking?"

Studying his stuck point log, he says, *"One of my kids will get cancer and die."*

"Yes." I wait for him to write. "Another style is blowing things out of proportion or discounting them as less important than they are. Do any of your stuck points fit this style?"

"Maybe…*I'm an egomaniac?*"

When a laugh escapes my mouth, his head pops up. "What? That's not an exaggeration?" he asks.

"It's a ridiculous exaggeration." *You're much humbler than my husband, at least.* "The self-reproach in your voice as you called yourself an egomaniac just struck me as funny."

"Oh." His smile looks relieved.

I tilt my head. "Where'd that stuck point come from?"

His smile drops, and the heavy feeling that pervaded our first sessions returns to the room. "The last words Kim said to me."

"Ah."

He looks out at the lagoon.

"Would you share them with me?" I ask.

He slides his hand over the Lowcountry Lionfish logo on his blue polo shirt. "We fell behind the group because my stupid shoulder was hurting." He turns to me. "That's why I should've brought fins on the boat, so I could keep up." A swallow bobs his throat. "I told Kim to go on ahead. She didn't want to, but…" His eyes flutter shut. "I snapped at her." He exhales. "I told her she'd better not gloat to my kids about how slow I swam, and she said… She said, 'Don't worry, I'll preserve your massive ego.'"

No wonder he's so full of shame. "Thank you for telling me that. You haven't done a worksheet on the egomaniac stuck point yet, right?"

He shakes his head.

"Is there any information your stuck point is leaving out?"

He shrugs.

"Did you and Kim ever tease each other?" I ask.

A harrumph lifts his chin. "All the time."

"Is it possible she was teasing you as a sign of affection?"

He scrunches his nose as he considers my question. "Maybe?"

"Is there any evidence she thought you were a narcissist?"

He glances out the window again. "She always told me I needed to be more confident, actually, especially as a coach. She called me caring and knowledgeable, said my swimmers were lucky to have me." He shrugs as he looks back at me. "I guess we'll find out soon, depending on how Mason swims."

I aim a gentle smile his way. "Are you perhaps overemphasizing the importance of one swimmer's performance in one swim meet as an indication of your entire coaching career?"

This time he laughs. "Touché. I'll add that one to the worksheet."

"Leaving out essential elements is our next style."

Jordan starts writing. "*I'm an egomaniac* fits this one, too, based on ignoring the fact that teasing each other was our jam."

He's back to his newfound lightness of spirit.

"Yes. Our next style is all-or-none thinking. For example, either Mason wins every race or the meet is a failure."

"Oh, he won't win every race. He's up against Olympians in this meet. He'll be lucky to finish in the top eight. But if he drops time like I think he will, he'll get on people's radars as one to watch." After glancing at his stuck point log, he says, "*I have no control over the future* sounds all-or-nothing."

I nod. Now that the fog of shame has lifted, he seems to grasp the concepts quickly. "Overgeneralizing is next. That's when we make broad, sweeping conclusions from one negative event. Like, if I get a C on a test and tell myself, *I'm too stupid for college. I don't belong here.*"

After some back and forth discussion, we choose, *I'm going to die and leave my kids fatherless* as an example of overgeneralizing. Just because it happened to his father doesn't mean it will happen to him.

"Mindreading." He announces the next style we'll explore. "Elena has accused me of that a time or twelve." He scratches his chin. "When I had my meltdown at practice a couple of months ago, I chewed out Mason — screamed at the kid." His face flushes. "Then he showed up in my office and asked for more work. I couldn't believe how brave he was. When I asked how he did it, he said he'd thought I hated him at first, but then he challenged his mindreading."

A glow of pride fills my chest. *I taught him that.*

"Mason told me how much you helped him." Jordan blinks at me. "And that made me pony up and schedule with you."

"I'm so glad you did. Keep working hard, and you'll keep healing."

After I give him the next practice assignment our time is up, but he lingers at the door. I brace myself for a dumb joke. Instead, he stares at me for several seconds. "Thank you, Dr. Avery. Thank you for helping me."

The warmth in his grateful eyes floods through me. "I'm honored to be on your team, Coach. But you're the one helping yourself. I'm just along for the swim."

He closes the door behind him, and I let out a long breath. Moments of deep connection between therapist and client are special, and I want to savor the fulfillment and satisfaction. Helping someone turn their life around makes me fall in love with my career all over again. I only wish I could connect to Brandon this way.

I touch my belly and whisper, "Can I give this all up for you?"

13. JORDAN

I arrive at Bluffton High School's pick-up circle an hour after my therapy session. There's sweat at the nape of my neck from rushing around to clean the cats' litter box before I packed the car. It's the least I can do to help Elena, who will be a single parent for the next five days while I'm at the meet. She plans to call from Hailey's school choir concert Thursday night. Though I don't want to miss our daughter singing, my secret hope is that Mason will qualify for a championship final to interfere with taking that call. It would save me the ear suffering of listening to the other kids screech like cats being sucked into a vacuum cleaner.

My swimmer strolls out of the high school with a scowl on his face. He tosses his backpack onto the back seat of my SUV and climbs into the shotgun seat. "You're late, bruh."

I suspect Mason's irritability stems from anxiety, so I don't call him out. If I were fast enough to make a meet like this — the TYR pro swim international series, which he qualified for after his stellar performance at junior nationals last summer — I'd be nervous, too. Especially at age fifteen.

"Sorry, bro." I start the journey north with the plan to enter the Knoxville pool's address into my phone GPS once we hit Columbia. "One of the cats decided his poop was litter-box optional."

Mason leans away from me. "Sheesh. Gotta be Jack. His aura's low-key sus."

Back in the day, Elena invited Mason and his mother to dinner so often that he almost knows my cats better than I do. But since Mason started high school, his visits have decreased. I've watched him spend more time with his teammates this year—as it should be for teenagers, I guess. And it's not like Mason has wanted to be around me since Kim died. I've been a self-absorbed mess. With that thought, I hear Dr. Avery's voice in my head. *"Is that an example of all-or-nothing thinking?"* Okay, I haven't been a *total* mess, but I've neglected my family for too long. I need to prioritize my time with Hudson before he gets older and wants nothing to do with his parents.

"Coach, Coach, Coach." Mason shakes his head. "What's with these unc tunes?"

I shoot him a look. One time when Mason told me I was being "unc" at dinner, Hudson translated for me that I was acting old. At least Mason didn't call me a boomer. "Coldplay? They're not old. They're timeless. Classic road tunes, son." I groove to the kicky chords of "Viva La Vida."

"When do I get to play *my* music?" he grumbles as he scrolls through his phone.

My hands beat imaginary drums on the steering wheel. "After you swim a best time, I'll let you play your music the whole ride home."

"Bet." After a second, he sits up. "Hey! My mom's driving me home."

I laugh. *Busted.* His mom has to work this week, but she'll drive to Tennessee to make Friday night's finals. My assistant coaches are also staying behind in Bluffton to coach the rest of the team, as Mason is the only Lionfish swimmer to qualify for this meet.

To get him off his phone, I ask, "How were your morning classes?" I would worry about most students missing almost four days of school for a meet, but Mason is smart. Too smart, sometimes.

"Boring." He pockets his phone and fidgets with the zipper of his team warmup jacket. "We could've left earlier, you know. What's this low-key stealth thing you had to do today?"

I'm not sure how forthcoming I should be. As the hypnotic rhythm of Coldplay's "Magic" thumps through the car's speakers, I remember how much Kim liked this song. I haven't listened to this playlist in some time.

"Don't mean to press." Mason breaks the somber spell that's come over me. "You don't have to spill the tea."

I glance over at his earnest hazel eyes and the endearing mop of fried, white blond hair that frames his face. He's no threat. "That's okay. You deserve to know." I take a deep breath. "I was meeting with Dr. Avery."

"No cap?" He tucks in his chin. "Since when?"

I look back at the road, relieved he didn't know. Dr. Avery kept my confidentiality like she promised. *Of course she did.* "Since you told me about your sessions with her that day in my office, back in February. That day...the day I had a meltdown at practice."

"You did crash out, yeah. You were trippin'."

I nod. "I was." Or maybe I still am. "She's helping me deal with some stuff. My sister..." I feel tightness creep up my throat. *Ten-percent responsibility*, I remind myself. *It's not all my fault.* "My sister's death. It's been rough, but I'm trying to get better. Trying to coach better."

"It's okay, Coach. I told Lexi's dad you're back to your old rizz self."

I look over at him again. "Mr. Redfield talked to you?" The board president asking my star swimmer about me can't be good.

He holds up his large hand, like he's attempting to soothe a feral cat. "He just asked if I wanted Gabe or Suzie to take me to the meet, that's all." He scoffs. "Of course I picked you." He gestures to the center console. "Even with your boomer music."

I feel a twitch of my upper lip. But then my shoulders tighten. If Mason doesn't swim well at this meet, I *will* get fired this time. But I hear my psychologist's words again: *"It's only one meet."* "Anyway," I say, "thanks for telling me about Dr. Avery. I wouldn't have gotten off my tired butt to schedule with her, if it wasn't for you. She's helped me a lot."

"She's a queen, right?"

The admiration in his eyes gives me pause. I was fifteen once. "Do you have a *crush* on her?"

He balks. After a beat, a small smile creeps in at the corners of his mouth, confirming my suspicion. "Low-key, she's a snack. I could see us together." He cringes. "It's a delusionship on my end, no cap, but a bro can dream." His lips press together. "Until she married that mog dog of a husband."

My eyes narrow. "She wasn't married when you started seeing her?"

"Nah. Not that I notice stuff like that, but Mom saw the rock on her hand—when was that, January? Mom asked if we should call her by her married name, and Dr. Avery got all flustered, saying the wedding had just happened. Said she hadn't thought through changing her name yet. Never seen her so stressy."

I could spill more tea and tell him our psychologist's now pregnant, but I won't. It seemed like she wouldn't have told me about her pregnancy if I hadn't gone mental in her office. But something Mason said bothers me. "Why'd you call her husband a dog?"

He hesitates. "Probs none of my business."

That may be true, but I want to hear this. I don't know much about Dr. Avery's personal life, but I trust her. I want good things for her—I want her to be happy. It's disheartening to think she might've married a jerk. But I can't push Mason too hard, or he'll shut down. He's a bright, strong-willed kid, and I've learned I have to balance every push with a pull. I aim for a lighthearted tone. "Can you believe how freaking neat her desk is?"

He snickers. "Slaps! Her whole office. Girl got OCD for sure."

"She's always anxious about time," I say. "She was late to our appointment once, and I thought she'd never forgive herself."

He grows quiet. I hear him fidget with his jacket again. *Zip. Unzip. Zip.*

For the next few miles, I lose myself in the music. *Where do we go…I'll never know.* Did God's grace put a smile on my face? Or did God let my dad and sister die? And if so, why?

"Does Dr. Avery ever take you on walks?" Mason asks.

"No." I give him the side eye. "She does that with you?"

He beams. "Only with clients she likes the best."

Punk. I don't feel offended, though. Mason's therapy is different from mine. There are too many handouts and worksheets for us to walk during our sessions.

"She stayed late one night to meet with me after practice," he says. "We went for a walk on this path near her office. When we came back to her building, it was getting dark, but I could still see this tall guy leaning against his boujee yellow sports car. His arms were crossed, and he gave us the bombastic side eye. I was like, Stalker Man Stan, what's your deal?"

"What did Avery do?"

Mason's hair sticks up for a moment after he runs a hand through it. "She like, freezes for a second, then we keep walking inside to get my mom and schedule the next time. But the guy calls out to her, and she tells me to wait. She goes over to him, and they start hissing at each other. I can't hear every word, but the dude looks *salty*. Dr. Avery says something like, 'It's not on me that you showed up early.' All the sudden he's out of pocket. He shrieks, 'It's not *my* fault you work all day and night! You *never* prioritize me!' Then he gets in the car and slams the door."

Whoa. "Did he drive off?"

"He just kept watching us from the car—total sus." Mason's jaw ticks. "I swear, she was, like, *shaking* when we walked back inside. I tried to apologize for making her stay late, but she said it was her husband's fault, not mine. She said she was sorry I had to see that."

Unease coils in my stomach as a memory comes back to me. "You said he was tall?" I picture the man in the waiting room who glared at me. "Black hair? Blue eyes?"

"No cap." Mason looks at me. "You saw him, too?"

I thought he was another schmuck like me who'd had to start trauma therapy, thus explaining his hostile vibe. But as I recount the scene through fresh eyes, it seems he was checking me out, competing with me for Dr. Avery's attention. A little contest to determine the alpha dog. "I saw him in the waiting room once." I rub my hand over my mouth. *She's having a baby with this man?* "I hope she's okay."

"Me, too."

Coldplay returns to my playlist, and we listen to "Something Just Like This" for the next few miles in silence. Mason's knee jiggles, and at first, I think he's jamming to the beat—I've won him over to my boomer music. But then I realize his nerves have set back in.

"Make sure to hydrate." I rummage behind me on the floor of the backseat for an electrolyte beverage in the cooler. I hand it to him, and after he takes a swig, I ask, "How're you feeling about the meet?" I wince as the words leave my mouth. I sound like more like a cheesy therapist than a coach.

But he doesn't clap back. He slumps in the seat. "What if I don't make the A final? I'll let everyone down."

I shake my head. "Newsflash, Mase." I glance over, waiting until he looks up. "You probably *won't* finish in the top eight."

He gawks at me.

"I don't care what place you finish." That's not entirely true, but I can't let the pressure I feel spill over to him. "It's your first big meet, and you'll be one of the youngest swimmers there. Just get a feel for it, experience it. Each swim is an opportunity to execute your race plan, to do your best. You've already put the work in — now's the time to let it flow."

His slow blinks as he looks up at me from his slouch remind me of his first year on my team. He was only eight — the same age as Hailey now. What he lacked in stroke technique, he made up for in muscle and grit. He won every race until one kid beat him in backstroke when Mason got tangled up in the laneline at an outdoor pool. I tried to talk him off the ledge after the race, but he kept sobbing.

I'd known then that I needed a way to lessen his intensity if he wanted to make it in the sport. I'd decided on a dramatic reenactment. After lining up along the deck chairs to my right, I'd windmilled my arms to mimic swimming backstroke as I stepped backward. Then I'd squinted and given a feeble cry, *"The sun's blinding me!"* as I careened into the chairs. I almost broke an ankle as I toppled over with one of them, but it was worth it to hear Mason's giggles. His tears had vanished, and he'd shouted, *"Do it again, Coach!"*

It's tough to reconcile the childish voice from my memory with the adult-sized manchild next to me now. "No matter how you swim in this meet, you could *never* let me down," I tell him. "We've been through a lot together these past seven years. And I hope we have at least seven more, if you come home to swim with me on college breaks."

He nods and sits a bit taller.

"It's just one meet," I add. "There'll be many more. One meet doesn't define you."

He smirks. "You sound like Dr. Avery."

That makes me smile. *Then I'm doing something right.*

We drive five more hours, stopping midway for Chipotle burritos, and when we arrive in Knoxville, we go to the pool first for a light practice, even before we check in to the hotel. The meet starts tomorrow night with a distance event, but Mason won't compete till Thursday morning.

As we head into the pool area, the smell of chlorine activates the butterflies in my stomach. I once again hear the grinding *zzzs* of a jacket zipper moving up and down, and I turn to see my young swimmer gaping at the expansive natatorium, colored in bright white and orange.

"Hey, Mase. What do sprinters eat before the race?"

His hand stills on the zipper. He tries to narrow his eyes, but a smile cracks through before I can get out the punchline.

"Nothing, they fast."

Electric energy fills the natatorium on Friday night as the finalists for the men's 200-meter freestyle emerge from the ready room. Whistles pierce through blaring rock music, and I watch my swimmer follow his competitors to take his place behind lane six. I'm standing about twenty meters from the blocks along the side of the pool, behind a rope that lines the length of the water, reserving the space for coaches. Not only did Mason qualify for the top eight, but his time from the morning swim was the fourth fastest. I'm still in shock. Countless coaches have introduced themselves and congratulated me for Mason's massive time drops. He finished tenth in the 100 free last night — not bad for an undeveloped fifteen year old who's still growing. His 200 fly was even better with a sixth-place finish.

But the 200 free might be his best event, especially since he's still ticked about getting beat at the high school state meet. Four lengths of freestyle, too long for a sprint but too short for a distance event, was also Kim's best race. She thrived on passing competitors in the third fifty before turning on her turbo kick to decimate them the last fifty. I've wasted Mason's legs in grueling kick sets over the years, and now he's fully rested and shaved. Thank God he seems to be hitting his taper just right.

"Nervous, Coach?"

I recognize the voice in an instant, and I turn to stare slack-jawed at my best friend. How is it possible for *Wyatt* to be here? His reddish blond hair and freckles look just like I remember. Without thinking, I grab him in a hug. I feel the vibration of his chest as he chuckles.

"What're you *doing* here?" I ask.

"I came to see you." His hand sweeps across the packed natatorium and gestures at the stopwatch I hold. "Witness firsthand you cosplaying as a successful swim coach."

Though the teasing is familiar territory for us, I notice the tension around his mouth, like he's nervous about my reaction. Wyatt and I have always had an easy friendship, but I've created the current strain between us. My avoidance has hurt a lot of people. "Where'd you get this?" I pinch the laminated credential hanging on a lanyard around his neck—a requirement for being allowed on the deck.

"Danielle." He motions across the pool to the University of Tennessee head coach, our former teammate. "I'm staying with her and her wife."

Just then, she looks up from the officials' table and waves at us. She points at Mason behind the blocks and gives me the thumbs up. Her kindness has floored me this week.

"I guess she's forgiven you for the Anna debacle," Wyatt notes.

"Guess so." The entire women's team hated on me for dumping our teammate, Anna, in college. "At some point, Kim was able to convince Danielle that it was just me being young and dumb, and it's all in the past."

"Well, you're no longer young," Wyatt says. "But that part about being dumb? That's lived on."

He has that so right that I don't even smile at his jab. Danielle cornered me in the coach's break room two days ago to tell me how sorry she was about Kim. I've never seen her cry before, and even now, recalling her fierce fight against tears constricts my windpipe. I clear my throat. "I talked to her earlier this week. She said life's short, that Kim...taught her that. She decided not to keep holding a grudge from twenty years ago."

Wyatt nods.

The announcer is almost finished introducing the finalists. I look again at my friend, who's a few inches shorter than me. We both swam the individual medley and trained in the stroke group for three years together. After our mediocre butterfly start to the event, I would surge ahead of him in the backstroke, and then he would catch up in the breaststroke. We'd both dig down deep and battle to touch the wall first after the freestyle leg. But no matter who won, we always stayed friends.

"Hey, Wy?" I wait until he looks at me. "I don't deserve it, but will *you* forgive me, too? Forgive me for disappearing after Baja?"

His smile spreads as the starter blows his whistle. The swimmers step up onto the blocks, and the spectators quiet. Wyatt reaches out to shake my hand. He pulls me down to whisper in my ear, "Why do you think I flew across the country to see you, moron?"

Mason rockets off the block, but he emerges from his breakout half a body length behind the taller, older swimmers in surrounding lanes. We'll have to add reps of plyometric exercises and the power tower to increase his explosiveness and underwater dolphin kick, especially for short-course high school meets that involve more flip turns and underwater push-offs. At his still-young stage of development, he's better at these long-course meets in Olympic fifty-meter pools. Fortunately, his long, smooth freestyle stroke looks older than his years, and he makes up a little distance on the field before he flip turns at the other end of the pool.

Ear-splitting whistles pierce the air and reverberate through my body. I mutter to myself, "Don't take it out too fast." I look at my stopwatch and blow out a breath of relief. He's within five one-hundredths of the split I want for the first fifty, even though a glance at the electronic timing board tells me he's in eighth place at the quarter point of the race. "Stay cool, Mase. Don't panic."

Wyatt shouts, "Goooooo, Mason! Get after it!"

Mason inches a bit closer to the competition as he heads back toward us, but he's only seventh at the hundred mark. He bursts out of his breakout and starts the back half of the race.

The adrenaline pulsing through me brings me back to my own races—the juxtaposition of chaos in my body and quiet underwater peace, the burning surge of energy in my lat and quad muscles. It's like it's *my* body rotating and gliding through the water, every move precise and powerful. *Kick it in the third fifty, Mase.* He seems to hear my silent plea. Whitewater gushes behind him, and he pulls even with swimmers in lanes seven and eight. The top two swimmers in lanes four and five are quite a bit ahead of him, but I wonder if Mason will be able to catch the third seed in lane three.

Wyatt bounces on his feet after Mason does his last flip turn. With emphatic finger points at the timing board, he shouts, "He's moved up to fourth!"

I'm vibrating with energy as I will Mason forward. *Mow them down, mow them down. Want it. Dig down deep.* It looks like he's still in fourth place with about fifteen meters left.

As the swimmers sprint to the finish, a barrage of sound deafens me. Mason barrels to the wall and touches the electronic timing pad at the perfect extension of his arm, just like we practiced. There's a pause in the auditory melee as everyone looks at the timing board to see the results. Then electric cheers erupt again.

Mason finished third after dropping almost a second from his morning swim. And his prelims time was already a two-second drop from his best—an amazing improvement at this elite level. It's a breakthrough swim that would qualify him for the national team at a selection meet. I'm still shaking as Mason rips off his goggles and pulls himself up to search the pool deck from the water. He finds me standing behind the rope, and he holds up a fist as he gives a cocky nod.

I nod back. I think this may be the first amazing swim of many we'll share at a big meet.

"What a baller!" Wyatt yells. He shoots his arms in the air in victory, and we grin at each other. "He swam that race just like Kim."

Our grins fade, but the sharp pain in my chest doesn't show up this time. Instead, a bittersweet sadness settles over me. The loss of my sister is a bitter pill, no doubt. But it's sweet to honor her legacy by coaching the sport she loved, infusing my top swimmer with her fierce determination to be the best.

Wyatt clasps my shoulder. "That's a well-coached swimmer right there."

I connect with his gaze, bowled over by his praise. It means even more given we both swam for the best coach in the country.

"You guys!" Danielle's orange shirt is easy to see as she dodges other coaches and swimmers to rush up to us. "What an exquisite swim, Jordan. You must be so proud!" She hops forward and scoops us both into a hug. I laugh at her infectious energy as I jump up and down with my former teammates. The moment feels just like twenty years ago when we celebrated our NCAA title after an emotional four-day meet. We're just clothed and dry now, instead of wearing swimsuits. Oh, and we're also old. And out of shape.

"Thanks for letting me crash your hotel room," Wyatt says as he takes his toothbrush into the bathroom.

I'm lucky my room has two beds. I tug a T-shirt over my head as I call, "It's the least I can do after you flew all this way." I slide under the covers, and exhaustion envelops me. I'm not accustomed to being in the spotlight for coaching a rising star, and I've received countless congratulatory backslaps from other coaches. My shoulder blades are almost sore from all the attention.

After Wyatt turns off the bathroom light, I ask, "What's Danielle's wife like?"

He crosses the room and sits on the other bed. His T-shirt has a logo from a sports medicine clinic in Seattle, where he works as a physician assistant. He took the red-eye last night and caught up on sleep at Danielle's house during morning prelims. "She's great. She's a nurse practitioner, so we talked shop. It's their five cats that made me want to get out of there." He holds up a hand. "No offense."

I think about Colby and Jack. I hope they're using the litter box, for Elena's sake. Then I realize I haven't checked in with Elena since she live-streamed the choir concert on her phone for me last night. I ended up being available for the third-grade choir's off-key performance between Mason's events at finals. I do feel guilty about not being there to keep Hudson in line, though. Elena said he threw a fit about having to attend the concert, which made them late.

I sit up in bed and reach over to unplug my phone from the charger. "Hold on a sec. I have to text my wife."

"No need," Wyatt says. "I called Elena while you were getting mobbed on deck. Told her how awesome Mason swam."

My head tilts. Wyatt was best man in my wedding, and of course knows my wife, but I didn't know they spoke on the phone. Then it hits me. "Elena asked you to come here."

He shrugs. "I planned to visit you this summer, even if you weren't returning my calls." One eyebrow cocks in a rebuke. "But Elena told me how nervous you were about the meet, so I moved up my trip."

Wow. "Thanks," is all I can manage.

"She also said there's some stuff you might want to tell me in person."

A frisson of dread prickles my spine as I realize the "stuff" Elena likely meant. "She did, huh?" To buy some time, I plug my phone back into the charger and make sure the alarm is still set. I plump my pillow and fit it between my back and the headboard.

When I don't say more, Wyatt pulls down his covers and stacks pillows against the headboard to echo my body position. He scrolls through his phone, probably reading texts from Cara, his girlfriend—a physician he met at work. Though they've been together six years, they've never married, despite our cajoling. Kim and I both liked Cara when we visited Seattle last summer.

I swallow. My mouth is dry, maybe from the salty fast food Wyatt made us eat after finals. I got a night off from procuring dinner for Mason since his mother took over babysitting duties when she arrived, and I was planning to go right to bed, but Wyatt said he was starved. When I bit into my cheeseburger, my stomach started rumbling, and I surprised myself by polishing off the entire burger and fries. I caught the surreptitious looks from my friend between bites, but at least he didn't comment on my weight loss. I bet Elena told him to make sure I got some food, in addition to hinting that I had something to tell him.

I stare at the ceiling for a few minutes. Should I tell him? My heartbeat quickens. *Can* I tell him? I glance at my friend and remember him rushing up to me at the Baja hospital. I didn't have the heart to tell him then. After a beat, I say, "Ever heard of gestational thrombocytopenia?"

"That's a big word for you, Coach." When I don't smile, he puts down his phone. "Hmm… We don't see many pregnant women in sports med, but I think so." His chin lowers as I keep staring at him. A long moment passes. Then he jerks up as his eyes bulge. "Kim?"

I nod.

"That's why she bled out." Once the information sinks in, he grabs his scalp. "Oh, God!" He pulls his head down to his knees. "Kimmy. Oh, Kimmy." His voice judders. "Poor Kimmy."

His grief rips through me, and I curse Elena for setting up this disclosure before I was ready. But who am I kidding? I'll never be ready to volunteer the details of my sister's death. Wyatt was there with us, though. He deserves the whole truth.

"Did she know?" Wyatt turns to face me. "That she was pregnant?" With a small shake of my head, I say, "Don't think so."

"Wait." His back straightens. "That guy. The, the guy at the funeral she was dating, the teacher, the mountain man."

I picture the teacher's bushy beard that almost hid the tremble of his mouth as he fought off tears.

Wyatt says, "He doesn't know he was going to be a father."

A heavy sensation pushes against my lungs.

"You should tell him, Jordan."

I grimace and press back into the headboard. That's the last thing I want to do.

"I'm serious!" Wyatt says. "If Cara got pregnant and something happened to her? I'd want to know."

I huff out a breath. "But would he? My *mom* doesn't even know!" My brain buzzes, and I close my eyes. "I wanted to tell you in the hospital. In Baja." I open my eyes to find Wyatt studying me. "But I couldn't — it made me sick to even think about it. I blamed myself."

His eyebrows form a deep V. "Why? It's not *your* fault." He looks down. "If anyone's to blame, it's me. Kim was vomiting on and off that whole trip. As a medical professional, I should've known she was pregnant. I should've watched out for her."

I blink at him as a calm blankets me. Maybe Wyatt needs a therapist too. I hear Dr. Avery's voice, *"When something bad happens, we second-guess our decisions. We blame ourselves to feel more in control."*

"Hey." I wait for him to look up. "It's not my fault, and it's not your fault. It's just an awful thing that happened. We got unlucky that day. We lost our best friend."

His face falls, and a muscle in his jaw jumps. Silence stretches between us. Then he says, "She would've been the best mom."

"That's exactly what I told my psychologist!" I freeze after letting that slip out.

He shakes his head. "Relax, I already figured out you were in therapy. At least I was hoping that's what Elena meant when she assured me you were working through your grief. It's why I didn't crash your doorstep sooner."

I'm not sure how I feel about Elena slipping him that hint. But I guess if it gave Wyatt some comfort, I'm okay with it. He deserves relief after what I've put him through.

"Is therapy helping?" he asks.

The drop in my symptom score says yes, but I'm still not back to myself. "It took a while to kick in, but my psychologist is great." I want to tell Wyatt that Mason also sees Dr. Avery, and she deserves credit for his performance as well. But that's not my story to tell. "At least I'm sleeping better." Just like that, a yawn overtakes me.

Wyatt nods. "I'll let you get some rest." He plugs in his phone, turns off the lamp on the bedside table, and we both slide flat in our respective beds.

I sink into the mattress, and soon, my breathing lengthens.

"Jordo?"

"Yeah?"

He pauses. "Thanks for telling me."

I picture the night of Kim's birthday in Baja, when Wyatt pressed in to get another piece of cake, leaving a blob of white icing smeared on her shirt. Remembering their laughter brings on a faint smile. "You're welcome."

A few minutes later, I ask, "Will you look at Mason's breaststroke during warmups tomorrow?"

He chuckles. "You got it, Coach."

14. AVERY

Jordan vibrates with energy on our walk from the waiting room to my office on Wednesday, and once we sit, he blurts, "Did you hear about Mason's swims?"

I'm vibrating too, but it's not excitement. It's nerves. At least there's no sign of Brandon's car in the office parking lot. I force a smile. "Even better — I watched the meet on TV." Or *tried* to. I need to stop thinking about the incident on my back deck, so I ask, "Did you complete the PCL this week?"

"Oh." Jordan knocks his palm against his forehead, and I'm pleased to see he left his ballcap at home again. "Forgot to fill it out in the waiting room." He accepts the clipboard I give him. "But what'd you think? Wasn't Mase impressive?"

I hesitate. One difficulty with a manualized treatment is that it doesn't leave time to process events in the client's life. "How about we proceed with session six and talk about Mason's meet at the end, if there's time?"

His shoulders slouch. "Oh, uh, sure." He picks up his pen and answers the first question about intrusive symptoms.

I hate that I've killed his coaching buzz. But I didn't shoot him down only because we need to stick with the therapy protocol. I'd rather not talk about Mason's meet. I don't even want to think about what happened after Brandon caught me watching it.

But my brain won't obey. As Jordan circles his answers, the sound of our back door opening last Saturday circles in my mind. I remember jolting in the deck chair before I lunged to press pause on my iPad's TV app.

I'd agreed to cancel my Saturday clients to accompany Brandon to the RBC Heritage, a professional golf tournament on Hilton Head Island. However, my morning sickness had other plans. I couldn't imagine walking a golf course, dodging throngs of spectators on an unseasonably hot day, in my condition. Brandon had refused to leave for the tournament without me, despite my nudging. Instead, he wanted me to sit with him and watch the TV golf coverage. I'd rather have stabbed an icepick into my eyeball, but I agreed. And my resentment grew when he'd then buried his face in his phone. He's not great at speaking my love language of quality time.

When I'd had enough of the golf announcers' hushed tones, I started cleaning the kitchen. But Brandon told me to leave it for the housekeeper on Monday. Then I decided to organize my desk and dresser in the guest bedroom. There are years of paperwork and other junk I didn't have time to sort through in the midst of the rushed move out of my townhome. But Brandon put the kibosh on that, too. He said he didn't want me touching anything in that room until the top interior designer he hired is available in a couple of months. He wants her to turn the space into a nursery around the time we'll learn the baby's sex. I'd been hoping we could decorate the room ourselves, even if we're not professionals.

Finally, Brandon had agreed to go to the tournament by himself. Scottie Scheffler was on fire, and Brandon wanted to watch him up close and personal. He told me to stay off my feet. Once I heard him drive away, I'd let out the longest sigh. Stress relief was what I needed, and I decided to go for a light jog. Brandon wouldn't like it, but my doctor said exercise was good for me. And the crackers and yogurt I'd managed to keep down would provide enough energy.

Running was always my escape from my parents. Losing myself in a long run had also been a reprieve from the cruel school cliques I encountered after every time we moved. And true to form, I felt so relaxed after a couple of miles. It wasn't until I showered afterwards that I remembered NBC was airing selected events from Mason's meet.

I'd poured sparkling water into a glass with ice, grabbed a protein bar, and turned on the TV. But then I'd wondered if Brandon might sneak up on me like he did when Nate visited. I didn't want to risk violating Mason's confidentiality if Brandon asked what I was watching, so I took my tablet from my briefcase and set myself up on the back deck. The dining table umbrella blocked the sun's glare, and ocean breezes cooled down the temperature.

After a women's race, the next event was the men's 200 freestyle—the same event Mason had bombed at the high school meet, leading him to start meeting with me. Despite Jordan's prediction that Mason might not qualify for the championship final, it had been easy to pick out his gangly gait in the line of eight swimmers walking to the starting blocks. He'd worn oversized headphones over his blue swim cap and a warmup suit with *Lionfish* printed on the back. I'd given a giddy clap of anticipation right before the glass back door to our house slid open.

I'd jabbed the pause button on the playback. Aiming for a bright smile, I'd looked over my shoulder. "*You're home early!*"

"*Your hair's wet.*" Brandon had approached the table.

I'd angled my head. "*Yeah? I took a shower.*"

"*Did you go for a run?*"

I remember wondering who he thought he was. My father? "*Why does that matter?*" I'd asked.

"*Just answer me, Avery!*"

"*Yes!*" I'd swallowed, trying to stay calm. "*My nausea went away. My doctor said running's good for me, as long as I feel up to it.*"

"*So you can go for a run, but you can't walk a golf course?*"

Ah. Then I'd understood his sullenness. I'd chosen running over him, and *he* wanted to be my number-one priority. "*I didn't feel up for the crowds.*" Despite him towering over me, I'd adopted a lighthearted tone. "*A woman retching in the gallery might distract the players teeing off.*" His cloudy expression hadn't lightened. "*How'd Scottie play?*"

His gaze had traveled from me to my tablet. "*What're you watching?*"

I'd tensed. "*A swim meet.*"

"*Thought you didn't like sports.*"

"*What gave you that idea?*"

"*You won't watch golf with me.*" His eyes had narrowed. "*But you'll watch a stupid sport like swimming?*" Before I could stop him, Brandon had stabbed the screen to press play. He'd then scraped a chair across the wooden deck and sat right next to me.

As the announcer had introduced the swimmers, my breath caught in my throat. I remember my rising panic, my whirling thoughts. *Should I hit pause again and try to distract him? Grab my tablet and run inside? How could I explain either without violating confidentiality?*

The announcer had introduced the swimmer in lane five as the bronze medalist from the last Olympics. Brandon had fidgeted next to me. "*We should go in and watch on the big screen. Why are you out here?*"

I'd shrugged. "*I love our backyard.*"

He'd opened his mouth to reply, but the announcer had interrupted him: "*In lane six, Mason McCall from Bluffton, South Carolina.*"

Brandon's attention had locked on the screen.

"*At only fifteen, Mason's having a breakout meet,*" the announcer had continued. "*He finished sixth in the two-hundred fly last night.*"

"*Hey!*" Brandon had pointed at the screen. "*That's the kid you meet with.*"

Everything in me had gone still as I'd felt his stare on the side of my face.

"*Right?*" he'd pressed.

"*That's private! I can't say.*"

"*C'mon, Avery. I'm not an idiot—just admit it.*"

I'd reached for my tablet. "*I'll watch this later.*"

But he'd pushed my arm away with more force than I expected. "*No. We're watching this. Let's see if you're any good at this sport-psychology thing. That's what he sees you for, right? Performance anxiety? Or...is he crazy?*"

I'd turned to him, unable to hide my disgust.

He'd held up his hands. "*Touchy subject. I apologize.*"

His voice rang in my ears even now. He hadn't meant that at all.

The electronic beep of the start had returned our focus to the race. A moment passed before I figured out which swimmer was Mason, but after that, I couldn't take my eyes off his beautiful stroke, powerful and fluid all at once. I'd wondered what must it feel like to surge through the water like that. No doubt it wasn't as effortless as it looked.

"*I wish I'd been on national TV at his age,*" Brandon had grumbled. "*He must get all the girls.*"

Maybe someday, I'd thought. *These days Mason seems far too anxious to ask someone on a date.*

"*Or not,*" Brandon had added after a moment. "*He's in last place—he's choking. You need to quit your day job, Dr. Clarkson.*"

Maybe he'd been aiming to joke with me, but I'd heard what seemed like contempt in his words.

I'd gritted my teeth, even as I'd willed Mason forward with silent pleas. *All your hard work, Mason. You got this. Do it for yourself. And your coach.*

Mason had seemed to hear me on the third length as he inched closer to his competitors. On the last stretch, cheers had swelled, and my heartbeat had kicked into overdrive.

Brandon had leaned closer to the screen. "*Wait a minute, he's pulling up to the field.*"

"*McCall's coming on strong!*" the announcer had boomed.

Mason had barreled toward the wall, and a gush of euphoria had hit me as he finished in third place. "*Yes!*" I'd leaped up and almost hit the underside of the umbrella.

"*Whoa.*" Brandon had looked up at me with a slow grin. "*The kid did good. You did too, Cute Stuff.*" He'd lifted his hand for a high-five. After a moment's hesitation, I'd slapped his palm. He'd clasped his fingers around my hand and spun me around before drawing me into his lap.

With my back pressed against his chest, I'd laughed in surprise.

"*What an exciting race!*" The announcer's voice had drawn our attention back to the screen. The camera had stayed on lane five, where the winner of the race had fist-bumped the swimmer in lane four before pivoting toward Mason in lane six. Mason had removed his swim cap and goggles, and the winner grinned as he knuckled the top of Mason's head in a gentle noogie. The winner had looked about ten years older than he was.

Mason had laughed as he ducked away, clasping the handles of the block to pull up and search the crowd. His chest rose and fell as he'd continued breathing hard from the race.

The announcer had chuckled. "*Someone's coach is pleased with his performance.*" The camera had scanned to three coaches jumping up and down as they hugged. When they separated, the tallest one filled the screen. *Jordan.*

Beneath me, I'd felt Brandon's muscular thighs tense.

"*Now I know why you're hiding out here.*" He'd pushed me up and off his lap. "*You wanted to see him.*"

I'd spun around. "*What?*"

He'd shot to his feet. "*You promised me! You said no handsome clients.*" He'd pointed at the screen. "*I ran into that guy in your waiting room, but I assumed he was there for Nadia. I didn't think you'd lie to me. But now I find out you did. You're seeing the coach.*"

"*I can't talk about any of this, Brandon.*" The thundering of my heart had vibrated my chest.

"*Can't or won't? Seems a convenient way to hide an affair.*"

My jaw had unhinged. "*I'm married! To you. I'm faithful to you. He's married, too.*"

Brandon's eyes had narrowed.

I'd thought sharing Jordan's marital status would calm my husband, but instead it had incensed him further. And I'd violated Jordan's confidentiality by outing him as my client. I'd searched desperately for a way to get out of the situation. "*Besides,*" I'd added, trying to quell the tremor in my voice, "*I would never do that with a client. Dual relationships are prohibited by my ethics code. I could lose my license.*"

"*Oh, we can't endanger your prized ethics,*" Brandon had mocked. "*But who cares about your code or your license? You're going to end all that soon.*"

His words had been a punch to the gut. When I'd been more tired and nauseated, I'd surrendered to the idea of becoming a stay-at-home mom. But in that moment, I'd realized I agreed with Nadia — I couldn't give it all up. Being a psychologist was part of me, part of my essence. My dysfunctional parents had messed me up in countless ways, but they'd also given me a gift: a deep sense of empathy and compassion that now drove me to help others. I would not let any man take that away.

My spidey sense of impending violence, just like I'd felt when my dad came home drunk, had tingled in my neck and back. But I was no longer a child. I'd planted my feet shoulder-width apart as I stared up at Brandon. "*No,*" I'd said, trying to swallow the ball of apprehension in my throat. "*I've decided I won't end my career. I love it too much.*"

His step toward me had sent chills up my spine. "*Love it or love him?*" he'd growled.

"*This is ridiculous!*" I'd thrown my arms up. "*I am not cheating on you.*" Then a sudden insight had frozen me. "*Though maybe* you're *cheating.*" I'd nodded as I considered that possibility. "*A classic case of projection — accusing someone of the very behavior you're guilty of.*"

He'd grabbed my left wrist and yanked me so close I could feel the heat of his breath on my forehead. "*Don't pull that psychobabble on me. You're deflecting, and you know it.*"

I'd tried to wriggle out of his grasp, but his hold was too tight, squeezing into the skin below my smartwatch.

"*You said you'd stop working to take care of our family!*" he'd huffed. "*Another lie. What else are you lying about?*"

"*Let me go.*" My breath had come in pants, while he'd seemed unfazed — so unaffected that he seemed dissociative, not fully present. As my heart raced, I'd considered what might happen if I kneed him in the groin or attacked with other moves I'd learned in the Navy. But I hadn't liked the potential outcomes. So I'd stopped writhing. "*Brandon.*" His blue eyes had darkened to the hue of a stormy sea. "*Look at me.*" I'd waited for him to focus on my face, even as my wrist burned from the pressure of his grip. "*I'm your wife. You're hurting me. You don't want to hurt me or the baby, right?*"

"*You're the one hurting me,*" he'd snapped, but he had loosened his hold. Then he'd pushed off my forearm to step back. "*You agreed, Avery! You agreed to stop working, to prioritize your family. You won't have anything left for us.*"

As I'd licked my lips, I'd forced myself not to massage my burning wrist. "*I'm sorry. I, I wasn't myself when I went along with that. The combined fatigue and nausea, well, it was hard to think straight. But I'm feeling better now. That's good, right? Good for our baby.*"

His jaw had remained locked tight.

I'd considered scooping his hand into mine to soothe him, like I had when Nate had visited, but I hadn't wanted to get that close right then, given the smarting of my wrist. "*Look, I can't predict the future,*" I'd told him. "*Maybe you're right. Maybe I won't be able to balance career and family. But I have to see for myself after the baby comes.*"

I can't promise that now. I trained ten years for this career. And honestly, I think I'll be a better mom and wife if I keep working."

He'd snorted a sound of disgust. *"How will we travel the world if you're working?"*

I'd squinted at him. *"How would we travel the world with a baby?"*

"I'll hire a nanny!"

"A nanny?" I'd said, incredulous. For all his talk about sacrificing my career to benefit the family, in that moment he didn't seem to care much about our baby's wellbeing. *"We can afford that?"* I'd pressed. When he didn't answer, I'd said, *"Even if we can afford a nanny, I don't want one. I want to raise our child, pour our love into the peanut."* He still hadn't responded, and I'd tried another tactic. *"How would you feel about giving up your career for the family? Giving up golf?"*

"I'd do it in a heartbeat."

Though he'd looked straight at me as he replied, I knew he was lying. He just wanted to win the argument.

"It's a betrayal, you changing your mind like that," he'd said. *"This discussion's not over. But the only way I go along with it for now?"* He'd gestured to my tablet. *"You stop seeing that coach."*

My chest had jumped as I'd pulled in a sharp inhale. *Was he really asking me to stop seeing Jordan in the middle of a CPT protocol, just as he'd begun to make significant progress?*

"Should be an easy decision, since you said he doesn't mean anything to you," Brandon had jabbed again. *"Your family or your client, kiddo."*

I'd already had an aversion to that word, but my husband calling me a child had bristled the hairs on my skin into needles. *"I can't stop seeing him in the middle of treatment. It'd be abandonment."*

"But you don't care if you abandon me."

I'd realized then what a narcissist he was. *How did I not see that earlier?*

"Refer him to Nadia," he'd hissed. *"I'm sure they'd hit it off."*

"I can't! She's not certified—" I'd blurted. I'd been about to say she wasn't certified in CPT, but I stopped myself. I'd already revealed too much about Jordan.

"Unbelievable. You choose strangers—people who don't matter—over me, your husband. Where are your priorities?" He'd seized the iPad off the patio table and shaken it over his head. *"This is all you care about!"*

I'd stopped breathing as he took quick strides to the deck railing and launched my iPad like it was a frisbee. Its sickening plop into the lagoon had seemed to resonate in the air. Shocked, I'd watched its quick descent to the depths.

The swish of a paper nearby rustles me out of the backyard scene, and I draw in a breath.

Jordan is looking at me oddly. "Dr. Avery? Here you go." He holds out the completed symptom checklist for me to score. I get the sense he had to repeat, *"Here you go,"* several times before I clued in.

"Sorry." I gulp as I take the paper from him. I tug down the left cuff of my jacket sleeve and swipe it across my sweaty forehead. I total the number and pick up my tablet to enter the score.

"You got a new iPad?"

Jordan's question freezes me. I couldn't order one and have it delivered in time for my Monday clients, so I had to drive two hours to the closest Apple store in Charleston on Sunday. The tech helped me transfer data from the cloud, and I'm grateful the electronic medical record stored my client information. "Yes."

"What happened to your old one? Did you get a good trade-in discount?"

When I stare at him, my mind scrambling for something to say, he holds up his hands. "Don't mean to get personal. I'm only asking because Elena needs a new one."

I frown, thinking about my poor baby on the bottom of the lagoon, likely covered in green mossy goo. "It got…wet."

"Oh."

"But don't worry, I can still access the chart tracking your progress." I tap the screen. "And your score dropped significantly again, all the way down to twenty-nine."

His eyes bug. "Whoa." A smile spreads. "I'll be your most-improved client ever."

I return his smile. "It's not a competition." Then my smile falters. My *husband* thinks it is.

How ridiculous that he sees Jordan as his rival. Brandon hasn't spoken to me since Saturday, though we've slept in the same bed. We haven't resolved anything. I should've recognized earlier his childish pattern of giving me the silent treatment when he doesn't get his way.

I should've known he would try to destroy my tablet, which to him represents my work—my autonomy, my freedom. I plan to keep my new one hidden in my office, away from him.

"Everything in life's a competition, Doc. Including Mason's next meet in June: US Nationals. I'm giving him a week off, but then we're back at it."

He's trying again to get me to talk about swimming, but I motion to his folder. "Do you have some worksheets for us to review?"

"Uh, yeah. Only had time for a couple. Hope I did them right."

I look over the beliefs he wrote as examples of unrealistic thinking styles. "Good job. The stuck point, *If I let someone get close to me, they'll die*—that fits with catastrophic thinking." I wait for his nod before I continue. "And you included examples of everyday thinking, like *I'm screwing up my kids*. How did you see that as overgeneralization?"

He shrugs. "You said this style is going from one to many, right? Whenever I mess up as a parent, I say that to myself. For example, I wasn't there to rein in Hudson when he acted like a little dictator at Hailey's school concert. He's been salty since I returned from the meet, and I don't know what to say to him. I'm screwing him up as we speak." He gestures at the worksheet. "Even though I'm a parent fail this week, I hope that's not always true." He smirks. "But it's all job security for you, huh? Hudson and Hailey will need therapy for sure."

"Just about every parent I've met has said the same thing."

My peanut will need years of therapy with Brandon for a father. But it'll be better than having divorced parents, right? Better to stay together than to fight him for custody in a legal battle he'll win with all his money? I don't want Brandon to be unsupervised with our child as a single father. Or even worse, as a father remarried to some stranger he meets while speed dating. The bruises near my wrist throb. I tug the sleeve of my jacket again and push down the fear climbing up my throat. I need to focus on my client.

"This is the halfway point of our trauma therapy, and given the decrease in your symptom score, you're making great progress." I gesture to his stuck point log. "If there are stuck points you no longer believe, you can cross them off."

His eyebrows bounce up. "Cool."

"And now it's time to introduce our last CBT worksheet. We'll use this one for the next five or so sessions." As I hand him a paper with a wordy, busy-looking table, I notice my breath has regulated. Another reason I love my career is that it takes me away from my own problems. "This worksheet brings together the prior skills you've learned to help you become your own cognitive therapist. Let's review the different sections before we practice with one of your stuck points."

He scratches his cheek as he studies the worksheet.

I take him through the columns that include the stuck point, questions to challenge it, thinking styles, and alternative beliefs. I wait for him to follow along. "Would you look at your log and select a stuck point for us to practice?"

"How about, *My sister would be a way better parent than me.*"

"That's relevant to our discussion." I nod. "But are there any starred stuck points that you still believe? One of those might be better for us to practice together." I want him to challenge a belief about why the trauma happened.

After a long pause, he deflates. "*God let my dad and sister die.* I've been, uh, thinking about my dad lately." He clears his throat. "Missing him."

No wonder we're talking about parenting. I shift in my seat as I consider whether to go forward with this. Beliefs about religion are tricky to prove, and I don't want to impose my faith (or lack thereof) on Jordan. But I'm not surprised that he's starting to process his father's death now that he's stopped suppressing emotions in general. I decide to follow his inner wisdom.

"Okay, write down the activating event. You could just put *trauma* or *Kim's death.*" He fills in that section. "Add your stuck point, but this time, also rate the strength of your belief from zero to one hundred. How strongly do you believe, *God let my dad and sister die?* Is it fifty-percent true to you? One-hundred?"

"I don't know," he says. "Ninety?"

I nod. "Now write how you feel and the strength of each feeling. What feelings come up when you think that God let your dad and sister die?"

He swallows as he writes. "Betrayed and…angry. And…confused."

"How intense is each feeling?"

"Betrayed, one-hundred percent. Angry and confused…they're each…" He rolls his eyes. "Sixty-three-point-five percent."

I let out a breath at his welcome humor. "Yes, it's tough to determine exact numbers here. Go for a ballpark. Let's ask questions about your stuck point. First, what leads you to conclude that God let your dad and sister die?"

His knuckles rub along his jaw. "God is powerful in all things."

"How do you know that for a fact?"

He stills. "I just…know. Don't you?"

I hesitate. *Should I share my beliefs?* I was trained to self-disclose only when it benefits the client. Though my parents took Nate and me to church near whichever Marine base we lived on, I don't practice an organized religion as an adult. But I do believe in God, who I view as a benevolent higher power. Who else would've directed me to this career I love so much? It's a calling—one I can't believe Brandon wants me to leave. Did God direct me to Brandon as well? I don't know. But I do know the baby growing in my belly, especially at my age, is a beautiful gift from above.

"Sorry for prying," Jordan says.

I look at him. "You can ask any question. I just want to keep the focus on you and your needs in here. How important is it for you to know my spiritual beliefs?"

He blinks. "I guess not everyone believes in God."

"I do." I decide to give a brief answer to show our common ground. "But people often disagree on the presence or nature of God. Would that be evidence against your stuck point?"

After he thinks for a while, he writes on the worksheet.

"If some people don't believe in God, would that be an exception to your stuck point that God let your family members die?"

"Yes," he says. "And if we can find a quick exception to the stuck point, it's not a fact."

I'm pleased by his absorption of CBT concepts. After he determines that his belief is repetitive, not factual, we explore the question about leaving out essential information. "Do you believe God gave us free will?" I ask.

"Definitely."

"How can God be powerful in all things if God gave us free will? For example, if a woman decides to jump off a building, can God suspend the law of gravity to save her?"

He frowns. "Probably not."

"Would God want her to die?"

"No way."

I nod. "Would God *let* her die?"

His eyes close, and he leans back on the sofa. "I see where you're going with this." His face relaxes as he seems to arrive at an understanding. "Maybe God didn't want, or *let*, my dad and sister die." His nods pick up speed. "Their deaths weren't under his control, since he gave us free will."

As he writes, I say, "You might be interested in the book, *When Bad Things Happen to Good People*. The author, Rabbi Harold Kushner, argues that very point. Death is a natural part of life—pain is, too. Maybe God can't stop the pain, but God can help us heal and grow stronger from it."

We review the rest of the questions and determine that his belief fits quite a few unrealistic styles of thinking, including mindreading. Jordan finds it entertaining that he mindreads even God.

"Okay, on to the next part," I tell him. "How else could you interpret your dad and sister's deaths? What else could you say to yourself?"

He rubs his fingertips up and down his forehead. "Okay, I've got one. God can help me become the man my family taught me to be."

"That's lovely." I smile at him. After he fills in that column, I ask, "How much do you believe that alternative thought?"

"It's true. One-hundred percent."

"Nice. Sometimes your alternative belief may not ring true because it's unfamiliar and unpracticed. But you came up with an effective new thought." I gesture at his worksheet. "Last part—*now* how do you feel? Do you still feel…" I look at my notes. "Betrayed?"

His head tilts. "No. *Huh.* But I'm still angry, maybe fifty percent? Still a little confused, though only twenty percent."

"Any new feelings come up when you tell yourself, *God can help me become the man my family taught me to be?*"

"Determined." He sinks a little lower on the sofa. "And sad."

"Sounds like a small change in thinking brought on a big change in feelings. What makes you feel sad?"

"Dad and Kim won't get to watch Mason swim in the Olympics one day. With you and me to coach him, he'll be unstoppable."

Guilt tightens my throat and warms my face.

Jordan studies me. "Which of Mason's events did you watch on TV?"

I try to remember. "The two-hundred freestyle?"

"His best race of the meet! You should've seen all the attention from college coaches, even though he's only in ninth grade. Think what he can do when he has a coach who's not going off the deep end all season long. And I hope you've cleared your schedule for the next few years, because Mase is going to need you."

The bruises near my wrist pulse again, and I make sure the left sleeve of my jacket hasn't ridden up. "It's hard to predict the future."

"Wait." He sits up. "You're not leaving, right?"

I hear the tremor of panic in his voice and realize I've activated his abandonment fears. "Well, I'll take maternity leave, of course."

"But then you'll come back."

I refrain from reassuring him. It's true I can't foresee the future, but the real wildcard is Brandon. I won't let him bully me to stop Jordan's trauma therapy midstream, even though I'm worried my husband will barge in on the appointment at any second. But I can't promise to keep meeting with Mason, since Brandon will view him as an extension of Jordan and therefore a threat. Also, if I reassure Jordan, his anxiety might lower for a second before shooting right back up. He needs CBT or other skills to address his anxiety long term.

"Jordan." I take a breath. "I'm thrilled that Mason had a great meet. You must be so proud. I'll do my best to be there for you both. In the future, though, I may need to focus on my family."

He presses his lips together. "Is this because of your husband?"

I flinch. *How does he know?* "Why...do you say that?"

"Why do you keep holding your wrist?"

I glance down and yank my hand away from my wrist. Have I been touching Brandon's fingertip bruises the whole time? I can't let Jordan see them. "I might've sprained it," I lie. "Listen, I see we're out of time. Your practice assignment is to complete one worksheet each day, okay?"

He's motionless for a long moment, but then he accepts the handout I've offered him. "See you next week."

I let out a long exhale after he leaves my office. *As long as my husband doesn't try to interfere.*

170

15. JORDAN

A day after my sixth session with Dr. Avery, I stretch a cramped calf muscle as I fill my insulated water bottle at the fridge. Spinning class with Elena at her gym this morning kicked my butt. I holler down the hallway toward my kids' bedrooms, "Leaving for practice in fifteen!" The lack of response confirms they're consumed by their tablets, catching up with their favorite games and videos after school. Allowing them to binge on screens is yet another parenting fail—another reason they'll need therapy one day.

"Every parent thinks that," Dr. Avery said. My jaw tenses. She did not look good yesterday. Though she perked up once we got into the session, her wan face and dull gaze concerned me. Elena loved being pregnant, but Dr. Avery's baby seems to be leaching the life force from her. Or maybe it's that tall jerk of a husband? How *did* she sprain her wrist, anyway?

"Daddy?" Hailey wanders into the kitchen. At first, I'm pleased that she left her screen behind to spend time with me. But then she pats my jacket pocket. "Anything in your snack holes?"

I grin. I used to stuff crackers or candy into my pockets to avoid overloading the diaper bag, and Hudson started referring to my pockets that way at age three. "No, ma'am, but let's get you a snack before practice." I open the fridge. "Grapes?"

She nods.

After I wash and pluck them off their stems, I give her a bowlful of green grapes. A wave of nostalgia hits me as I recall how Elena used to slice the grapes in half to avoid a choking hazard when the kids were younger. I bet Hudson is hungry, too, so I prepare some for him. "Anything else?"

She raises her shoulders and dips her chin as she bats her eyelashes at me. "Golden Grahams?" Her tactics for procuring sweets are top notch. And adorable.

"Too bad. We just ran out." That's not quite the truth. Elena threw out all the sugary cereal last night. She also vowed never to buy cereal again after reading it has a high glycemic index that spikes blood sugar. Once she finishes this nutrition book she's reading, I'll look it over. I want to help Mason improve his fueling before the next Olympics.

Another shrug from my daughter. "Cookies?"

Hailey knows I'm the weaker link in the parenting chain when it comes to feeding her sugar addiction, but I don't give in. I don't want Elena mad at me. "Pretzels and Nutella," I tell her as I open the pantry. Still a lot of carbs, but at least she'll get a little protein.

As she hoovers in the pretzels, I walk back to Hudson's bedroom. His door is closed, and I pause before knocking. Since getting off the school bus this afternoon, Hudson hasn't said one word to me. I have no idea what to say to him, either. I was hoping to work on my parenting skills with Dr. Avery once I finish the trauma therapy, but now I can't count on her being available in the long term. My neck feels tight as I lift my fist to knock. I'm on my own now.

When my knocks go unanswered, I open the door to find Hudson wearing noise-canceling headphones as he plays a game on his tablet. He's lounged on his bed, and his head jerks up at my entrance, but he soon returns to jabbing at the controls.

My chest clenches with irritation. "Hey." I point at the shoes he's wearing—a no-no on his bed—but he's still ignoring me. I tap the inside of his knee, and he looks up. I gesture at his shoes as I shake my head. He lets out a long sigh before toeing off the shoes. A funky odor wafts up from his socked feet, and I'm glad he'll be doused in chlorine soon.

I try to tell him about the grapes, but he can't hear me. Exasperated, I lift one large headphone away from his ear. "I have a snack for you."

Hudson shakes his head. "Not hungry."

"It's a good idea to eat something before practice."

"Not going."

My mouth drops open as he returns his attention to the game, and I slide the headphones off over the back of his head to rest around his neck. "Turn that off, please." He doesn't respond, though I know he can hear me. "I want to talk to you."

His next sigh is more forceful, but he does stop the game. I nudge his legs toward the wall to create a space for me to sit on his twin bed, facing him. "What's this about not going to practice?"

"I don't wanna go."

I fight the urge to snap back and order him to go. Instead, I take a breath. "Since when?"

He scowls. "Why isn't Mom driving us?"

So, it's not about swimming—it's about me. He doesn't want to spend time with me? "Mom's at a listing appointment. I get to drive you today, since the gold group has a week off."

"But you'd rather be coaching *your* group."

I look at him. Where'd he get that idea? I remember all the times my dad drove me home from practice. Even if I was grumpy after a tough day of school and swimming, he could get me to open up by sharing funny stories from his swim career. I wish I could feel that close to Hudson. "No, I'd rather drive you and your sister."

"Right." He rolls his eyes.

Jeez, he seems cynical. How has a ten-year-old boy become so jaded? It's not like one of *his* parents died. I'm right here. "Okay, Huds." I pat his thigh. "What's going on? Seems like you've been mad at me for a while now…maybe since I left for Mason's meet. Is that true?"

"Like you care," he sneers. The defiant set of his jaw softens as his upper lip trembles, revealing hurt beneath his angry façade.

That trembling lip breaks my heart. I have to make this right. I study his profile as he stares at the wall. "I *do* care."

He turns to glare at me. "You don't care about me. You only care about Mason." He blinks double-time as his trembling voice grows louder. "You wish *he* was your son, not me!"

My vision expands. "That is so not true! What makes you think that?"

"You talk about him all the time. I wish I could swim as fast as him, but I suck. I embarrass you. You hate me." His eyes glisten.

I'm so stunned that it's hard to breathe. How could he believe that?

Hudson keeps railing. "And Mason hates me, too. He stopped coming over because I'm slow. I'm stupid. He doesn't want...to hang out...with me." Tears leak from the corners of his eyes despite his furious blinking, his breathing erratic. "And when he stopped coming over...we never saw you...anymore." He sniffs. "You only want to spend time with Mason."

Through the fog of shock and guilt created by my son's words, I'm able to glean one source of clarity: his thoughts are irrational stuck points that need to be challenged. And the reason I know this is because I've also worried that everyone hates me, especially since Baja. But how can I make Hudson see how wrong he is? I'm not trained as a therapist. I don't have Dr. Avery's insight.

All I know is I want to hug him, if he'll let me. I scoot forward on the mattress and lean down toward him. When he wraps his arms around me, I almost start crying, too. His acceptance of my comfort is more than I deserve. "I'm so sorry, bud," I whisper in his ear as I squeeze him tighter. "I've hurt you and our family these past...six months. I owe you the deepest apology."

As he cries it out, I wonder how my dad would've responded in this situation. I keep patting Hudson's back, trying to figure out what to say. "You never got to meet your Grandpa Perry. He died before you were born." After I swallow, I tell him, "I was only twelve when he died."

Hudson pulls back and blinks up at me. "You never talk about him."

I close my eyes for a moment. "Something else I'm sorry for." I shake my head. "I shoved away those memories because they...hurt so much. I did the same thing after your aunt died." My cheeks blow out with an exhale. "But I'm learning I can't avoid my feelings. I've got to deal with them. And the more I let myself remember, the less it seems to hurt. Your grandpa... He was such a wise, kind person, just like you. You have his eyes."

Those big, brown eyes, still wet from the sheen of tears, lift to mine. "I do?"

I nod. "And what a swimmer he was. He almost made the Olympic team. Did you know that?"

Hudson's mouth opens.

"Let's visit your grandma in Cincinnati soon. We can look at some of Grandpa's medals and trophies." Maybe in August, after the summer swim season. "I felt so insecure compared to my dad. I was nowhere near the caliber of swimmer he was. But that didn't matter to him. He just wanted to share his love of the sport with me and Aunt Kim—to share the joy of moving through the water, pursuing excellence, improving, making friends." I think about the boys who swim in Hudson's lane. "You don't *have* to go to practice today, but will you miss your bros if you don't?"

His mouth twitches with a suppressed smile, probably from my lame attempt to speak his language. "I guess."

"If it's okay with your mom, we can invite Lucas and Elijah for a sleepover this weekend."

A small smile cracks through.

"Listen, Hudson." I clasp his wrists. "It doesn't matter to me how fast you swim. I just want you to learn skills that will make you strong, skills to face the hard things that happen in life."

I let him absorb that as I consider those hard things. I can't keep hiding from the pain. "My dad got sick, and he died…from cancer. Lymphoma." When I see Hudson's questioning look, I add, "I'll explain it more to you and your sister one day. They're trying to find a cure." I exhale. "Anyway, when Dad died, I think I blamed myself. I thought God was punishing me…for being mean to Aunt Kim, or not swimming fast, or not getting good grades."

A crease forms between Hudson's eyebrows as he wiggles out of my hold and raises his hands. "But that's dumb. It wasn't your fault."

I nod. "You're smart—smarter than me. I'm trying to learn that now, bud." I rub my jaw. "Aunt Kim's death wasn't my fault either." Each time I say that out loud, it seems more believable. "I think you may be doing the same thing? Taking responsibility for stuff outside your control? You're blaming yourself for the way I've acted since Aunt Kim died."

He looks away as his tongue sweeps across his lower lip, confirming my suspicion.

"But me yelling at you, saying awful things I don't mean—that's not on you. That's on me. And I'm trying to improve myself." *I've got a long way to go.* "I'm seeing a psychologist to help me understand my thoughts and feelings better. I can't promise I won't get angry with you—just like you'll feel angry at me sometimes—but I'll do my best not to go hulk-smash again."

One eyebrow elevates as he turns back to me.

"That." I point at the slanted brow. "That's another thing you do just like your grandpa. He could arch one eyebrow and put me in my place in an instant."

"Bet you deserved it," Hudson says.

I huff out a breath. "Kim deserved it more than me." My tone sounds childish, and I sigh. "Her death, on top of my dad's, well, it hit me hard. You see, she got me through that time, through our grief. She made sure we kept swimming, where we could cry into our goggles and no one would know."

Hudson gives a quick nod as he sniffs, and I wonder if he's done the same thing.

As I'm talking, I realize something. "I guess…I'm always try-ing—I always tried—to repay Aunt Kim." My voice hitches. "To… thank her for helping me through our dad's death. I wanted to save her the way she saved me. And when I couldn't, it messed me up. Made me aggressive and on edge."

Hudson seems to be thinking hard. His serious expression reminds me of the time a few years ago when he told us a neighbor boy had been mean to Hailey. His eyes had held both disbelief at the neighbor's words and a determination to protect his sister. It was a cruel loss of innocence. Now he seems to waver about accepting my apology. I worry that unpredictability and harshness from the very man who's supposed to protect him has stripped away even more innocence.

He is so precious to me. That familiar fear seizes my gut—what would I do if any harm came to my little guy? "I've been terrified that something might happen to you, or Hailey, or Mom. I've been holding on to life with a crushing grip. But none of that is on your shoulders, Huds."

He sinks back into his pillows.

Has my explanation landed? Will he stop blaming himself for my screw-ups? I study my son. As his face has lengthened, his apple cheeks have lost their roundness, and the side part in his light-brown hair brings more prominence to his forehead. His teeth are straight, though of course the dentist told us he'll need braces in a few years. It seems like his skinny legs take up more real estate on the bed every time I come in his room. He's perfect in every way. I should've tried to talk to him sooner, but I couldn't see past my own pain.

Back in November, Elena told me her mother had given her a book about helping kids through grief. The book said it was important to speak in concrete terms about death. Elena gathered Hudson and Hailey together and explained how Aunt Kim had stopped breathing, and her heart had stopped beating. But I've avoided any mention of my sister to my kids. Maybe I should move the urn with her ashes out of its closet hiding place.

"It must be painful not to have Aunt Kim around," I say.

Hudson looks down at his tablet, which has gone dark.

"What do you miss about her most?" I ask, unsure what to say next.

His finger traces the edges of his tablet. "Body surfing."

At once, I smile. Kim loved taking the kids to the Hilton Head beach on spring break or summer visits. The times Elena and I tagged along, we marveled at Kim's nonstop energy to swim out with Hudson and help him select the perfect surging wave to ride in, showing him how to sprint freestyle to keep ahead of the break. Hailey used to join them, but a jellyfish sting two summers ago made her more interested in building sandcastles with other girls she met on the beach.

A rustling noise draws my attention to the doorway, where Hailey stands with a smear of Nutella at the corner of her mouth. *How long has she been eavesdropping?* But I'm glad she's here. She needs to hear my apology as well.

Hailey says, "T-shirts."

It takes me a moment to understand her comment. "You miss Aunt Kim buying you T-shirts?"

She gives a solemn nod.

"She bought the best shirts. C'mere, baby girl." I pat the mattress, but she walks in and backs onto my lap instead, snuggling into me.

"You've got poop on your face," Hudson says.

She jerks back. "Dad! He can't say that."

I shake my head and decide not to intervene in their sibling squabble. It just feels good to hang out with them in a moment of normalcy. We haven't had that in a long time.

Hailey scrapes the hazelnut spread off and licks her finger. "This poop's yummy." She sticks her tongue out at her brother.

I cradle her in my arms. "I love you two so much." I look over at Hudson. "And as far as me loving Mason *more* than you, that's hooey bunk!" Hudson still looks skeptical. "I'm sorry I get all obsessed with swimming, and sometimes I pay extra attention to Mason because he doesn't have a dad. But you two are my kids, my *blood*. Your mom and I are so blessed to have amazing kids like you—smart, funny, creative, and kind. You two are precious gifts from God. The world's a better place since you were born."

Hailey tilts her head back onto my chest as she relaxes. But Hudson's gaze still seems wary.

"Huds, you blame yourself for Mason not coming over as much. I bet that stings, but it's not because he doesn't like you anymore. You'll see, once you start high school, your friends become more important than your family. That's why I'm so glad you opened up to me today. I want to spend all the time I can with you before you discard me and your mom for your friends." I sigh and adopt a dramatic tone. "You'll drop Mom and me like old shoes thrown in the trash."

"Old, *smelly* shoes," Hailey pipes up. After a beat, she asks, "Are we still going to practice?"

I look at my watch. "We'll be late, but I'll cover for you with Coach Gabe. What do you say, Huds? Want to go?" Hailey scrambles off my lap, and we both stand.

He tilts his head. "As long as you don't play your unc tunes in the car."

I thump my fist against my chest in a stabbing motion. "Ugh, stick the knife in deeper, bro. Just for that, I'll play the slowest, nerdiest songs I can find."

As I back out of the room, Hailey asks, "Is there a serial killer in the house, Daddy?"

I freeze. Maybe I shouldn't joke about knives. Or maybe this is a sign she's grieving Aunt Kim—fears about safety, perhaps? "What... makes you ask that?"

She scowls. "Somebody ate *all* the cereal. They killed it."

My widened eyes dart to Hudson's, and we can't help it—we both crack up.

"Why're you laughing?" Hailey demands, which makes us laugh harder.

The following Wednesday, Dr. Avery's tired eyes smile at me. "You're killing it, Jordan." She holds her iPad aloft. "Down to twenty-one today."

I've dropped over forty points since we started this therapy! But it's tough to feel excited when Dr. Avery seems so down. Smudges darken the hollow above her cheekbones. "I should've trusted you more from the get-go," I tell her. "You really know what you're doing."

"Thank you for saying that, but your buy-in and hard work are the factors driving your success." She pauses. "It's interesting you mentioned trust, as that's one of the themes we'll cover soon. Trust often takes a hit after trauma."

That rings true. I can't believe I thought Gabe was plotting against me, given how much fun we've had coaching together this week. He came up with all kinds of clever uses for pool noodles to teach proper technique, like the "Chariot" drill. That had Hudson balancing on a kickboard while three swimmers pulled him with stretch cords belted around their waists. I couldn't stop laughing when Gabe gave him a pool noodle to beat on the water like a whip, urging his swimmer horses forward.

After we review the week's worksheets, Dr. Avery says, "You've come up with successful challenges to many of your stuck points. And you crossed off the ones you no longer believe?"

I nod and show her my log with lines drawn through many of my starred beliefs, including *Kim's death is all my fault because… I'm selfish, I have a huge ego, I abandoned her,* and *I was out of shape.* It felt good to strike through those beliefs.

"For the second part of this therapy," she continues, "we'll focus on five types of beliefs affected by trauma: safety, trust, power and control, esteem, and intimacy. Session seven typically covers safety, but since you're making great progress, I suggest we combine sessions seven and eight to cover both safety and trust today. How does that sound to you?"

Is she trying to speed this therapy along to get rid of me? Kick me out so she can stop working and leave Mason and me out in the cold? My paranoid worries are probably a sign I need to work on trust. "Let's do it," I tell her.

She gives me the safety handout. "Let's explore your beliefs about keeping yourself and others safe."

I read how negative safety beliefs can increase irritability, anxiety, and edginess, all of which sound familiar. When she asks me to review my stuck point log for any relevant self-safety beliefs, I identify *If something bad happens to me, my kids' lives will be ruined,* and *I'm going to die and leave my kids fatherless.*

"Curious," says Dr. Avery as she looks over my stuck point log. "I don't see any beliefs about others threatening your safety. Instead, your stuck points are all about *you* keeping *others* safe. For example, *I showed zero concern for others' safety,* and *If I let someone get close to me, they'll die.*"

"Is that unusual?" I ask.

Her eyebrows tug together. "Nooo, not necessarily. It tracks with your experiences prior to the trauma, when you felt safe for the most part. Sounds like your parents did their best to create a loving, supportive home." A faint blush colors her cheeks. "Not everyone has parents like that." She shifts in her chair.

Is she hiding something? "Well, *I'm* the one who's been the safety threat in my family. Elena already knows how sorry I am, and I finally apologized to my kids for being such a PTSD tyrant."

"I bet that meant a lot to them." She crosses her legs. "It takes, um, a confident man to say he's sorry." She looks away.

Avoiding eye contact is uncharacteristic for her. I'm not sure what to say next.

"So." She gives a tight smile, and I fight the urge to squirm. It's the first moment of awkwardness between us that I can recall. "Your relationship has improved with your son and daughter?"

I shrug. "My daughter will forgive anything as long as I ply her with sugar."

A hint of a smile plays on her mouth.

"My son's a tougher sell. He's missing his aunt, and I think I could help by taking him to the beach like she did."

Her head inclines to one side. "But no swimming in the ocean since Baja, huh?"

I frown and shake my head.

"Any pool swimming?" she asks.

I look down. I need to get over this fear. "At least my shoulder doesn't hurt anymore." As I stare at my flipflops, I remember my sprint to the panga after Peter shouted Kim's name. My shoulder didn't hurt then, either—too much adrenaline coursing through my blood. The choppy waves buffeted my body as my arms and legs churned, my pulse and ragged breaths thumping in my ears, each swell clouding the turquoise water as I sliced through it... I look up with a start.

"What is it?" says Dr. Avery.

My eyes must look wild, and I blink a few times. "I just remembered—I hit coral, too, that day."

She looks confused.

"When I was racing to the boat, my hand..." I look down at my left hand and lift it to peer at my unblemished fingertips. "I brushed against coral. But it didn't cut me." As I exhale, I feel my heart rate begin to descend. "I wasn't hurt."

"I'm not surprised you're remembering more from that day as you process it. What does that memory mean to you?"

"I was...lucky, I guess." An ache fills my heart. "And Kim was unlucky."

Silence settles between us as she gives me some time to think.

"Now that you've stopped blaming yourself, you're searching for other causes," she says eventually. "How does it feel to attribute Kim's death to bad luck?"

I shake my head. "Doesn't sit right. I know bad things can happen, but chalking them up to luck... It just seems so arbitrary."

"I feel you." She sighs. "When I was young, I used to wear a necklace with a little ladybug charm that my mom gave me. I thought it brought good luck." There's a melancholy to her voice. "But then I wised up and tossed it out." Her gaze seems far away, and her faint smile fades as she rubs her wrist. "Maybe I should've kept wearing it." With a quick shake of her head, she inhales, pressing her lips together. "I think our concept of luck is just an attempt to control the uncontrollable." She touches the hollow of her neck. "As much as I wanted it to, my ladybug necklace didn't stop bad things from happening."

She seems so sad, and I wish I could help her feel better. *What are those bad things? Has she been through trauma as well?*

"But I'm getting ahead of myself, talking about power and control," she adds. "We'll cover that next session." She glances at her smartwatch. "Let's move ahead with the trust theme."

The next handout uncovers quite a few of my issues. I don't trust myself to make good judgments, as evidenced by my anxiety, indecision, and harsh self-talk. My stuck point, *I never should've booked that trip*, is an example of a negative trust belief.

It appears that I also struggle to trust the promises of others, particularly that they won't abandon me. I cross off the stuck point, *You can't trust Gabe at all. He will try to steal your job.* But I'm still wary of trusting the Lionfish board, and I keep the stuck point, *If you want something done right, do it yourself.*

My next practice assignment for the week ahead is to complete challenging beliefs worksheets focused on safety and trust stuck points. I'm going to lower my score below twenty next week—I can feel it.

Dr. Avery walks me out of her office, and as we turn the corner, she hesitates. I turn to see what held her up, and her hard stare is fixed on the empty waiting room. She notices me watching her, and she plasters on a smile. "Great work, Jordan. See you next week."

A joke seems inappropriate, and I can't think of one, anyway. I grimace as I walk to the lobby of the building. She was weird today.

I'm not surprised by the blinding late-April sun, and I slide on my sunglasses as I stride to my car. But I *am* surprised by the sports car parked next to mine. A yellow, *boujee* sports car. I stop short as the driver's door opens and a man climbs out. Once he reaches his full height, he towers over the low-profile car. His mouth is a slash of antagonism beneath his sunglasses. When he approaches me on the sidewalk, my heart presses up into my throat.

"Jordan, isn't it?" He holds out his hand. He flashes his white teeth in a smile that seems fake.

I don't accept the handshake. How does Dr. Avery's husband know my name? Does she talk to him about me? Tell him my secrets? She wouldn't do that. "Do I know you?"

His smile vanishes as he retracts his hand and slides it into the pocket of his gray pants. Combined with his crisp navy polo shirt, Italian loafers, and jet black hair, his vibe is sharp and powerful. "No," he says. "And you don't want to know me. That's why I'm here."

I wish I was wearing something more professional than a Lionfish T-shirt, shorts, and flip-flops. "You don't want me to know you, yet you…introduce yourself?"

A muscle in his jaw ripples. His car barely makes a sound, but I can tell he left the engine running from the heat drifting my way. I hope that means he intends this standoff to be brief.

"I'm here to give you a message," he says. He steps closer. "Stay away from my wife."

My right hand twitches, and my fingers curl toward my palm. Other than preteen skirmishes with neighbor boys, I haven't ever had a fistfight. But this guy's posturing ignites a desire for violence in me. I don't want to be aggressive, though. I'm not that man anymore. To de-escalate the situation, I play dumb. "Dude, I don't know who *you* are. How would I know your wife?"

"Avery Brown," he snaps. "The therapist you were seeing."

I know he intends to humiliate me by outing me as a therapy client, but I don't care about this jackhole's opinion of me. All I can think about is Dr. Avery. How has she let this man into her life? Is she in danger? Then the echo of his words snags my attention. "What do you mean, the therapist I *was* seeing?"

"She's giving up her practice because she's pregnant."

From his smug smile, I gather he thinks he's telling me something I don't know. But I keep my face neutral. "Congratulations…" My eyes wander down. "To your…swimmers."

His jaw muscle ticks again. "You think it's funny."

I don't know what to say, so I shrug and look away. I see a path through the trees. *Is that where Dr. Avery takes Mason on walks?*

"You think it's funny her job is killing her baby?"

My gaze zooms back to him. "What?"

"She's so stressed out from her clients that she started spotting."

I freeze.

"The doctor told her to stop working, or she'll lose the baby."

Her baby! My heart jumps a beat.

"But she won't stop!" He raises his hands and plows them through his hair. "I've been pleading with her, *begging* her, but she says she won't stop working. She refuses to abandon you." He pockets his sunglasses and rubs his palms over his eyes. "She said *you're* her most troubled client—the one she worries about." He lowers his hands to reveal piercing blue eyes. "Once you're done with therapy, she's promised she'll go on leave. But she won't abandon you."

She thinks I'm troubled? Her worst client? She told me I was making good progress. Was that a lie? Does she wish she could stop seeing me? She has seemed to want to rush through our last sessions.

Her husband's voice lowers. "Avery's selflessness is what made me fall in love with her. She always puts others' needs ahead of her own." His eyes turn sad. "This time, though, the stakes are higher. If she doesn't take care of herself..." He lets out a shaky breath and steps back.

His energy seems to shift from dominance to something else... devastation? As I study him, his eyes begin to glisten.

"I'm terrified, Jordan." He shakes his head. "Terrified of losing her or our baby. She's so stubborn—she'll work till she collapses. She won't stop seeing you or her other clients." His voice wavers, and he swallows. "*You're* the one who has to save her. You've got to stop therapy to save her and the baby."

This is on me? Why hasn't Dr. Avery told me any of this? We just talked about trust—doesn't she trust me with truth about her health? "We're almost done with the treatment," I say. "I can't just ghost her after everything she's done for me. I need to talk to her first."

"No!" His eyes beseech me. "You can't tell her we spoke. She'll deny everything so you won't worry. She hates when people worry about her. Just don't show up next Wednesday. That'll let her know she can step back and go on bedrest like her doctor ordered."

My phone buzzes in my pocket. I pull it out to see that Elena is calling—the perfect excuse to get away from this confusing man. It's unsettling that he knows way more about me than I do about him. Is he telling the truth? Am I the reason Dr. Avery's unwell? Or is *he* the one hurting her? I make a beeline for my car.

"Please, Jordan," he calls as he wipes his eyes. "Please save Avery and her baby. I'm begging you...from one father to another."

He knows I have kids? I hustle into my car and let Elena's call go to voicemail as I back out of my parking space. From my rearview mirror, I see him watching my car as I drive away.

16. AVERY

The bustling weekend crowd in Harbour Town missed the memo that it's only early May and tourist season hasn't started yet. Brandon scowled at the diners waiting for a table at Sea Pines' Quarterdeck restaurant before he slipped the hostess a fifty. I'm unsure if the cash or his charming smirk scored us a table on the upper level, but here we are, admiring the iconic red and white stripes of the Hilton Head lighthouse.

After we order drinks, Brandon fixes his gaze on the boats bobbing in the calm waters. I study his chiseled face. I watched him shave three hours ago, but the beginnings of a five o'clock shadow already encroach along his angled jaw. Sunshine reflects in his eyes, lightening their deep blue. He's so handsome. I still can't believe he's my husband. A mottled scar near his left temple is the only blemish on his perfect face. I asked him about it once, but he didn't answer. I realized, after the conversation, that his deft change of topic had distracted me. And he still hasn't shared anything about his work in investments, despite my pointed questions.

For the hundredth time, I wonder if I should stay married to him. I've always wanted a companion for lazy Sunday brunches like this one. I've harbored a tender longing to share my life with a partner—to vent about the hassles we encounter, to lift each other up during the hard times, to share the delight of joyful moments. To create a tiny, precious baby and teach him or her to navigate the potholes on the road of life.

But the downsides of marriage had always stopped me from committing in the past. The burden of responsibility for my husband's well-being, the dread of feeling lonelier within the relationship than living on my own, the fear of a spouse curtailing my freedom to do whatever I want, when I want... My insides tighten just thinking about it. Have my worst fears come true?

The needy man across from me is indeed beautiful, but I worry his beauty is only skin deep. A darkness shrouds his inner self. Will he ever let me see inside? Based on a little over six months together, I'm losing faith. I also *hate* when he tries to control me.

I'm so stupid and impulsive. I should've vetted Brandon more thoroughly before jumping into a life with him. And the intensity of our relationship will only increase when we have to co-parent. I look down at the elastic waistband of my skort, which now presses against my small bump. Good thing I'm feeling more energetic in the last few days since I'll need to shop for maternity clothes soon. But if I leave Brandon, will I have enough energy to raise a child by myself? Will divorce be better for our child than growing up with married parents? Nadia usually helps me sort through questions like these as we dive into psychological research. But for now at least, my shame over the sad state of my marriage has prevented me from turning to her.

Brandon gestures to a couple on the dock below who are talking to a charter fishing boat captain. "Striking watercraft."

"The Chris Craft launch thirty-two?" I ask.

He turns to me with a surprised smile. "Sometimes I forget you were in the Navy. You don't talk about it much."

That's because I associate the military with my father.

After silence spreads between us, Brandon says, "I'll have to take you fishing one day."

I tilt my head. "You like to fish?"

"I used to fish all the time...in California." He swallows.

"What stopped you?"

He looks out at the boats again. It appears I've asked another question he won't answer.

A waitress sets our drinks on the table—club soda for me, scotch and soda for him. She leans in closer to Brandon. "I told the bartender to make it a healthy pour, sir."

A slow grin spreads his mouth. "I *knew* I liked you."

As the waitress giggles, I marvel at the two of them. Does he remember that his pregnant wife is right here watching this little flirtation tableau?

He picks up his menu. "I'll start with Clams Casino, then the South Carolina Grouper Rockefeller. The lady will have a hamburger, medium-well, with a side salad and vinaigrette. Bring her salad with my appetizer."

I gawk at him.

"Very good, sir." The waitress takes his menu and reaches for mine.

"*Not* very good." I clutch the menu with a death grip. "I'll order for myself, thank you."

Brandon's face falls. "But you've been craving burgers, and you can't eat raw fish."

How in the world does he think it's okay to decide what I want without consulting me first? "That was last week—" I halt. I don't want to argue in front of this young server. I focus on my exhale. But my ire flares again as I scan the menu and notice Brandon's meal costs over $60, whereas the one he ordered for me is $20. "I'll take the Thai crunch salad, and…" I consider ordering the most expensive entrée on the menu, but that's too much food for a stomach irritated by my husband. "The salmon." That will be good brain food for my baby.

"Our salmon is my favorite entrée," says the waitress as she accepts my menu and makes a wise exit.

Brandon takes a long pull of his amber drink. As he sets down the tumbler, the tension around his eyes communicates his reproach. "You won't let me take care of you."

He seems to confuse caring with controlling. It's like he gets off on trying to dominate me. I search for a non-aggressive response so I don't stoop to his level.

With a shake of his head, he says, "I thought you were going to work on your avoidant attachment style."

My eyes flutter shut as I suppress a groan. Why did I share that with him? I should've known he would throw it in my face later. I open my eyes to catch a faint uptick at one corner of his mouth. He enjoys winding me up.

"You won't let me in," he adds.

"I'm letting you buy me an expensive meal," I counter.

A muscle in his jaw ticks. Too late, I remember that he gets cranky when I bring up any mention of money.

"You agreed that I'm better with finances than you are," he notes. "But you still haven't given me your bank account password."

Excellent decision on my part. I don't want Brandon to know that I've paid my brother's rent for two months. My left wrist still stings if I move it the wrong way. And Nate texted last week that his wife, Morgan, had started a new job. I hope they won't need more money.

"And you haven't changed your last name yet," he adds.

I almost protest that Nadia didn't change hers, either. Many established female professionals keep their names when they marry. But my husband bristles whenever I mention my best friend.

"Do you know how that makes me feel?" he says. "People will think you're embarrassed that I'm your husband."

I'm not surprised he's making this about him. "It's not like *your* attachment style's so secure," I retort.

He leans back in his chair. "What do you mean?"

"You say *I* don't let you in? I feel the same stonewalling from you. For example, why don't you fish anymore, Brandon?"

After he takes another sip of scotch, he crosses his arms in a classic defensive posture. One hand lifts to scrub his mouth, then slides over his chest. He sighs. He fidgets. He forces a swallow. Then he looks straight at me. "Because my wife died in a boating accident."

My jaw drops. *Finally.* He finally told me. And no wonder he's withheld her cause of death. He's been through trauma, too. "That's awful." I have so many questions, but I need to proceed with caution, or he'll clam up again. The chatter of the other diners falls away as I select my next words. "Were you...on the boat as well?"

With a taut press of his lips, he looks away. His head bobs.

My mouth is dry, so I take a sip of club soda. *What happened on that boat?* Does he blame himself for her death? Does he experience intrusions of the event? I haven't woken up to him thrashing in the throes of a nightmare, but I have caught him awake in the middle of the night, watching golf on TV as he plays a mindless game on his phone. I've seen his irritability, jealousy, and attempts to control me as signs of narcissism. Might they be PTSD symptoms instead?

There's a quick rise and fall of his chest as he stares at the water, reminding me of Jordan in my office. But he's my husband, not my client. I don't want to interrogate him. I soften my voice. "You must've been through so much pain."

After a long pause, he turns to me. Sorrow swims in those deep blue pools, and the tiny creases at the corners of his eyes also suggest guilt. Self-blame, guilt, and shame. Here I am congratulating myself for helping clients heal from trauma while I miss a big, fat case of PTSD right under my nose. There's no way I can abandon him now. If the loss of one wife has crippled his sense of peace and self-worth, the loss of another would destroy him.

"I'm…here," I say, a lame offering for what he's endured. "I'm here when you want to talk about it."

His breath comes out in a blast. "I'll never *want* to talk about it."

Poor choice of words on my part. "I hear you. It's so painful to remember, you can't imagine how processing it could help." His breathing seems to slow a bit. "Too bad that locking away the memories prevents you from healing."

His eyes slant in a look of anger.

"Too bad avoiding the past keeps you stuck in the past," I add. "You *can* get better, Brandon. You don't have to talk to me. But I hope you'll talk to someone who can help you process what happened."

He scoffs. "No way you'll get me to see Nadia."

"That would be a bad idea for sure. First, as your wife's best friend, it's unethical for Nadia to be your therapist. Second, she's not trained in CPT like I am."

"CPT?"

I sense a slight lowering of his defenses. "Cognitive processing therapy for trauma, if that's what you need. It's amazing. I can find you a CPT therapist, easy. And it's only a few months of sessions. You'll be back to yourself long before our baby arrives. You could truly experience the joy of being a father." I fold his hand into mine. "You can heal and move forward. I've seen it happen with many of my clients."

He studies me, then yanks away his hand. "Like the swim coach?"

My heart jumps. Why is he still so obsessed with Jordan? If I stay with Brandon—and at this point I have to give him the chance to overcome his trauma before I'll know if that's feasible—I can't keep avoiding the Jordan issue. I need to grow a backbone and stop tiptoeing around my husband. "There are some things I can't, and I won't, share with you about my work. But I'll be straight with you about one thing." I remind myself to breathe. "The coach is still in therapy with me. I'm going to finish our sessions no matter what you say." I brace myself for impact.

But Brandon doesn't clench his jaw or thrust forward to get in my face. He doesn't hurl accusations that I'm cheating on him. He doesn't even seem surprised. He sits with a blank expression, unmoving.

Maybe he's exhausted from the adrenaline rush of disclosing how his wife died. Or…maybe he already knew I'm still meeting with Jordan? But how would he know?

The next morning, I arrive at the office only to find that my 9:00 client hasn't shown up for her appointment. I'm often irritated by no-shows, as they mess with my income and my schedule, but today I relish the quiet as I suck on a peppermint and scroll on my iPad.

Last night I dreamed about towering waves of sea water swamping a boat, drenching the deck with fearsome power. Just before the boat capsized, I woke up. Despite my panting breaths, Brandon's soft snores continued. He looked so serene in the faint moonlight filtering through the curtains. I wondered if he'd ever had nightmares about the accident that took his first wife. What was her name? What was she like?

Resigned that I'd never discover the answers, I'd turned over on my left side, just like my doctor instructed. From behind me, Brandon had stirred. His strong arm had encircled me and drawn me into him. Our spooning position, with his large hand resting on my belly, had comforted me. I'd begun to drift back to sleep. But after a while, his body heat had seeped into my skin, lighting me up like a furnace. I had to fling off the covers and scoot away from him.

Now in my office, my internet search explains the engulfing night sweats: older pregnant women are more likely to experience hot flashes. *Wonderful.* We're also more prone to headaches, cramps, emotionality, and nausea—especially after dreams involving seasickness. Thinking about boats, I remember my urge to look up something yesterday. I'd sidestepped it because Brandon was nearby. But now I'm all alone.

Should I investigate, or should I wait for him to tell me when he's ready? My fingers decide for me. I open a new window and type *boat accident California.* There are multiple news stories about a deadly capsizing in Lake Tahoe, but that accident occurred after Brandon and I had married. Adding his name to the search doesn't turn up any leads, either.

"Knock, knock."

I flinch at Nadia's voice. She stands in my open doorway holding two Starbucks to-go cups. "Hi!" I set my iPad face-down on my desk.

"Organic herbal raspberry tea?" She holds one cup aloft.

I stand and accept her offering. "I was just reading about the benefits of raspberry tea for pregnancy. Thank you, my friend." I gesture to my sofa. "Want to talk for a bit?"

"Your nine was a no-show?"

"Yep." I return to my seat. "When's your first client?"

"Ten. I have a little time." She brushes her hand under her skirt to smooth it as she sits. Her long, blond hair is styled in a neat bun, and her makeup is flawless. "How'd you spend your weekend?" she asks.

I learned my cruel, controlling husband might have PTSD is on the tip of my tongue. I'm too embarrassed to tell her how he's treated me, though. I'm even more mortified to admit I'm staying with him despite said treatment. I recall my grad school advisor's study on secrets in therapy. She found the number-one secret clients kept from their therapists was returning to an abusive partner. I wonder if that research finding extends to secrets between friends.

"Brandon golfed on Saturday," I tell her.

"Shocker." She smiles.

"Then we went to Sunday brunch at Sea Pines."

"Oh." After a pause, she says, "We'd love to join you some weekend. We could go to the early church service and meet you later."

Her shoulders shrug. "But maybe you don't want a seven year old disrupting your meal."

Guilt weighs on my chest. "I would *love* to see Charlotte! Martin, too. Sorry I didn't let you know." Given the strain in my marriage, I didn't even think about inviting Nadia and her family. I doubt Brandon would've been up for it, anyway.

"Char's been missing her Auntie Avery. And Martin wonders if he'll *ever* get to meet your husband." Her slight laugh seems like a cover-up for her hurt.

"I'm sorry, Nadia." With growing alarm, I realize I haven't spent any time with Charlotte since I met Brandon. I need to rectify that soon.

She sips her coffee before looking down. "I'm starting to wonder if Brandon dislikes me, actually."

He definitely does. But I could never tell her that. Maybe I'll confess everything after Brandon heals in therapy, but for now, I don't want to malign him to my friend. How can I explain without raising suspicion or hurting her feelings? "It's not you, Nadia. It's just been…tense…between Brandon and me."

She looks up. "Tense? How?"

I blow on my steaming tea. "I told him I'm going to keep working after the baby."

"Thank God." Her perfect posture sags. "I've been so worried, but I didn't want to pester you. How'd he take it?"

"He…" I search for the right words. "He says my job steals too much from me, says there's not enough left for him. He wants me to be free to travel the world."

Her forehead wrinkles. "With a *newborn?*"

I feel my eyes grow big. "That's what *I* said!"

"He needs Martin to talk some sense into him. Sounds like he has no clue about being a father."

Or a husband. Since Brandon entered my life, I've been a bad friend, and I try to think of a way to make it up to Nadia. "Are you and Charlotte free to shop this weekend? I need maternity clothes, and I want to buy my favorite girl a new swimsuit for the summer."

Her face lights up, but before she can answer, my phone rings.

I look at my phone. "Oh, this is my OB's office."

"I'll let you get that." She takes her coffee and closes my door on her way out.

When the receptionist asks me to reschedule my three-month checkup from Tuesday to Wednesday, right during Jordan's session, I start to tell her that won't work. Then, I reconsider. Changing Jordan's session time might be helpful to throw my obsessed husband off his scent, if necessary. After agreeing to the rescheduled time, I call Jordan.

He answers on the second ring, and I can hear him breathing hard. "Are you canceling our session?"

I squint. "*What?* No. I mean, I need to reschedule, but why'd you think I want to cancel?"

His rapid breaths are his only response. I hear peppy music and a harsh female voice in the background.

"Are you having a panic attack?" I ask.

"Possibly. This witchy Peloton instructor's killing me…one climb… at a time." The insistent voice jumps in volume, and Jordan swears.

I grin. It's good to know he's exercising — the best antidepressant out there. "Something came up during our Wednesday time." I glance at my calendar. "Could you make Thursday at ten or eleven instead?"

Again, he doesn't answer.

I'm booked Wednesday and Friday, but maybe I could squeeze him in on my lunch hour. "Or if Thursday doesn't work, Friday at noon?"

"Thursday works," he wheezes. "It's just…are you *sure* you want to keep seeing me?"

What's his deal? "Yes, I'm sure. I want you to get the full dose of CPT and keep kicking trauma's butt. Are *you* having doubts?"

"No, no. I…" A long pause. "Forget it. Eleven on Thursday?"

"Yes. Thanks, see you then."

"*If* I'm still alive after this workout. Bye, Doc."

I frown at the unlit blue light on my desk. It's 11:07 on Thursday, and still no sign of Jordan. Was his weird vibe on the phone trying to tell me something? Has he decided to drop out of therapy? He wouldn't be the first client to stop showing up without a word, but ghosting me at this late stage of CPT would be unusual.

Finally, the light clicks on, and I exhale. I go out to the waiting room to find Jordan's back to me as he peers out the window at the parking lot.

"Anything exciting out there?" I ask, hoping there's not a Sao Paulo yellow BMW M4.

He spins around and breathes out his nose. "Bluffton's *never* exciting. Sorry I'm late."

After we settle in my office, he completes his symptom checklist, and I total his score. "Do you want to guess your number today?"

He brushes one hand across his jaw, which appears freshly shaven. "Nineteen?"

"Even better. Seventeen." I look over his answers. "You scored lower on intrusions, avoidance, and negative thoughts and feelings… Though there's still some elevation with feeling jumpy and on-guard." I look up to find his dark brown eyes on me.

"Sounds about right," he says, his tone wary.

What is that look? Is he still worried my morning sickness will make an unwelcome entrance and trigger traumatic memories?

We review his worksheets on safety and trust beliefs. As usual, he's done great work. I give him the next worksheet. "This exercise challenges the idea that trust is all or nothing. There are different types of trust, and the same person may be worthy of trust in one area but not another. For example, my friends trust me implicitly to be on time."

His quick laugh surprises me. "What?"

"Mason and I have talked about your obsession with time," he says. "You were probably having a cow when I was late today."

I'm more bothered by him and Mason talking about me than his tardiness. Trying not to squirm in my chair, I ask, "Traffic?"

His smile vanishes. "No. Just had…something on my mind, I guess."

The awkward weirdness is back. When he doesn't elaborate, I go on. "While my friends trust me to be on time, they don't trust me to be blunt with them. It's hard for me to be direct if I think I might hurt their feelings. I'm a bit conflict averse, I have to admit."

He nods. "How much do your friends trust you to take care of your needs, even if it makes it harder for them?"

"Where did *that* question come from?" It's like he can see right through me.

"Just..." He shrugs. "Curious."

I need to redirect our focus. "Is taking care of one's needs important to you when it comes to trust?"

He rolls his head around in a circle as he considers. "Ssssure."

Further confused by his unconvincing response, I decide to soldier on. "With this worksheet, you'll consider different types of trust, like being reliable, on time, or supportive. Then you choose one person to rate on those types of trust." I show him the sample worksheet.

Jordan looks over the sample. "Got it. I think I'm going to rate Elena."

"Okay. What's important to you in trusting someone? You can write each type of trust on the worksheet."

He taps his leg. "Reliable, honest, doesn't gossip..." He looks up from writing. "That must be something you're good at, huh? Keeping secrets confidential."

I hide a wince as I recall the debacle of watching the swim meet when Brandon discovered Mason *and* Jordan as my clients. "I do my best," is my feeble reply.

He hesitates, then finishes the list. "Elena's great at all of these. Well, except for being nonjudgmental. She doesn't have the same difficulty with bluntness as you do." His smirk tells me he loves her all the more for it. I wish I felt such fondness for my spouse.

"You can finish this worksheet as part of your assignment this week," I say. "Let's move on to our next theme: power and control. Trauma survivors often believe they're totally powerless, yet they also believe they have to control everyone and everything to feel safe. That impossible combination is crazy-making."

"Huh. I felt that way after Baja. But then I realized I can't control *anyone* around me...even the cats." He shakes his head. "*Especially* the cats."

With all the military moves, my family didn't own pets, much to my brother's disappointment. As an adult, my status as an honorary dog-aunt to Nadia's golden retriever has been enough. Belle's size and energy are enough for two households. But I could revisit the idea of getting a dog now that Brandon and I live in a huge house. Is it possible that he and I have never discussed whether he would even want a pet? Yet another thing I don't know about him.

I give the next handout to Jordan. "You've already crossed off power-and-control stuck points like, *If I'd kept up with Kim, she would've never hit coral* or *If I didn't insist on finishing the swim, she would still be alive.* Do you still believe, *I need to be perfect to be in control?*"

"Ooh." He blanches. "That one still hits deep."

I can relate to that as well. I scan down the page and feel ill upon reading that passivity and submissiveness—apt descriptions of my behavior in my marriage—are symptoms of negative power/control beliefs. Am I ceding control to Brandon, letting him walk all over me? Or am I just aiming for healthy compromise? I can't have it my way all the time, right?

Willing myself to focus, I ask Jordan, "Any other stuck points related to power and control?"

"*There's no point in trying to fight against authority,*" he says. "I had that thought during the meeting with the board president. I'm lucky Suzy prodded me to fight for my position, or I'd be unemployed."

"How secure does your job feel now?" I ask.

His mouth twists to one side. "Better, but I still have to rebuild trust with the board."

"I know you can do it." I look at my watch. "We're almost out of time, so we'll cover esteem and intimacy next time, and then we'll wrap up with our last CPT session in two weeks." I hand him the practice assignment for session nine, but he doesn't take it from me.

He skims his hands down his thighs in what appears to be a nervous gesture. "You said I'm making great progress, right?"

I draw the paper back toward me, wondering where he's going with this. "Yes?"

"I think we're good here. I don't need the last two sessions."

"You…" I feel my eyebrows inch inward. "You *are* making great progress, Jordan. And there's more you can achieve by finishing the therapy. We didn't get a chance to discuss preparing for termination today, but I want ending therapy to be a mutual decision."

He blinks at me. "I was a mess when I came in here—I needed this. I needed you to guide me. But I'm better now. Other people need you more than I do."

I've heard clients tell me something like this before, protesting that they aren't worthy of my time. But I sense that's not what he's saying here. What *is* he saying? "Jordan, what's going on? First you thought I wanted to cancel today's session, and now it seems like you can't get out of here fast enough." Maybe I can reach him through an attempt at humor. I lift the collar of my shirt to sniff it. "Do I smell?"

He doesn't crack a smile. "How are you feeling, you know, with the...pregnancy?"

I stare at him. Why did I have to barf during one of *his* sessions? He knows too much about me.

"It can't be easy to take care of all these clients when you're feeling sick," he adds.

"Listen, Jordan. Thank you for your concern. It makes sense that you worry about my pregnancy. But I have people in my life looking over me, taking care of me. You don't have to worry." This supports my hypothesis that Jordan has an anxiety disorder in addition to PTSD.

The lines around his mouth stiffen.

"I just saw my doctor yesterday," I disclose. "And she says everything looks good."

"Really?"

Exasperated, I raise my hands. "Do you want to read her note in the chart?"

I'm not proud of my immature sarcasm, but at least he backs off.

"Sorry." He slumps on the sofa.

"If you truly want to stop therapy, you can. But *I* would like to see this thing through, finish what we started." I decide to introduce an element of session ten's homework early to entice him. I hold up the piece of paper again. "I'm adding something special to this practice assignment. Would you like to hear it?"

"Somethin' somethin' special?" His chin tilts with interest.

I nod.

He sighs and flops out his hand to receive the paper. "Fine."

"In addition to practicing the worksheets on power-and-control beliefs, I want you to do one nice thing for yourself each day, and not because you achieved something. Also, give and receive one compliment a day before we meet again."

He grimaces. "How can I control whether or not I receive a compliment?"

"You can't." I shrug. "But the assignment will help you notice compliments better. I'll give you one right now."

He sits up in anticipation.

Though it's not part of the manualized therapy, complimenting my client after session ten is one of my favorite parts of CPT. I try to honor to each client's unique gifts and strengths. "You told me how much your college swim coach means to you." He meets my eyes. "It's also clear how your dad and sister guided you. I really admire how you took their mentorship and funneled it into your coaching, Jordan. You've taken what they taught you and used it to become your own person—effective, smart, and fun-loving. I know Mason thinks the *world* of you. And I bet all your swimmers think they've hit the jackpot when they start swimming for you."

He falls completely still for what has to be ten seconds. *Does he believe me?* A slow, gradual grin forms. "Could I get that Hallmark card in writing for the Lionfish board?"

I should've known he'd make light of a serious moment. "Get out of here, Perry. See you next week."

17. JORDAN

A week later, I'm in the parking lot of Dr. Avery's office building for my next-to-last session. I like to arrive early and gather my thoughts before the tumult of therapy. Last week, though, I waffled so long about whether to go inside that I ended up being late.

Today I sit in my car with the windows up and A/C cranked. Not only is it a humid eighty-six degrees at 10:30 am, but I also don't want my psychologist's husband sneaking up on me. I'm grateful there's no sign of his ridiculous muscle car. Compensating much?

When my phone rings, *Mom* flashes on my car console. We went for months without talking, but now this is the second time in two days that she's called. I guess it helped when I actually answered the phone yesterday. *Hey, hey, Dr. Avery! Check out how I no longer avoid emotional conversations.*

"Hi, Mom."

"Jordan! Is this a good time?"

I look at my watch. "You've got twenty minutes before Dr. Avery shrinks my brain." I still can't believe I told Mom about my therapy. But after she started crying the moment I answered yesterday—crying because of how worried she's been about me—I felt compelled to reassure her.

"I'm so glad you have someone to talk to, honey. I think, well, I think *I* might need therapy, too."

My eyebrows lift.

"I was up most of the night thinking about…Kimberly," she explains.

I shake my head. Kim tolerated Mom, but no one else, calling her by her full name. Mom insisted it was so beautiful that it was a crime to shorten it.

"Bill and I had a long talk this morning," says Mom, referring to my stepfather. "He got to spend more time with Kimberly than with you, since she lived closer. But still, he regrets not visiting her in Columbus more often. He barely knows *you*, Jordan."

I sigh. Mom didn't meet Bill till I was in college, and I haven't lived at home since then. But it's spot-on that I've kept the man at a distance. It appears I was avoidant long before Kim died.

"And it's devastating for me to be so far away from my grandkids," Mom adds.

I suppress the growl that starts to rumble in my throat. My choice to live in the South is a personal affront to my mother, as if I moved away just to spite her. I can't help it that I met my wife here, or that Ohio's weather is cloudy and gross. "I told you we'll visit at the end of the summer."

"I'm grateful for that. But it's not enough."

What more does she want from me? The compact summer swim season consumes almost every weekend—I can't make it there before August.

"So…" She pauses. "Bill and I decided we're moving to Bluffton."

My jaw unhinges.

"Would that be okay with you?" she asks.

Realizing I'm a mouth breather, I dart my gaze around, relieved that no cars have pulled up next to me. "*Okay?*" A grin lifts my cheeks. "That would be *amazing*, Mom! Hudson and Hailey will be over the moon."

"Oh, good." She lets out a breath. "We're thinking of moving this fall, once it cools down. When you visit in August, we'll ask Elena to highlight some properties in our price range, and we'll caravan back south with you to tour houses." High-pitched barks from their yorkie rise in the background. "Quiet, Ainsley!"

Given Elena's happiness when she heard me talking with Mom yesterday, I think she'll be okay with her in-laws moving to town. We've commiserated about not having family nearby, since her parents live overseas. Throwing in a real estate commission will seal the deal. "That's a big change for you, Mom," I note.

"Sixty-seven years in Cincinnati. Bill's lived here even longer. But there's not much holding us here now."

Now that Kim's gone. Bill was divorced with no kids when Mom met him.

"When you visit Cincinnati in August…" She falters. "Will you drive me to Columbus?"

I pause. *Where is she going with this?* "Sure. Why?"

"I want to…" Her voice trembles. "I want to visit Kimberly's school and her condo. I know someone else lives there now, but I guess I want to be where she was. Try to feel closer to her." She sniffs. "Maybe it's silly."

"I get it," I say.

"And I want to talk to that nice man we met at the funeral. Xander's his name?"

My heart skips a beat.

"You said Wyatt wants you to tell Xander about the pregnancy," she continues. "I'm not sure I agree. I fear Xander might blame himself for Kimberly's death, just like you have." She hesitates. "Like I have as well. I didn't tell you this, but I've felt so guilty about letting you two go on that swimming trip to the middle of nowhere. I was nervous about it, but I didn't want you to yell at me if I said something."

I nod. That's exactly what our response would've been. Mom is a championship worrier and overprotector.

"I do want to get to know Xander better," Mom says. "Invite him to be part of the family. We can make a game-day decision about how much to tell him."

I smile at the sports reference. Though Mom never understood our family's infatuation with swimming, she played volleyball in high school and now joins Bill in cheering for the Cincinnati Bengals.

"I think that's a great idea. We can rock out to The Eagles on our road trip."

She takes in a sharp breath. "Oh, Jordan." She grows quiet, then she sniffs. "It's so hard losing them both."

An ache fills my heart. My dad loved The Eagles.

"You've grown much stronger this past year," she adds. "Your father would be so proud of you."

Would he? As an ache builds into my chest, I realize she just complimented me. "Thanks, Mom." Now I want to return the compliment so I can complete my homework assignment for today. "Dad would be proud of you, too, for not giving up on me when I kept pushing you away." I feel a lump in my throat. "For offering to move down here to keep your family together. And for finding another man—a good man—to spend your life with."

She sighs. "Bill *is* a good man. I regret taking seven years after your father died to get back out there. It was a dark time, but you kids kept me going."

I press my hand over my heart. "Kim helped us both get through it."

"She did." Mom sniffs. "Kimberly was the glue of our family, and now you and I need to stick together. Learn to rely on each other."

I nod silently. I want that, too.

"Do you think…" She stops. "Do you think I could meet with this psychologist of yours after I move down there?"

I consider that a moment. "Seeing family members might be against her professional ethics. She's very serious about the rules. Besides, she's pregnant. I'm not supposed to know this, but she might leave her practice once she has the baby." My stomach knots as I scan the parking lot.

"Oh, that's too bad. She's really helped you."

"And one of my swimmers," I say. I should stop there, but racing thoughts propel me to add, "Her husband's *shady.*"

"What do you mean?"

My heart rate kicks up. "He approached me after my session a couple weeks ago. It's unclear how he knew I was her client, but he seemed quite sure of himself." *More like arrogant.* "He said Dr. Avery's supposed to be on bedrest, but she won't stop working. She won't tell her clients because she doesn't want to worry them. He insisted I'd put her baby in jeopardy if I showed up for my next session."

Mom gasps. "What did you do?"

"I agonized over it, and I decided to stop therapy. But then Dr. Avery called to reschedule, and she said of course she wanted to keep meeting with me. I talked to Elena, and she thought I should trust the person I know—Dr. Avery—over the person I don't." *Her shifty husband.* "So, I went last week, and she knew something was up, but I decided not to tell her what happened. She's got enough on her plate already."

"Oh, that's a hard situation," Mom says.

"She's not showing yet, and my therapy will conclude next week, so I hope it'll end up okay." *If* her husband's telling the truth about the risk to her health. One of them is lying, and my money's on him.

I look at my watch. "Hey, I gotta run. Awesome news about you moving down here! You made my day." I think about her purse dog. "Just be careful walking Ainsley near the lagoons. She's a perfect-sized snack for a gator."

"*Jordan!*"

I've missed the sharp tone of her appalled reprimands. "Love you, Mom."

"I love you, too, honey. I'm happy I'll get to see you every day soon."

I wince. Do I want to see her *every* day?

Ten minutes later, in the waiting room, I hand my completed symptom checklist to Dr. Avery. "Fifteen today," I tell her as we walk to her office. "I scored it for you since your math skills are sus."

She rolls her eyes as she sits. "You've been hanging out with Mason."

"Five weeks till US Nationals. He's swimming great. Maybe too great."

She writes on her tablet then lifts her tired eyes. "*Too* great? Is that a thing?"

I look her over. Her face isn't as pale. I hope that means she's been jogging and enjoying nature. But there are still smudged depressions beneath her eyes, and her energy seems low. "Nah, just me worrying."

She reaches for an insulated tumbler on the desk and takes a sip. "We all worry from time to time. Do you think worry has interfered with your coaching?"

"For sure. I've always had trouble sleeping before big meets."

"Just like Mason," she says with a smile.

I incline my head. He's never told me that before. I wonder if improved sleep at the TYR meet helped him swim so fast.

"Did worry hurt your school performance?" Dr. Avery asks.

"I got stressed out before tests, but my grades were pretty good." Though Kim's grades were always better than mine.

She writes on her tablet. "Did either parent worry excessively?"

I give an emphatic nod. "My mom. Why are you asking these questions?"

"Well, I've wondered about generalized anxiety disorder as a possibility for you, maybe preceding the PTSD. We all have anxiety and worry. But sometimes people experience unrelenting worry that causes significant distress and interferes with their functioning. Do you think that might fit you?"

My mouth presses down as I remember sleepless nights before the high school state meet in Canton, Ohio. Maybe that's why Mason drives me crazy sometimes—he reminds me of myself. "Sounds quite plausible."

"When did you first notice your trouble controlling the worry?"

That ache hits my chest again. "After my dad died. I worried all the time that something would happen to Mom or Kim. I think Mom's anxiety increased then, too."

"The world felt much less predictable and stable after your dad died."

I nod. *Exactly.*

She gestures to the PCL-5 I completed. "These anxiety questions relate to our trauma therapy, I promise. Remember that picture of a brain I drew to explain the neurobiology of PTSD? Similar pathways are involved with anxiety disorders, to a lesser degree. When you worry, your amygdala fires, and your prefrontal cortex becomes less active. It's not that you're *choosing* to worry. It's just brain structures under- or over-firing, which can be partly genetic. People with anxiety disorders are more likely to develop PTSD after a traumatic event."

I scoff. "Lucky me." *Thanks for passing down the neurotic anxiety gene, Mom.* But Dr. Avery's explanation helps. Teachers and coaches have always told me not to worry—if only I knew how.

"The good news is that CBT can balance the emotional and thinking brain for anxiety *and* trauma," she says. "Though your PTSD symptom score might not decrease much more since some of the questions overlap with anxiety."

I glare at her. "I won't get down to zero? I want to ace that thing next week."

"You might be even *more* competitive than Mason, if that's possible." Her soft smile smooths the worry lines on her face.

But if I tell her about her husband confronting me, those lines will return, pronto. I don't want to upset her.

We review my worksheets challenging power-and-control stuck points. I only completed three, but she seems satisfied. "How'd it go with doing nice things for yourself?" she asks.

"About time you gave me a *fun* practice assignment." I glance at my notes. "I took a nap with the cats two of the days." I'd curled up on my side on the sofa. "Colby likes to chill behind my knees, but Jack tries to sleep on my head, which is not so nice."

"I'm guessing they're orange cats from their names?"

"Yep." I remember when they were just little orange balls of fluff, chasing and attacking each other in a feline wrestlemania. "They're brothers, so we wanted matching names. One day Hailey slipped the kittens some cheese, and when they snarfed it up, their names became clear. Jack has a whiter belly than Colby."

"Cute."

"Elena called me lazy when I napped, but I told her it was my therapy homework. That shut down her nagging real fast!"

She smiles back at me. "Any other pleasant activities?"

"I took the kids to putt-putt when Elena was at her open house on Saturday. I've found that inviting a couple of their friends along is key for preventing arguments. Hudson made his first hole in one, and we had a great time."

"Glad to hear it. How was giving and receiving compliments?"

I tap my thigh. "A little uncomfortable, if I'm honest. I felt like I didn't deserve it."

"That's a normal reaction. We'll get into that with the esteem theme. When did the stuck point pop up that you didn't deserve the compliment?"

"Just this morning." I blow out a gust of air. "Mom said Dad would've been proud of me for going to therapy and getting stronger."

Her eyes expand.

"Yep, I've talked to her twice in two days. I told her about Kim's pregnancy. Today she shocked me by saying she and my stepdad are moving down here this fall."

"Whoa." She chews her lip. "How do you feel about that?"

"Excited." Dr. Avery leans back, like my response has surprised her. "I'm excited for Hudson and Hailey to have grandparents nearby."

She waits for me to make eye contact and says, "You opening up to your mom like that, being vulnerable with her—I bet that invited her to move here. You've decreased self-blame and grown more confident, which enabled you to be honest with her. In turn, she wants to be closer to you."

I let that sink in, and I realize she's right. Mom would never move down here if I'd kept all my walls around myself.

"That's the perfect segue into our last two themes: esteem and intimacy." She passes me a handout on esteem. "You're obviously familiar with the concept of self-esteem. You also have beliefs about others' worth. It's important to have realistic views of others, to challenge perceptions of others as totally perfect or completely horrible."

I nod, though I think Dr. Avery is pretty close to perfect, at least from what I know about her. But that guy she married? He gives off bad vibes. Maybe her taste in men isn't so perfect. Or maybe he's not as rotten as he seems, if she picked him. I wish she would tell me more about him.

"Do you struggle with any of the symptoms on the handout?" she asks.

I examine the page. My guilt, shame, and cynicism are now relics of the past. "Not really."

"I think you've crossed off all the esteem stuck points as thoughts you no longer believe." She opens my log on her iPad. "Including *I'm an egomaniac* and *I'm cuckoo for Cocoa Puffs.*" She snorts.

Does her little chuckle indicate she's up for a joke? I'm still bummed no one laughed at the one I wrote on the whiteboard at practice yesterday: *I was going to tell a time-traveling joke, but you guys didn't like it.* With their access to nonstop short-attention-span videos, Generation Alpha is a tough crowd. "Hey, Dr. Avery. When does a joke become a dad joke?"

Her chin lowers in a look of dread.

"When it becomes apparent."

She groans.

"Why can't you hear a psychologist use the bathroom?"

She shakes her head, but a smirk lifts one corner of her mouth.

"Because the P is silent."

"Stoohhpp!" she laughs. "The last thing I need is you bringing more attention to the baby pressing on my bladder."

I grimace. "Sorry. You need to use the restroom?"

She looks at her watch. "We're almost done. I can make it. Here's the intimacy handout. First let's talk about your ability to soothe yourself and cope with emotion. Do you still believe that if you get angry, you'll cause damage?"

I realize I haven't thrown a temper tantrum for weeks. "Nope." I read over my stuck points. "But like we talked about earlier, I keep going into anxiety spirals and can't talk myself out of them. I'm already nervous about nationals, and the meet's over a month away."

"Which reminds me, we need to plan for the future. After our last CPT session, we'll schedule a follow-up visit one or two months out to check your progress."

I freeze. Won't she need to stop working by then?

She's focused on opening her iPad calendar and doesn't seem to notice my consternation. "Some clients are done with therapy at that point. For others, if they have remaining goals to pursue, like managing anxiety, we keep meeting." She frowns when she sees my face. "Is something wrong?"

"I thought we'd be done after next week."

She blinks at me. "That's what you want?"

No. Mason and I both need her. But is she throwing her health under the bus for our benefit? "You said you need to stop working to focus on your family."

Her eyebrows lower. "I said I was thinking about it, when…" She rubs the back of her neck. "When Brandon, my husband, wanted me to take a break." Her smile is tight. "He worries about me. He gets overprotective."

Brandon is his name. *Overprotective?* That's what she calls his threatening behavior?

"He wants to be extra careful, maybe because we'll be older parents. And he's been through…a lot. But I told him how important my career is to me, and he's coming around."

I nod. It's true that he didn't stalk me and try to prevent me from attending my appointment today. I'd better not see him when I leave.

"It's always a compromise in marriage, right?" She doesn't wait for me to answer. "Anyway, Jordan, I'm here for you if you want to keep meeting. Let's talk about it more next time, okay?"

"Okay." I exhale. She's right that I worry too much, and I need to stop analyzing the situation between her and her husband. It's not my business, and she's a big girl who can take care of herself.

We finish reviewing intimacy, and she gives me my practice assignment—a doozy. Not only do I have worksheets on esteem and intimacy, I need to keep working on pleasant activities and compliments, *and* I have to write a new impact statement about what caused the trauma.

"Jeez," I grouse as we stand. "You'll probably make me read it aloud next time, too."

"Accurate prediction."

Her smirk has earned her another dad joke. "Knock, knock."

Her eyes narrow. "Really? I have to pee!"

"Knock, *knock*," I repeat.

She places her fists on her hips. "Who's there?"

"Control freak." I cut off her next line by jabbing my finger toward her as I shout, *"Now you say control freak who!"*

After a few stunned seconds, she cracks up. "That's your best one yet."

18. AVERY

I examine the man seated across from me in my office. It's been less than three months since he straggled in wearing disheveled clothes and a ballcap that hid his face. Today, for our last CPT session, the shipshape cut of his brown hair emphasizes the bright mischief of his eyes.

"You're all dressed up today," I tease, pointing at his collared shirt and khakis.

He puffs out his chest—another sign of improved self-esteem. "Elena's taking me to The Bluffton Room for lunch. We're celebrating my graduation from therapy." He hums a few bars of "Pomp and Circumstance."

"Swanky." I finish scoring his PCL-5. "What progress has she seen in you?"

He ticks the list off on each finger. "No more aggressive outbursts with her or the kids. I'm contributing more to the family. I sleep and eat better. And, I'm back to the gym."

I nod. His tanned face doesn't appear as gaunt, and the muscles of his upper body fill out his shirt better.

"But my biggest change, according to Elena? I'm more…" He air-quotes. "Present."

"Less dissociative or stuck in the past," I say.

"Less zombie-like," he agrees.

Jordan and I have been through a lot since February. Discovering I was pregnant not only rocked my world but unlocked a secret about his sister that had stalled his recovery. Once he could process the loss of his unborn niece or nephew, in addition to the huge vacancy Kim's death created in his life, he started to heal.

I'm feeling better about my unborn child as well. My morning sickness has eased, and I can't wait to feel the baby kick in another month or so. Most important, though, are the changes I've seen in Brandon. He started therapy, and he seems less agitated. I can now visualize us making it as a family.

I hold up Jordan's symptom tracker on my tablet. "Your score reflects those positive changes. Check out that massive improvement! A score of sixty-seven in February, all the way down to twelve. Well done."

He grins.

I send the score sheet to him through the electronic chart and set the tablet on my desk. "Not only are you more present, but you also seem more optimistic about the future."

"That sums it up." He bends forward. "Did you hear the one where the past, present, and future walked into a bar?" He waits a beat. "It was tense."

I shake my head. "How does Elena feel about the return of your jokes?"

"Eh, somewhat less excited." He laughs.

Mason has griped about his coach's thirsty, cheugy (whatever that means) jokes, but at this point I know the complaints are more about Mason getting nervous and salty before his big meet than disdain for Jordan. Mason said life's easier since board members stopped peppering him with questions about his coach's anger management. In our recent session, we shared a sincere moment when Mason thanked me for returning "the most fire coach in the country" to him and the team. He said he was grateful I'd helped his coach get back to his boomer self. It was the best validation for CPT I've heard.

We review Jordan's last worksheets on esteem and intimacy stuck points, and I remind him that his continued success depends on diligent CBT practice in the future. I ask him to read his new impact statement. This time, he doesn't balk.

"Why did my big sister die?" He sighs. "I may never know. Life is full of mysteries, and death is even more opaque. After Dad died, Kim insisted he was up in heaven, watching over us and loving us from afar. When I confessed that sometimes it hurt too much to believe in God or heaven, Kim said the agony of grief is when we need faith the most. She said if I struggled with the traditional concept of heaven, we could create something new: a bottomless pool in the sky where Dad kept swimming laps and called out advice like *'Keep your head down'* or *'Balance your position'* or *'Treat your teammates with kindness.'*"

What a clever idea to help a boy through grief, I think.

Jordan reads on, "Now I know both Dad and Kim are up there, swimming together, splashing each other, laughing. They're both healthy and strong, no longer in pain." He clears his throat. "She stands on his strong shoulders and launches into a front flip, just like when we were kids at the hotel pool on Hilton Head."

I didn't know Jordan and his family had vacationed on the island, though I could've predicted it. Since Lowcountry beaches are some of the closest to Ohio—only a one-day drive—Buckeyes seem to overrun the place. I've seen bumper stickers on Hilton Head Island roads that say *O-HHI-O* as well as the derisive *NFO (Not From Ohio)*. No wonder Jordan chose to make this area his home. His warm vacation memories of hotel pools and palm trees likely help him feel closer to family, especially now that his mother has decided to move here. I listen as he continues.

"I take refuge in knowing Kim died doing something she loved: swimming. My dad introduced us to the sport, but Kim is the reason we stayed. She kept us chlorinated for life. She introduced me to Wyatt and encouraged me to become a coach, which then led me to the blessings of Elena, Hudson, and Hailey. We're all better off for having known her."

My nose begins to burn. Kim has come alive in the memories Jordan has shared, and I regret missing the chance to meet her.

He continues reading. "I'm striving to be kinder to myself and others so I can be a better father and coach. I shouldered all the responsibility for Kim's death, but that was just another example of being too hard on myself. As I grappled to understand how something so awful could happen, I looked in the mirror and decided that sad sack was the one at fault. But I've realized I'm not the only one jumping to self-blame. Wyatt and Mom have done the same thing, and I hope they can also learn the facts of that day."

He looks up at me for a moment. "What *are* the facts? All I wanted was to give Kim the best birthday of her life—one she truly deserved. And before its horrific ending, I had achieved my goal. We were so happy on that Mexican island, Isla Espíritu Santo. I looked up the translation: Saint Spirit Island. Kim's spirit lives on in bodies of water and the hearts of my family and me."

I shift in my chair as tears fill my eyes. This is the first time I've cried at a client's statement, and I try to blink away my emotion. Then I recognize that stuffing down my feelings makes me a hypocrite. *It's okay to cry*, I remind myself. *Crying is coping.*

Jordan keeps his gaze on the page. "I'll do my best to keep Hudson and Hailey safe, but I don't want to become a helicopter parent. I want my kids to take risks and grow. I want them to know how precious they are to me. I need to express more gratitude to my wife as well. This whole trauma shindig has revealed what an amazing life partner I have. Elena has proven she'll be there for me at my worst, and I can trust her to handle *all* of me, even my dark side. She's my sky full of stars.

"I want to loosen the reins of control, especially as a coach. To swim fast, you can't muscle through the race. Instead, it's essential to move *with* the water, to trust your training and let your performance flow. I hope to push my swimmers to be exceptional, but they have to want it first. Mason has that fire in his belly, and I trust him to take me along on this journey, wherever it may lead. I've always looked up to my dad and college coach. While they continue to inspire me, I know I have to be my own man. I need to parent and coach with my own style."

Jordan stops reading and looks up. He does a double take when he sees me crying.

I feel my cheeks flush as I pluck a tissue from the box. *Are my tears helpful or hurtful to his therapy?* "Sorry. Pregnancy hormones."

He nods.

I cringe as I realize I'm still avoiding emotion. "That's not the whole truth. Your beautiful statement is what brought me to tears, actually. Your relationship with your sister—it was a special, deep, *rare* connection. You motivate me to try to repair my relationship with my brother."

"Thank you." He pauses. "Weirdly, I don't feel like crying."

"That's okay." I wipe the tissue under my nose. "I'm crying enough for both of us."

He chuckles.

I let out a shaky breath as I find a file in his chart. "Okay. Now is the time for me to read your original statement—once I get ahold of myself—and then we'll compare and contrast."

His forehead lifts. "*Oh.* This should be interesting." One corner of his mouth quirks. "*You* have to read aloud this time."

His apparent delight at revenge helps me regain control, and his neat writing makes the statement easy to read. "Why did my sister die? I've asked this question over and over." I keep reading until I get to the most impactful part of the statement—his self-blame—and I meet his eyes before I resume. "Why did the smartest, most competent, most caring person I've ever known have to die? How is that fair? How is it fair, especially after our dad died so young? How could God let this happen twice? All I know is the common denominator between my dad and my sister. *Me.*"

He goes on to describe his sister, ending with, "She was the best aunt to Hudson and Hailey. She loved those kids, almost like they were her own." I remember him breaking down at this point. "I robbed her of having children of her own. She helped me so much, but did I help *her?* Where was I when she needed me? Nowhere to be found. I never should've booked that swim trip for her birthday..." Then he concluded, "I'm so self-absorbed."

Jordan cuts in, "Jeez, I was a wretch."

"Indeed. But wait, there's more." I keep reading, "Why did Kim die? Look no further than her selfish brother. I'm an idiot for choosing a trip on a remote island with no cellular service. I showed zero regard for others' safety. If I had kept up with Kim—if I'd been in better shape—she never would've hit that coral." He continues listing his many perceived failings before ending with, "I'm such a petulant child. My last words to her were so cruel—I'm a horrible brother." I pause for a moment to emphasize his next words. "It's all my fault she died."

I read the rest of his diatribe, including predictions of death, mistrust of his employer, lack of control over himself and others, guilt about his irritability, and feelings of detachment. After I finish, he gapes at me.

"You're sure I wrote all that?"

I smile. "Hard to believe, huh?" After a beat, I ask, "What do you notice about the two statements?"

His face falls. "It's like a different person wrote that. I was so full of self-hatred..." He chews the inside of his cheek. "I don't feel that way anymore, though. I didn't know it was possible to change so much in such a short time." He looks at me. "You tried to tell me how powerful CPT was, but I didn't believe you."

"I remember. But even with your skepticism, you made the brave choice to face the pain."

"Not sure how much of a choice it was—my life was swirling down the toilet, and I had to find a way to stop flushing. I'm grateful you convinced me. Now I want *everyone* with PTSD to try this therapy."

I sit forward in my chair. "Me, too! Every time I read a book with a traumatized character, I want to yell at them to go get CPT. I want to tell them, *you* can *get better!*"

His eyes crinkle.

"Anything else you notice from the before-and-after statements?"

He rubs his right shoulder. "At least my shoulder no longer hurts. That's what happens when you don't swim for seven months."

"How much do you miss swimming?"

His mouth presses into a line. "A little." His frown deepens. "Elena's realtor friend is part of a boat club, and she and her husband invited us to Daufuskie Island next weekend. I told Elena I'm not ready."

I nod, wondering what it will take to get him back to the water.

He skims his hand through his hair. "But I *am* ready, finally, to deal with Kim's ashes. We decided to spread them in the Atlantic Ocean. Her favorite Cincinnati and Columbus places, too."

"That sounds meaningful." After a moment I add, "Have you given more thought to future therapy?"

He leans back against the sofa and looks away. "Thought I graduated from therapy," he tells the window.

What just happened? We were sharing such a happy moment, reveling in his progress, and just like that, he seems so far away. "You'd rather not keep working on anxiety then?"

His gaze darts around my office. "I think I'm good for now, Doc."

"Okay." Despite his evasiveness, I choose to trust him to know what he needs. I open my calendar. "For our follow-up visit, do you want to schedule in one or two months?"

"No follow-up for me."

I recoil. "No?" He's still not looking at me. "A follow-up visit is part of the CPT protocol, like a booster shot. I recommend it to keep your improvement going."

His eyes meet mine for a millisecond before they dash away again.

An insight straightens my spine. "You're worried about me—my pregnancy. Is that it?"

He gives a tentative nod.

"I can't predict the future, of course." I touch my bump. "But I'm feeling strong. I'm feeling hopeful for my...family." I don't want Jordan's anxiety to prevent him from getting the care he deserves. "Your brain might be telling you to worry about me, but that's not your job in here. Therapy is about *your* needs. I've got people in my life to take care of my needs, like my husband."

Now he stares right at me. "Did you tell him about me?"

My heart jolts. *"What?"*

"Your husband—he knew I was your client."

"He..." Chills prickle up my back. "Brandon *talked* to you? Where?"

"In the parking lot." He gestures toward the waiting room. "Did you tell him about me?"

"No." My breath quickens. "But he found out you were my client. I'm so sorry, Jordan." The confession tumbles out of me. "Brandon caught me watching Mason's meet. I couldn't turn it off without raising suspicion, and then the camera panned to you going nuts after the race." Guilt grips my heart. "He said he'd seen you in my waiting room." I don't say the next part aloud: *He accused me of cheating with you.*

Jordan's nods gain speed. "Yes. That makes sense."

"I'm so sorry," I repeat. There's a quiver in my chest. "If you need to report me to the state psychology board for breaching confidentiality, I understand."

He gawks at me. "No! That's not why…" A deep line puckers his forehead. "I wasn't going to say anything, but it's our last session. I feel…I feel like I have to warn you."

Warn me?

"Brandon told me your doctor ordered bedrest, that you would lose the baby if you didn't stop working. But you wouldn't say anything to your clients because you didn't want them to worry."

I stare agape at him, unblinking. Jordan's next words sicken me even more.

"He said I was your most troubled client, that I had to stop seeing you or you'd lose the baby. He told me to back off." He sees my open mouth and shakes his head. "I figured out later he was lying."

I married a monster. My stomach flips as I realize the depths of Brandon's manipulation. In an effort to eliminate his imaginary competition, he betrayed me, my client, and my profession. He betrayed my trust. Whether or not he has PTSD no longer matters. I can't let my guard down with him ever again. A new thought repulses me. *Has he confronted any more of my clients?*

"Maybe I should've told you sooner," Jordan says. "Or maybe I shouldn't be telling you now. You're a private person, and I don't know the particulars of your marriage. But I thought you needed to know. You're having a baby with this man."

I'm having a baby with this man. Oh, God. I'm going to throw up. I try to breathe through my nose. "Thank you…for telling me. I'm deeply sorry this happened." My voice trembles. "I apologize for my husband hurting you and your therapy."

"It's not your fault," he says.

Tears spring to my eyes again, not from sadness this time, but from horror. My own fight, flight, or freeze moment. *I can't believe Brandon did this.*

"I'm doing great, Dr. Avery." Jordan scoots forward on the sofa, reaching his hands out, like he wants to grasp mine, before pulling them back. "You healed me. I'm strong now. I'm so lucky I found you and this therapy. You changed my life. But now you need to focus on yourself. You're a good person, and you deserve good things… good *people* in your life."

This role reversal is so wrong. My past supervisors would be aghast.

He looks at his watch. "I have to meet Elena for our lunch date." He stands. "I can't thank you enough for what you've done for me." "Wait." I scramble to my feet. This abrupt ending, right after the bombshell about Brandon detonated our therapy relationship, feels off. But Jordan said he's done, and he needs to leave. Is forcing him to keep talking for his benefit or mine? "My mind is swirling right now. It's hard to think straight." I lick my lips. "You've made fantastic progress, and I see how much stronger you've become. I want you to keep options open, though, if therapy might benefit you in the future."

The rustle of his hands in his pockets conveys his eagerness to leave.

"How would you feel if I call you next week to discuss those options?" No way I can continue as his psychologist after Brandon obliterated all therapy boundaries, but I want to give him some referrals.

"Okay." He glances at my bump. "Please be safe, Dr. Avery." His eyes hold mine for a long moment. Then he leaves.

The door closes behind him, and I stand stock-still as the atrocity of my situation settles over me like a gossamer wedding veil. A *tainted* veil, shredded and soiled. I keep it together long enough to rush into the hallway. When I see Nadia's open door, my knees almost buckle. Sobs rip through me as she notices me shaking in the doorway.

"What happened?" she cries.

"My husband…" Hyperventilated breaths make it hard to speak. "…is a monster."

19. AVERY

Brandon's sports car purrs as he pulls into a shaded parking spot near Harbour Town. Though there are open spaces closer to the restaurant, he picks one farther out to prevent dings from other car doors. He's explained this to me before. I expected the golf clubhouse to be busier on a Sunday afternoon, four days after my final session with Jordan. Maybe the remaining storm clouds have kept away the crowds.

It rained most of the day yesterday, preventing my husband from golfing as well as screwing up my plans. The jittery feeling that began for me yesterday has continued into this morning, including my sharp edginess on the drive here. Every time I looked at Brandon's phone charging on the center console, my heart shuddered. But no notifications lit up the screen.

I bolt out of the car before he's even turned off the engine so I can take in big gulps of air, a fresh mixture of grass and sea. The scent of his aftershave, which pervades the car's interior, used to turn me on. Now, the cloying stench makes me want to vomit. With any luck, I'll never have to be stuffed into a small space with him again.

"What's your deal?" He scowls at me as he rounds the hood.

It takes effort to manage a smile. "Nausea. Didn't want to get sick in your car."

He glances at his precious vehicle and then up at the ancient water oak tree. "Birds better not mar my baby's paint job. I just had it washed." He looks back at me. "*Told* you we should've taken your car."

My breath catches. Our argument over which car to take almost blew up my plan before it even started. I scan the area. "Then you wouldn't attract so many admirers, like I promised." I incline my head toward a man ogling the sports car from a distance. Just as I hoped, my husband's chin lifts a notch, and he forgets our squabble.

"You're always looking out for me, Cute Stuff." Brandon drapes his arm over my shoulders, and I hold my breath for as long as I can. A swimmer would be better at this than a runner. "Including picking this restaurant," he adds. "I've asked you ten times to try Links, but you were too busy with work."

I've had zero desire to chum around with his rich golfing buddies at a fancy restaurant overlooking one of the Sea Pines golf courses. But today, I'm hoping the presence of those same boujee golf bros will keep him on his best behavior. I know impressing them is foremost on his mind.

After we walk up the stairs and enter the restaurant, his mouth grazes my ear. "I've been wanting to show you off."

To avoid shivering from his touch, I focus on the hostess. She asks us where we want to sit. "There," I blurt, pointing at a nearby table.

He shakes his head. "Not a good view." He looks at the hostess and orders, "By the window, overlooking the course."

"No." My sharp tone widens the hostess's eyes, so I lower my voice as I look up at Brandon. "I told you I'm not feeling well. I need to be near the ladies' room. *And the exit.*"

He looks behind us, where another couple waits. I bet he doesn't want to make a scene. He taps my bump. "Okay, mama. We'll do it your way."

He's already ruined the terms *cute stuff* and *kiddo* for me. I'll have to banish the sound of his voice saying *mama* from my memory. I won't let him tarnish that beautiful word, too. As we follow the hostess to the table, I cradle my little bump. The baby gives me courage to stand up for us both. Too bad courage isn't the absence of fear. My quaking insides corroborate that.

As our drinks arrive and we order food, I frown at my quiet phone in my lap. I wish I'd worn a lighter outfit than this scoop-neck shirt and stretchy yoga pants. I take a tissue from my cross-body purse and dab sweat off my forehead.

Looking cool and composed, Brandon arches an eyebrow. "I wanted to show off my hot wife to my golfing partners, but maybe it's a good thing they aren't here today." He sips his drink. "So proud of my hot *flash* wife."

Though I often enjoy well-placed sarcastic remarks, right now his tone flusters me. I once read that sarcasm is a sign of hidden anger, but there's no hiding his hostility at the moment. When I reach for my water glass, I manage to knock it over. We both spring from our chairs to avoid getting wet, and the commotion draws stares from other diners. "Sorry!" I cry.

The waiter swoops in with extra napkins. After we mop up the mess, he leaves to get me a fresh glass of water. I'm thankful Brandon's scotch and soda is still intact.

He stirs his drink as he studies me. "What's *with* you today?" When I don't answer, he says, "First, you make me wait in the car so you can run inside to get your sunglasses—not that you'll need them today—and then you order *mac 'n cheese?*"

Is that what I ordered? I don't even remember, but it sounds plausible since I need a heavy dose of comfort right now. The curl of his lip shows his disgust. I guess it's no bistro steak like he ordered.

"And then you make a spectacle of us by spilling your drink everywhere."

I exhale. "*Get yourself together, Clarkson,*" my father's voice tells me. "*You're just like your mother. You can't do anything right. God, your mother's so weak. Don't listen to her. Don't be anything like her. You have to be tough like me to make it in this world.*"

From there an image rises of my lieutenant from Officer Candidate School. He's tipped forward after a never-ending fitness run (at least the longest one I'd ever attempted), hands on his knees, his chest heaving, a look of wonder in his eyes as he squints up at me. "*That motor inside you won't quit! You persevere like no one I've seen. You're fierce, Clarkson, much stronger than you think.*"

Later, when his words had bounced around in my brain at mile eighteen of my first marathon, I somehow kept going, despite the burning lactic acid in my legs. "*Persevere, Clarkson. Just keep running,*" *just keep running.*" A year after that, as I'd studied for my arduous psychologist licensing exam, I'd heard my lieutenant again. *"You're stronger than you think."* I finished in the top ten percent on the test.

"Do you need to go home?" Brandon's condescending tone mimics the way a parent would speak to an errant child.

You're fierce, I tell myself, though my heart pushes toward my throat. *Don't let this narcissistic fraud push you around.* I clasp my wrist, which still twinges with certain movements. *Stop him from hurting you again.*

Nadia hasn't texted yet, but I can't stay quiet any longer. "That's not *my* home, Brandon. Not anymore."

He doesn't move.

"That will never be my home again. *You* are not my home. I'm leaving you."

His jaw muscles ripple. "This is some sick joke."

"No." The dryness of my mouth makes it tough to swallow. Pregnancy has swollen my fingers, but I'm still able to yank off my wedding ring. I place the ostentatious diamond next to the salt and pepper shakers between us.

Just then, our waiter returns with my water. "Oh," he says, noticing the awkwardness of the moment.

"Leave us," Brandon barks. "My wife is having a psychotic episode."

I almost laugh as the waiter scurries away. Brandon using my professional jargon to insult me is comical. The *true* psychotic behavior would be staying with him after recognizing all the red flags he's been flapping in my face.

"This is about Jordan Perry," he seethes.

"No." Actually yes, in a way. But not the way he thinks. *Thank you for helping me see the truth, Jordan.*

Brandon's eyes squeeze into slits. "You're cheating on me. I knew it."

"Oh, Brandon. *No.* Why are so obsessed with him? He has nothing to do with us."

He shakes his head. "You keep denying it." He gestures at my bump. "But we'll see what the paternity test reveals."

My mouth drops open. "Your paranoia knows no bounds. You need help."

Breath snorts out his nose in a scoff.

I incline my head as a realization dawns. *I've been such a fool.* "Good thing you're already in therapy. Remind me, who're you seeing?" "You don't know him. I already asked."

"What's his name?" I press.

He turns away. "I want to keep it private."

How do I catch him in this lie? "What kind of therapist? What're his credentials?"

He shrugs, still looking away. "A psychologist, like you."

"On the island?"

"Of course."

Gotcha. Nadia and I scoured the Psychology Today website a few days ago, looking for psychologists to whom I can refer my clients. After I leave town to get away from Brandon, I may need to stay away for some time. "There are only thirteen psychologists in the area, all of them female." I don't mention the one male psychologist we found, because he does assessment only—not therapy. "You're lying, Brandon. You never started therapy." Before he digs himself deeper in the lie, I add, "You're projecting, just like I thought—calling me a liar when *you're* the one trying to manipulate me. What else are you lying about?"

After a swig of his drink, he shakes his head.

"How many affairs are *you* having?" I demand.

"None." His drink sloshes out as he thumps it on the table, and I'm thankful the thick tumbler doesn't shatter and send us on another hospital trip. "I'd never do that to our child. But you, you're tearing the family apart before the baby's even born. Mother of the year. Stellar future that kid's going to have, bouncing back and forth like a pinball between divorced parents."

Based on his wounded tone, that scenario sounds personal, like he experienced it himself. Were his parents divorced? *I don't even know!* This is what you get when, on impulse, you marry a total stranger. One who won't get *near* my baby, if I have anything to do with it. "Divorce is not ideal. You're right." My stomach twists. *You're fierce,* I remind myself. "But unless you get therapy, with receipts this time, our child will *not* be 'bouncing over' to your house."

His eyes flare. "You'll *never* get full custody."

It's true that he'll hire a high-priced attorney to try to squash me, and I'll have difficulty proving his manipulation in court. But I try not to think about that now. I have to focus on getting away from him first.

"No court will keep a father from his child," he adds. "Especially when the mother is unemployed."

What does *that* mean? I press my back against the chair as his smug smile fills me with dread.

He leans over the table toward me. "What will your psychologist board do when they learn you're having an affair with a client?"

His threat freezes me. I didn't anticipate Brandon going there, though I should've known he'd stoop that low—scrabbling to find any way he can to interfere with my career. I have truth on my side, but an investigation could spell trouble for my license, especially after my carelessness at protecting Jordan and Mason's privacy.

My lack of response seems to empower Brandon. He scoops up the ring and thrusts it toward me. "Stay with me, and I'll forget we ever had this conversation. I'll forgive you for what you've done. It'll be tough, but I'll do it for our baby. I'll be the bigger person." His hand trembles as he holds the ring out to me. "I know being pregnant has made you crazy, but soon you'll be back to yourself. Back to us, to our marriage. Please, Avery."

Why is he so frantic to keep me? He seems to hate me and my autonomy. I will never be the docile woman he wants. There's a wild energy in his gaze, a desperation to change my mind, or perhaps a PTSD intrusion taking over his brain. Every muscle in my body tenses, sending my heart rate into overdrive. For a second, I wonder if he'll throw the ring at my face. He likes to throw expensive objects.

Over the pounding heartbeat in my ears, I keep asking myself, *where is Nadia?* She should've texted by now. The diamond is still inches from my face, sparkling in its illusory splendor—the same deceptive beauty my husband used to entrap me. *Placate him*, I think, well aware that abusive partners become more dangerous when you try to leave. I pluck the ring from his grasp and push it onto my finger. I can get rid of it later.

"That a girl," he says, rewarding me with a full smile.

Does he truly believe I'm taking him back, just like that? *What a psycho.*

"I didn't come clean about therapy because I didn't want to disappoint you." A sheepish shrug lifts his shoulders. "But it's only because I don't need it. *You* healed me, Avery. You're such an amazing psychologist that you've already healed my PTSD."

What rubbish. Does he think this transparent ploy will get me to stay?

"I need to show you." He beams at me. "I want to show you how much you've helped me. Just over there." He points in the direction of Harbour Town. "Will you let me show you?"

I study him. *What's his angle?*

"We'll come right back, just as our food arrives," he promises. "I have to show you what you've done for me. I hear you. We have some things to work on. But no matter what happens between us, I need you to see how you've given me my life back."

I look at the harbor, which bustles with people. My phone buzzes in my lap, and I massage my forehead to hide my downward glance as I read Nadia's text:

Done. M on way.

I almost cry with relief. Nadia's husband, Martin, will be here in twenty minutes to take me to their place, where Nadia has driven my car, which she stuffed with as many of my belongings as she could fit. My fumbling attempt to disable our smart home system during my sunglasses retrieval appears to have worked.

My legs bounce beneath the table with keyed-up energy, just like I felt before high school track races. I want to run now, but I need to wait for my rescue. Maybe going with Brandon will lull him into thinking I'll stay? Maybe it could even facilitate my escape. I'll tell him I need to use the restroom when we return. Then I'll slip out to meet Martin at the rendezvous spot.

Brandon stands and extends his hand. "Come with me?"

Is it possible to keep stonewalling him for twenty minutes? All I know is I can't stay seated anymore with tremors ripping through my body. "Okay," I say.

He motions to our waiter, who arrives in a flash. He's probably been gawking at our marital soap opera from the drink station. "We'll be right back," Brandon tells him as he slips him a large bill. "Keep our table for us."

"Yes, sir."

I follow my husband out of the restaurant toward the harbor. It's about a five-minute walk to the round marina, but we don't stop there. He leads us around the circumference of the harbor, all the way to the left. As we pass slip after slip, a spring in his step quickens his pace, whereas my feet start to drag, weighed down by growing apprehension. Where is he taking us? He turns to jog down a ramp toward the last row of boats and looks back at me, circling his hand with impatience. "C'mon, slow poke! You're going to love this."

I paste on a smile as I descend the ramp and stop short on the concrete dock. He has already boarded a sizable fishing boat, sleek white with black trim, and he waves at me from the deck. "Look at what I just bought!"

My eyes bug. He *bought* this?

"Bet you know the name and model, Navy girl."

The oversized logo near the motors confirms my guess. "It's a Black-fin, but I don't know the model." I think it's a newer one. It's gorgeous.

"The three-thirty-two CC," he says. He reaches out for my hand. "Come on board and check it out."

Despite my curiosity, I back away a step. "Morning sickness and boats don't get along."

"Aww." He scowls. "Don't rain on my parade. Look at this!" He spins around with his arms to the side. "I used to be terrified of boats, after what happened to Diana."

Diana was his wife. What a pretty name.

"But you inspired me to face my fears. I'm getting back on the water, finally. I'm going to fish again." His eyes shine as he holds his hand to his heart. "It's all because of you, Avery."

I'm not sure what to say. I'm glad he'll no longer avoid an activity he loves, but it doesn't change the horrible things he's done.

"Did you know this has an insulated baitwell?" He points at port side. "And nine-hundred horsepower!" He ducks under the T top and starts the two motors before hustling back to me and extending his hand again. Over the roar, he hollers, "You got to feel this power!"

His energy is frenetic, like he's in the throes of a hypomanic episode. Does he have bipolar disorder? Whatever's going on, there's no way I'm getting on that boat.

In a flash, he lunges for me, seizes my wrist, and yanks me toward him. A sharp sting shoots up my left arm as I tumble forward off the dock and feel the sickening sensation of falling. I scream. Before I can orient myself, he's wrapped me in his powerful hold, my back slammed against his chest with his hand clapped over my mouth, suffocating me. I writhe in his hold as I try to stomp his foot or bite his hand.

"Stop," he hisses in my ear as he squeezes me tighter. "You did this. I saw Nadia's text on your watch. You will *not* leave me. You won't steal my baby away."

A shock of pain hits the side of my head, and all goes black.

20. JORDAN

Wispy gray clouds swirl in the sky, just like on the day Kim died. My throat feels constricted. It's hard to swallow. Standing on the concrete slab of the dock, I watch Captain Bobby help my kids step over the gunwale to the deck of a charter boat. Even their minimal weight causes the small boat to dip toward the dock. When Bobby takes Elena's hand, I inhale a sharp breath. The ramp leading back up to the lighthouse and restaurants isn't too far away. Should I make a run for it?

This is a bad idea. Our Sunday started with a service at The Church of the Cross and brunch at First Watch before driving to Sea Pines for our boat reservation. The plan is to spread Kim's ashes in the ocean. But first, I have to board this boat. Egg frittata flutters in my stomach and threatens to make a reappearance. When Bobby reaches for me, I hesitate. Deep lines on his face, weathered by the sun, wrinkle as he nods. The kindness in his eyes reassures me, and I grasp his hand.

The boat sways beneath me, and I shoot a longing look back at the dock. My kids explore the seats and gadgets, intrigued by their first time on a boat. My only thought? It'll be their *last* boat trip. Storms could blow back in without warning, or we could capsize, or…

I try to convince myself that I'm being crazy. I picture a worksheet to challenge the stuck point, *We're all going to die*. Evidence for the belief? Kim's ashes in Elena's handbag. There's no evidence *against* our impending demise, at least what I can come up with while fighting chest pain and ringing in my ears. Before I know it, I've scampered back off the boat.

Elena sees me back on the dock, and she must notice my heaving chest. I scowl as I shake my head. She gathers the kids and whispers to them. Hailey crosses her arms in an apparent pout. I hope she doesn't throw a tantrum. Hudson, however, looks back at me with sympathy. He drapes his arm over his sister's shoulders and guides her toward me. Each accepts my hand to pull them back onto the dock.

"It's okay, Dad," Hudson says as he stretches up to pat my shoulder.

"Thanks." With a quivering arm, I pull him close. "Sorry I couldn't stay on the boat."

On my other side, Hailey snuggles in, and I wrap her in a side hug as well. Feeling their bodies next to mine, I can breathe again.

"Mom said we'll take the Sea Cat another day," Hailey says.

"The Sea Cat?" I ask.

She meows as she points at the lettering on the side of the boat. "Can we bring Colby and Jack next time?"

Hudson scoffs. "Cats don't like water, Hay."

Elena finishes talking to Bobby before she joins us on the dock. She studies me. "How're you doing?"

"Better." At least my panic attack was brief. I sigh as I gesture to her handbag. "Sorry I'm not ready."

"Totally understandable." She clasps my hand. "That Bobby's so nice. He offered to give us a refund, but I wanted to pay him for his time. So, we compromised on half price." She points toward a dock farther from the harbor and lowers her voice. "We're supposed to get three nautical miles from shore before we spread the ashes. But he said he'll look the other way if we want to do it now."

As proof, Bobby starts walking past us on his way toward the ramp. "Have a good day, folks."

"Thank you," I call after him. The docks around us seem deserted, and I don't want this melancholy task hanging over my head any longer. I've waited long enough. I think Kim would be okay with it, too, as she joined us at Harbour Town plenty of times to enjoy the serene views of the lighthouse and marina. "Let's do it," I tell my family.

We walk to the fourth row of docks, which I hope is far enough that people at the restaurant or nearby pier can't see us. It helps that a couple of larger, empty boats are moored on either side. I lower to sit on one end of the dock with Elena on the other and the kids between us. We dangle our feet toward the water.

At my daughter's request, I cue up "In My Blood" on my phone and set it on the dock behind me. I've avoided Shawn Mendes, Kim's favorite artist. But his song seems to strengthen me now. He refuses to give up. When the walls crumble around him, giving up isn't in his blood. I stare at the dark water. I hope it's not in *my* blood, either.

We've filled two scattering urn tubes with a portion of Kim's ashes, and Elena hands them to me. I give one each to Hudson and Hailey.

After the song ends, Hudson asks, "Is it time, Dad?"

I glance at the turquoise tube he holds, then at Hailey clutching her own. She leans into her mother at the end of the row. I meet Elena's eyes, warm and forgiving. She smiles at me, and I nod. After my scan of the area confirms no witnesses, I take Hudson's tube, slide off the lid, and perforate the tab before handing it back to him. "Anything you want to say about Aunt Kim?"

He slumps his shoulders. "She was the best body surfer ever."

"She was," Elena says.

Hailey pipes in, "She taught me how to swim butterfly."

Not Kim's most shining moment, I think wryly. *Your stroke still needs work.* I exhale a long breath. "The water was Kim's home." I nod at Hudson. "Let's bring her home, bud."

His mouth presses tight.

A scream pierces the air, and my hand shoots to Hudson's elbow. I look over at Elena. "Did you hear that?"

She's already clambering to her feet, and I push up to stand on the dock. Across the water, on the other side of the harbor, there's a commotion on a boat. It's hard to make out...a man and a...woman? My breath catches as the tall guy restrains the woman against him. She thrashes in his hold, and he tries to subdue her. I flinch when he cracks a vicious punch to the side of her head. The dark-haired woman's body slides to the deck, and the man's frantic looks around him reveal a glimpse of his face. I gasp. "Oh my God, that's Dr. Avery's husband!"

"No!" Elena rushes to my side.

I'm frozen, my heart in my throat. "He's going to kill her."

Clutching a tube of her aunt's ashes, Hailey cries, "Who, Daddy?"

As Brandon lunges to untie the ropes from the cleats, I snap out of my stupor. "Call nine-one-one!" I yell as I sprint down the dock, keeping my eyes on the distant boat. Before I get far, though, it roars away toward the open water.

I stop short and spin around. Elena and the kids have started to follow me, my wife with her phone pressed to her ear, but they're still twenty-five yards down the dock. What do I do? I can't think. I head back toward them, but then I halt as I reach a familiar boat slip. "Forgive me, Captain Bobby."

I bend to whip the ropes off the cleats before I jump onto his boat and try to orient myself. Elena's realtor friend let me drive his boat a time or two, and the Mexican boat captain showed off the inner workings of his panga, but this model is new to me.

"Jordan!" Elena shouts.

I rejoice that Bobby left his key on a red coil in the ignition. When I turn it, there's a soft revving of the motors behind me. I shift up the throttle and surge forward. I'm lucky the other slips around me are empty, but I'm going too fast, and I come close to a yacht before I straighten my steering.

"Hey!" a man hollers from above.

Sorry, Bobby. As I push up on the throttle, I shoot past my family jumping and yelling on the dock. I'm so focused on clutching the steering wheel and trying not to slam into the other boats that I don't have time to look at them. All I can think about is Dr. Avery. *I have to save her.*

No Wake Zone, the sign says as I zoom by. Well, if Brandon's not following the rules, neither will I. I push the throttle up another notch, and the thrust of the propellers plunges me back into the captain's chair. Once I'm out in open water, my stomach drops. Where are they? I slow my pace to get my bearings. I see one, no two, sailboats far to my left. Despite the clouds, there's still a glare, and I flatten my hand over my eyebrows to scan the horizon.

Then I notice a blur of white speeding away from me to my right, and I gun the motors again. I'm breathing hard, my heart jack-hammering in my chest, but I don't let my gaze stray from that boat. It calls to me like a beacon, and a vision of Dr. Avery's huge eyes fills my mind. *"Brandon talked to you?"* she cried in our last session. *"Where?"* I'd never seen her scared like that before.

"Please be safe," I'd told her then. *Please be safe,* I think now. But how can she protect herself if she's knocked out, unconscious? I *knew* her husband was dangerous. I clench the wheel. I shouldn't have let her out of my sight!

Focus, Perry. The boat's so far ahead of me that I may never reach it. But it's not like I have a plan if I do manage to catch up. Brandon's taller than me. Meaner, too. I wouldn't put it past him to have some sort of firearm on board. I need to call Elena to check on police backup. But when I slide my hand into my pocket, my heart sinks. My phone is still sitting on that dock.

Giving up isn't in my blood. I keep the throttle at full speed, the wind whipping against my body. Bobby gassed up before our cruise, right? My arms ache from my vise-like grip on the wheel. After I roll my shoulders and stretch my neck from side to side, my breath halts. I'm closing in on the boat—it must have stopped. I wait to shorten the distance between us before I throttle down.

As I near the boat, I confirm it is indeed Brandon glaring at me from the deck. I shift into neutral. There's no sign of Dr. Avery. *Is she still alive? Is the baby okay?* I force down a swallow.

"Unbelievable!" he shouts. "What're you doing following us, Crazy? I *told* you to get the hell away from my wife!"

"Where is she?" I yell back as I scan the deck. The boat's too far away for me to see over the sides.

He steps up on something and keeps shouting. "None of your concern, but she's down below. She doesn't want you! Give up your crazy, psychotic fantasies, man! She's not yours. She's mine."

"Just let me see her, make sure she's okay. Then I'll leave!" *Like hell I will.*

He hops back to the deck and steers the boat toward me. Though his clip is slow, I tense at his approach. Might the plastic shield in front of me be bulletproof? He pulls his boat at an angle to mine, closer this time. "Check yourself into a facility, Jordan." His voice is icy calm, as he no longer needs to shout. His eyes blaze with contempt. "You need help."

I step up onto a cushioned bench near the motors and fill with dread when I see Dr. Avery lying curled on the rear deck. Her lack of movement, along with the smear of blood next to her body, send chills up my spine. I thrust my arm toward her as I scream at Brandon, "I saw you! I saw you hit her! We called—" The motor's roar cuts me off as Brandon speeds toward me at full throttle. I look to the helm of my boat, but there's no time to maneuver out of the way. Right before impact, I dive into the ocean.

Even underwater, I can hear the sickening crunch of one boat crashing into another in a snarl of metal and plastic. I surface in the cool, wavy water to face the shock of a gaping gash in the Sea Cat, which now tilts toward Brandon's boat. Will she sink? How will I get back to land? My short sleeve button-down shirt billows up to my elbows, and my shoes make it hard to kick and keep myself afloat. I toe off each of my loafers while treading water.

Brandon reverses away from the crash. There's not even one scratch on his boat. As the gleaming white hull beneath the bow swings around to point at me, it takes too long for me to realize Psycho Husband's next move. Fast as I can, I dive down as the boat zooms over me. I feel a swirling rush of pressure near my feet and rotate in the murky water to watch the churning propellers of two motors pass over me, mere inches above my body. *He almost killed me!* I may join my dad and sister sooner than expected.

Salt stings my eyes, and my lungs burn for air. But I can't surface, since I know he'll come for me again. The dwindling drone of his motor confirms my fear—I bet he's sweeping the boat around for another attempt at murder. I'm not sure how long I can stay under, but I know I have to slow my racing heart to conserve oxygen. *Easy and relaxed*, I tell myself, staying deep as I swim toward the dark shape of the Sea Cat that hovers in neutral. *Just like underwater repeats at practice.*

His next roaring pass is not so close due to my advantage of invisibility. *Air, I need air.* But he circles around again, this time jabbing some sort of pole into the water to try to impale me. *He's insane!* My body starts to convulse from lack of oxygen, and I take desperate kicks up to the side of the Sea Cat farthest from his boat, making sure to steer clear of the idling propellers.

As I suck in glorious gulps of air, I listen for a change in the sound of his motors. All I hear are manic shouts and curses—I don't think he can see me. "I hope you drowned, Crazy! A fitting end for a swim coach!" He laughs. "But if not, I'll be back for you. You'll face justice for what you did." His motors rev, and I pull myself up to peek over the side of my boat. Brandon's back is to me as he steers, and I catch movement behind him—a flash of short, dark hair ascending as Dr. Avery pulls herself up from the deck. *She's alive!* Too soon, the boat zips away.

I *have* to follow them. My heart thunders as I haul myself up over the gunwale to survey the damage. Ocean water spills onto the deck from the gaping laceration on the other side of the boat. It's clear in an instant that the Sea Cat has lived all of her nine lives. Without hesitation, I ease back into the water and wriggle out of my billowing shirt. I dive under the hull. When I emerge on the other side, I start sprinting freestyle, following the path created by my target's wake. There's no way I can catch a speeding boat, but there's also no way I'm just going to float here and do nothing. Not when the life of another woman I care about hangs in the balance.

All I can hear is the sound of my labored breaths as I thrash through the water. Each time I lift my head to sight, the boat seems farther away. I don't stop. I consider removing my pants, but my belt is holding tight, and I don't want to waste time. The swells lift and lower me with each stroke. *"Keep your head down,"* my dad advises. Longing for goggles, I keep my irritated eyes closed when I'm not sighting. The next time I lift my head, though, I gasp to discover the boat ahead of me has stopped. My pace quickens as I churn my legs in a swift six-beat kick.

As I swim closer, I make out streaks of shadowy motion and shouts on the boat. Twenty strokes later, I halt. This time, I hear only the quiet hum of idling motors. *She's dead.* Despair catches in my throat. *He's killed her.* I curl into myself, feeling the roil of anguish in my gut. *It's happened again. I should've never left her side. I should've saved her.* Grief and horror press down on my shoulders, threatening to drown me.

I turn my face toward the sky, barely keeping my head above the waves, panting as I float. I wipe my stinging eyes, and a new thought pops into my head: *It's not your fault.* I blink as I consider that fact. *It's* his *fault.* I feel a stirring of energy surge within. Then my blood froths with a seething rage, a thirst for justice. I glare as I look at the boat. I don't care if he tries to hurt me. *If there's any chance she's still alive, I have to save her.*

I swim head-up breaststroke the remaining distance, still hearing no sound from the boat, and quietly unfold the metal ladder near the motors. After I creep up the ladder, I halt. It's not Dr. Avery's motionless body I see on the deck. It's Brandon's. He's coiled on one side, and a silver pole lies next to him. She stands over him, hyperventilating, blood dripping down one side of her face and round bruises blooming across her neck. When she catches my movement, she aims a red gun at me. I raise my arms.

"Jordan!" she cries. "What're you doing here?" Then, she crumples to the deck.

I rush to her side and help her into a white leather chair, keeping close watch on Brandon, whose face is also bloodied. "Is he dead?"

"Think so." She continues panting. "I knocked him over…with the dock push pole."

That's what that evil thing is.

"Then I smashed his head…with this flare gun." She winces. "I went too far." She shivers. "I couldn't feel a pulse."

The way her body is shaking, I question the accuracy of her read on his pulse. "Good," I tell her, trying to head off her guilt. "He deserved it. He tried to kill us both." No matter what I say, though, I know she'll blame herself for what happened. Her gaze seems unfocused, and I wonder how much blood she's lost. I nod at the gun she still grasps. "Nice job, Sarah Connor." I hope Brandon doesn't reboot like *The Terminator*. "Keep an eye on Psycho Spouse while I hunt for a first-aid kit."

She tells me where to find it. I sit next to her and press gauze to the cut on her temple. It was only eight months ago that I did the same thing to Kim's wound. There's nowhere near as much blood this time, but Dr. Avery *is* pregnant. I try to quell the tremor in my hand as the boat rocks in the gentle waves.

"Thanks, I got this." Her hand replaces mine to apply pressure to her head.

Though I'm sickened that Brandon did this to her, he may still be alive and need first aid as well. I also have to make sure he doesn't hurt her again. I hover over him a few seconds before I crouch to check his pulse. I look up to find her watching me, and I nod. "He's gone."

A look of torment crumples her face. "I've made so many mistakes." Her sob splits the silence, and I take the chair next to her. I reach out to cup her shoulder, wishing I could give her the same comfort she's given me. She starts at my touch, looks at my hand, then at me. "How did you get here?"

I drop my arm. "Remember my plan to spread Kim's ashes?"

Her wobbly hand covers her mouth.

"We were supposed to be out here on a boat just like this one."

Her gaze moves to the trail of open water beyond the motors. "The boat Brandon smashed into?"

"You were conscious for that?"

A line creases her forehead. "I think the crash is when I came to. Brandon was losing it, screaming at you like a madman." The line deepens. "You distracted him long enough for me to form a plan. You gave me a chance to fight back." She draws in a breath. "Wait—your *family* was on that boat?" She looks frantically at the water around us.

"No." I sigh. "I panicked. I made everyone get off. We were on the dock when I heard you scream. I watched Brandon hit you, hard…" I shudder. "And you went down. I stole the boat we were supposed to charter to follow you." I gulp. *The boat that's on the bottom of the ocean by now.*

Her eyebrows pull together as she seems to notice for the first time my bare, wet chest and lack of shoes. "But how'd you get *here?*"

"I swam." I shrug, like it's the most normal thing in the world to swim in pursuit of a speeding watercraft in the middle of the ocean, especially after getting crushed in a high-stakes game of bumper boats.

She meets my eyes. "You got on a boat, and you swam." She tilts her head, like she's trying on the words to see if they fit. "You got on a boat, and you swam." Her chin dips as she exhales. "Despite your fear, you got on a boat, and you swam. Well done, Coach Perry."

I absorb her praise. I *did* do that. "Thank you, Dr. Clarkson." I sit up. "But really, you're the one who healed me. You saved me."

Her eyes fill with tears. "You saved me right back. If you hadn't taken the risk to get on that boat, I wouldn't be here right now." She sniffs. "You did it, Jordan. You saved me." She cradles her bump. "You saved both of us." Tears slip down her cheeks. "Thank you."

The distant drone of an engine grows louder, and we both rise to see a US Coast Guard boat speeding toward us. We stand shoulder to shoulder, a swim coach and his psychologist, as we watch the first responders approach. Time to face the aftermath. I killed a boat, and Dr. Avery killed a man. I guess we've both been through trauma now.

21. AVERY

My heart pounds like I'm running up Heartbreak Hill on mile sixteen of the Boston Marathon. Is this how my clients feel in the waiting room? No wonder they don't always show up for their sessions. Despite my anxiety, the little kick I feel low in my abdomen brings a smile to my face. "Hi, sweetheart," I croon. My ladybug bracelet jangles as I cradle my five-month bump. She must wonder what that telltale-heart thump is in there.

The *Connect* button for the Veterans Administration Hospital telehealth session keeps waiting for me to press it. I pat my bump. "I'm doing this for you," I whisper. After a moment, I add, "And for me." I shift in my desk chair and touch my iPad screen.

For a long minute or two, it's just me in the video visit. Then the screen fills with a man's face. His short gray hair and beard, along with his wire-framed glasses, give him a cool, professorial vibe. But his wholehearted smile seems warm and kind.

"Avery, is it?"

I almost reply, "Yes, sir," but we're both civilians now. I nod.

"Good to meet a fellow psychologist. I'm Jack Prentice." He shares his work history at the VA, reviews the limits of confidentiality, and verifies my location. "Please call me Jack, and know that Bluffton's not too far from me in Charleston, if you'd like to meet in person for a future visit."

I consider that. "My brother lives in Charleston. Maybe we can schedule something the next time I visit him." But I'm glad our first meeting is over video so I'm surrounded by the comforts of my office.

"Is your brother older or younger?" Jack asks.

"Two years younger."

"What's he up to in Charleston?"

Nadia encouraged me to tell Dr. Prentice everything, so here goes. "He's in rehab for alcohol-use disorder." Rehab that I'm paying for. Correction — that Brandon is paying for. Correction — that Diana's family is paying for.

"Okay, then. Sounds like we have much to discuss."

You have no idea, Jack.

"I like to start by asking about prior therapy experiences to get a sense of your preferences," he explains. "What's been helpful in the past, that sort of thing. What would you like to share?"

"Nothing." I cringe. "This is my first time in therapy."

His eyebrows shoot up.

A nervous laugh bubbles out. "My best friend, Nadia, had the same reaction. She's also a psychologist, and she said she can't imagine being a therapist without sitting on the other side of the couch. I presume you've had therapy, too."

He nods. "My graduate program required it, actually."

Mine encouraged it, but I skirted the issue. "This is why I'm here, Dr. Prentice: my avoidance." I take a deep breath. "I've avoided therapy because I didn't want to talk about my dad's physical and emotional abuse. But I've since realized that my avoidance trapped me in an abusive marriage — one I barely survived."

"Wow. It's rare for a patient to be so direct about her life and what she's looking for."

"I feel like an idiot admitting all of this, but I'm tired of avoiding, I guess." I look down, then back up. "And time is ticking. My baby's due in four months. I've got to clean up this mess before I become her mom."

One corner of his mouth quirks. "Two strong motivations to heal and grow stronger—you and your daughter. I wonder if you're selling yourself short, though. Your former CO spoke quite highly of you. He thought we'd be a good match, by the way."

"He's not the only one. Nadia also likes you."

"Yeah?" He tilts his head. "How'd I earn her approval?"

"She told me I need an older male therapist to work through my daddy issues."

He snorts, and I'm relieved he doesn't seem offended. "She sounds *bossy*."

I chuckle. He's got her number, and he hasn't even met her. But I must admit my gratitude for her bossiness. I couldn't bring myself to stay in Brandon's mansion after his death, nor did I want to be there as police culled through our belongings. Nadia invited me to live with her and her family, and I've been there the past six weeks.

Staying with Nadia is only temporary, though. A realtor helped me list the Hilton Head property while I look for a home to buy in Bluffton. Though I miss the majestic birds and wildlife of the lagoon, my lower-middle-class upbringing isn't a good fit for the ritzy island. And it's been lovely to be part of seven-year-old Charlotte's life again. Nadia's daughter ramps up my excitement about having one of my own. Their huge golden retriever also provides a sense of safety and support.

"Where would you like to start?" Jack asks.

I consider that a moment. My birthday is next month. How do I encapsulate forty-two years into one session? "I'm not sure. You pick."

"You mentioned barely surviving your marriage. Is that literal or metaphorical?"

The spike in my heart rate every time I think about what happened still surprises me. "Let's put it this way. The Fourteenth Circuit Court solicitor determined that I acted in self-defense when I killed my husband." I can't believe those shocking words just came from my mouth.

"Whoa," says Jack. "No wonder you want a trauma specialist."

I nod. I administered the PCL-5 to myself years ago and only scored nineteen. But I wonder if I minimized my answers to avoid facing the truth. And that was *before* I met Brandon. "My husband was in a jealous rage. He planned to kill me and dump my body in the ocean." I swallow. "He'd done it before, to his first wife."

Jack doesn't move as I relate the events of May seventeenth. After the Coasties boarded Brandon's boat, two remained onboard while the others returned Jordan and me to land, where paramedics tended to my cuts and bruises. The Beaufort County Sherriff's Department took statements from me, Jordan, his wife, a few onlookers, and Nadia, who Martin had called when I hadn't met him at the rendezvous point. After several hours, Detective Kennedy had let Nadia and Martin take me home with a stern warning not to leave the jurisdiction while the investigation proceeded.

"Before they determined it was self-defense, how worried were you about being charged?" Jack asks once I've finished.

"I…" I lick my lips. "I was panicked, even though it was obvious he tried to kill me."

He nods. "I invite you to share what happened on that boat."

I like the way he worded that statement—an invitation I can accept or decline. I know it's supposed to help to talk about what happened. I just wish the memories of that day didn't bring such terror. My head was still hazy when I picked myself up off that boat deck…

The thrum of the motors fills my ears as I skulk toward Brandon, clutching the silver pole I found discarded on the deck. He's focused on the GPS screen, probably looking for a deep ocean trench to leave my body in a watery grave. From my flashes in and out of consciousness, I gather that he just tried to kill Jordan, increasing the odds that he murdered his first wife. I know I'll become his next victim unless I can stop him.

Though our speed must be over thirty-five knots, I've had plenty of practice keeping steady on a boat in worse conditions. I swipe blood away from my eyebrow. I swing the pole to my right and muster all the force I can to thwap it against his skull. He careens to his left, but he catches himself before he hits the deck. He pushes off the railing and darts out from under the T top toward me. His dark eyes glint.

As I back toward the motors, I feel a sliver of satisfaction at the blotch of blood near his ear. *"You murdered your wife!"* I yell.

He shakes his head derisively. *"You think you're smarter than me, with your fancy PhD. But you're so easy to manipulate."*

He's not wrong about that.

When he lunges at me, I swing the pole again. He anticipates my move and catches it mid-air. My heart nearly stops as we wrestle for control, pushing and pulling. He uses his strength and height advantage to yank me forward. I scream as he grabs me, and the pole clanks to the deck. He whirls and wraps me in a suffocating grip, just like at the harbor. Only this time, he's wrapped his hands around my throat.

I shove my sandals against the slippery deck as I tear at his long fingers, pressed into my neck. I lift my knee and drive my heel into his shin, drawing a grunt from him. Without decreasing his death grip, he lowers us so I lie on top of him, my back to his chest. My frenzied kicks and punches only tighten his grasp.

"Your lover's dead," he pants as he squeezes my windpipe. *"Soon you will be, too."* Black spots encroach on my field of vision. As I claw at his hold, desperate for air, warm blood trickles into my eye. My blood or his blood? *His blood.* A memory flashes in my mind. I focus the force from both of my hands onto the outside of his right palm, digging my fingernails deep into that tender scar.

His groan of pain releases his pressure on my throat for a second, which is all I need to wriggle out of his hold. I spin and rise onto my knees as I whip the flare gun from the pocket of my yoga pants. Just as he scrambles to sit up, I shoot the gun straight at his heart. A red-hot spark of phosphorus bounces off him into the water.

"Aaaaggh!" he yells, scooting away from me as he clutches his chest. The darkening splotch on his chest has got to burn like hell, but I doubt the wound's fatal, even at point-blank range. I grip the butt of the gun and crack it onto the top of his skull. His body slithers to the deck.

"What do you notice in your body?"

Jack's voice brings me back to the video visit. I've related the horrific events to the police on several occasions, and each time feels a little less intense. Still, my breaths come in quick rasps as adrenaline courses through my body. "The whole sympathetic nervous system… thing," I say. "You know."

He stares at me for several moments. "Using a flare gun as a weapon—so creative. I don't know if I would've thought of that."

He must not harbor the same murderous impulses. Does he judge me for killing a man?

"How do *you* view your use of the flare gun?" he asks.

Warmth floods my face as I think, *I killed my baby's father.* Aloud, I say, "I should've stopped after shooting him."

His smile is gentle. "That belief could use more examination in the future."

It's a stuck point, in other words. I should know enough by now not to buy into my own stuck points. Whoops, there's another one.

"So," Jack says. "Jealousy was your husband's motive?"

"As far as I can tell," I say. "He kept quite a few secrets, and I didn't know him all that well. But he was for sure jealous—another reason I'm here. I'm on leave from my practice until I'm fit to see clients again." I blow out a breath. "I need to improve my ethical decision-making. You see, the man my husband accused me of cheating with was one of my clients."

Those gray eyebrows fly up again.

I hold up my palms. "I wasn't having an affair, I promise. But behind my back, my husband confronted my client, lied about the health of my pregnancy, and told him to stay away from me."

"Whoa," says Jack.

"Horrific stuff." I shake my head. "When my client told me what had happened in our last session of CPT, I knew I had to leave my husband." I tell Jack about my therapy with Jordan and how he played a significant role in saving my life. In the midst of Brandon trying to kill Jordan, I snuck the flare gun from the compartment under the T top.

"In the end, it was Jordan's statement to the police that exonerated me, along with what they discovered about my husband." I make air quotes. "*Brandon Brown.* His real name was Leander Floros." A beautiful name for an evil man. "The detectives interviewed his brother, Andrew, after they found his contact information hidden in our house. According to Andrew, he and Leander grew up without a dad, and their mom was a drug addict. Andrew had been best man in Leander's wedding to a woman named Diana Wilmington." At least my husband had told me her real name—probably because he'd planned to drown that secret along with me.

"There's evidence he killed her?" Jack asks.

"Diana's sister in California thinks so. Her family's loaded—something to do with software development. The family loved Leander at first, but when Diana started avoiding them after the wedding, they blamed him for isolating her. Leander took Diana on a yacht off of Greece, and he was the only one who returned to land." I cringe. "They never found her body."

Jack shakes his head. "It's frightening to imagine that could've been you."

If not for Jordan. "Yes, but Leander wouldn't have gotten away with it this time. Too many people knew I was on that boat, and he didn't have the chance to make a getaway plan so quickly after I sprang the divorce on him."

"He would've tried to charm his way out of it, though."

I feel a chill at the back of my neck. "He was a good actor." I picture his tears when Nadia and I stumbled upon him at the beach after speed dating. My body tenses. How was he right there, right then, in our path? *I bet he followed us from the restaurant.*

"They couldn't pin Diana's disappearance on him?" Jack asks.

"They tried. Leander took plenty of cash from their joint bank account, but the investigation had to clear him before he could access the sum left to him in her will. US authorities had a tough time investigating a murder in a foreign country, though. Leander left California at some point, but they had to wire millions to his account when they couldn't prove his guilt." I've realized that his so-called "investment hitting big" in February coincided with them closing the case.

Diana's sister, Alice, has become the one blessing bestowed by this trauma. She and her family are so thankful that I helped them find justice for Diana that they've gifted me the Hilton Head house and enough cash to serve as a nest egg for my daughter. I've already put some of that money to good use, helping my brother with rehab and Captain Bobby with boat repairs. The Coast Guard was able to rescue his boat before it sunk, but Bobby told Jordan he'd better not see his face near the harbor ever again.

"You've been through quite a trauma," Jack notes.

The VA's expertise in evidence-based treatments for trauma is a big reason I'm here. "What EBTs for PTSD are you trained in?" I ask.

"CPT, PE, and EMDR," he says.

"Nice." He's certified in Prolonged Exposure and Eye Movement Desensitization and Reprocessing — two steps above what I can provide. "I'm only certified in CPT."

"That's my favorite. Since you're so familiar with CPT, though, we might want to go with a different treatment. But let's take it slow, Avery. As you know, we should wait three months after the trauma before even thinking about PTSD. Your symptoms may resolve on their own before then."

Maybe, I think. But I still have a lot to process from my childhood. Next, I answer Jack's questions about my family background, substance use, medical history, social life, and goals for therapy. We agree to meet weekly once he can squeeze me into his schedule.

He nods at me. "Well, you survived your first therapy session."

I made it. I feel a flutter in my lower abdomen, and my daughter's kick feels like a tiny fish swimming in my womb. I'll be sure to enroll her in swim lessons one day.

"Was it as bad as you thought?" he asks.

"Much better than expected," I tell him. I'm surprised I made it through the first session without crying. "I actually feel a sense of hope."

"Me, too. I think we're off to a great start. I've enjoyed meeting you, Avery." He smiles. "I'm grateful you're still in this world."

A lump lodges in my throat at his compassion. Maybe Nadia's right—over time, Jack could become a father figure, the type of father I never had. "Thank you," I manage.

After I click off the visit, I collapse in my desk chair and let out a long breath. Then I realize my bladder's about to burst. I'm on my way back to my office from the bathroom when I pass the waiting room and stop in my tracks. Jordan sees me and hops up from the chair.

"You're back?" he asks.

"Not yet. I came in to take care of some stuff in my office." I touch my neck, relieved the bruises have faded. "Gotta do some work on myself before I resume my practice."

He nods, and there's an awkward moment of silence. "Mason's been asking when he can schedule with you again." He shrugs. "At least he liked his first video visit with the USA Swimming sport psychologist."

I heard Mason qualified for the Pan Pacific team at Nationals last week—quite the accomplishment. While I agreed to meet with Mason when I return, I've remained firm that I can't be Jordan's therapist after such blurring of our boundaries. "You're here to see Nadia?" I ask.

"Yep." He waits a beat. "She's no you."

"She's *better* than me," I counter. "More objective and self-aware. I hope you give her a chance."

He scowls. "She won't let me tell dad jokes. Says I'm deflecting."

"That must *kill* you," I tease.

That look of mischief is back, dancing in his eyes. "Today I had someone knock on the door, asking for small donations toward the local swimming pool."

I brace myself.

"I gave him a glass of water."

NOTES & ACKNOWLEDGMENTS

Since earning my psychologist license in 2000, I've strived to help clients recover from trauma. But it wasn't until 2019, when Dr. Kate Chard taught me Cognitive Processing Therapy for PTSD, that I truly developed skills to change lives. I've never encountered such a powerful therapy. Countless clients not only stop experiencing PTSD, but also learn CBT skills to improve important areas of their lives like relationships, work, school, and sport performance. Every time I read a novel featuring traumatized characters, I want to yell at them, "Go get CPT! You can get better!"

Patricia Resick, PhD, Candace Monson, PhD, and Kate Chard, PhD authored the manual, *Cognitive Processing Therapy for PTSD*. I asked Dr. Chard to review the therapy sections of this novel to ensure fidelity to the treatment without copying her well-researched protocol. I appreciate the time she devoted to my little novel, and any remaining errors are mine. I'm sure I join countless trauma survivors in expressing heartfelt gratitude to Drs. Resick, Monson, and Chard for creating this masterpiece of a treatment.

At the small publisher that released my first four novels, I was fortunate to find a stellar writing team: Nicki Elson (critique partner), Jessica Royer Ocken (editor), and Coreen Montagna (book designer). Fellow Omnific Publishing author **Nicki Elson** has critiqued my writing for over eleven years. Sending her a chapter at a time keeps me motivated and on track regarding plot and characterization. Plus, whenever she updates me on family, friends, and current events, she cracks me up!

Editor **Jessica Royer Ocken** is a dogged dustbuster to my belabored writing efforts. *Low Water* is my tenth novel, and JRO has edited them all, wow! I still have fond memories of joining Jessica at the U2 concert at Soldier Field—an event that inspired the ending of my psychological thriller, *Twin Sacrifice*. Creative **Coreen Montagna** whips up beautiful book covers and interiors that are both professional and pleasing to the eye. Thank you, writing teammates!

Whenever I stray outside of sports or psychology, readers better watch out. Therefore, I'm thankful to my subject-matter experts. Fellow Kenyon College swimming alumna **Niki Watson Book, MD**, who joined me and our former teammates on swimming vacations much like the one Jordan and Kim attended, provided helpful medical information. I'm grateful, Dr. Book.

After moving to the South Carolina coast in 2023, I have yet to learn much about boats. I'm lucky a local friend, **Robert Flax**, shared his insights about fishing boats and potential makeshift weapons onboard.

Regarding the setting of this novel, I adore my new home in the Lowcountry. I grew up in Cincinnati, Ohio, and after graduate training in Indiana and Washington State, I settled in Columbus, Ohio for twenty-four years. As my only children are the fur variety, my sisters have welcomed me into their families (much like Jordan did for Kim.) Though I traveled to Chicago often, I wish I could've been more involved in my three nephews' upbringing. Now, I'm thrilled to live near my seven-year-old niece in South Carolina. She hasn't let me teach her freestyle, yet, but we have a blast in outdoor pools. And, we team up to hunt for cereal killers.

ABOUT THE AUTHOR

Psychologist/author (psycho author) Jennifer Lane invites you to her world of sports romance and romantic suspense with a psychological twist!

Jen fell in love with sports at a young age and competed in swimming and volleyball in college. She went on to become the Honda Award Winner for Division III Athlete of the Year. She still gets high from the smell of chlorine and the satisfaction of smashing a beautiful volleyball set.

In Jen's tenth novel, *Low Water*, a swim coach and his psychologist team up to heal from trauma. *Rivals* features a romance between coaches from rival universities, Ohio State and Michigan. Her *Blocked* trilogy also explores the transformation from hate to love. One of Jen's favorite themes is finding common ground.

A romantic suspense trilogy (The *Con*duct Series) and a psychological thriller (*Twin Sacrifice*) complete Jen's collection of stories. She calls South Carolina home and shares writing space with her two trusted feline collaborators: Tuxedo and Tessa.

Whether writing or reading, Jen loves stories that make her laugh *and* cry. In her spare time, she likes to exercise and visit her amazing sisters in Chicago and Hilton Head.

Visit Jen at:

Website: http://jenniferlanebooks.com

Twitter: http://x.com/JenLanebooks

Facebook: https://www.facebook.com/JenLaneBooks/

Goodreads: http://www.goodreads.com/author/show/2798441.Jennifer_Lane

Instagram: http://www.instagram.com/jenlanebooks/